I0553927

A Cold and Quiet Place

Copyright © 2020 Alison DeLuca

First Edition

All rights reserved. Except as permitted under the U.S. Copyright Act of 1976, no part of this publication may be reproduced, distributed or transmitted in any form or by any means, or stored in a database or retrieval system without the prior written permission of the publisher.

This is a work of fiction. Names, characters, places and incidents are products of the author's imagination or are used fictitiously and are not to be construed as real. Any resemblance to actual events, locales, organizations, or persons, living or deceased, is entirely coincidental.

ISBN-13: 978-1680630794
USBN-10: 1680630794

Cover Image: Ana Marinovic | bit.ly/chupova

Myrddin Publishing

unique electronic & print books

Published by Myrddin Publishing
Contact us at myrddinpublishing.com

A COLD
AND
QUIET
PLACE

Other books by Alison DeLuca

CROWN PHOENIX: *Night Watchman Express*
CROWN PHOENIX: *The Devil's Kitchen*
CROWN PHOENIX: *Lamplighter's Special*
CROWN PHOENIX: *The South Sea Bubble*

Also by the author:
Christmas O'Clock

*This book is dedicated to wonderful
and loving fathers everywhere,
especially Richard DeLuca and Carlos Alfaro.*

It is also dedicated to all victims of abuse.

A COLD
AND
QUIET
PLACE

1.

Lily is about to jump into freezing water. It's 5:30 in the morning, a numb and silent time devoted to her training schedule. Nothing is worse, she thinks, than early practice when all of her friends are still sleeping in warm beds. They didn't stay up late to finish homework the night before, working on assignments that didn't get done due to a hectic training schedule.

The huge natorium is silent, as though everything is waiting for that first and dreaded cold plunge. In a moment it will be just her and the underwater black line painted on the bottom of the pool for lap after exhausting lap.

• • •

Yet months later Lily will remember this as the last moment when she truly owned herself, one final tiny fragment of freedom before her world crumbles away like sand from a clenched fist.

• • •

She's been awake since her phone blared an alarm at 5, yanking her from deep sleep into autopilot. Yasmin, her roommate, muttered a few curse words as Lily felt blindly for swim stuff and her sports bag before stumbling out of their dorm.

A tiny voice at the back of Lily's mind whispers, "It's cold out there. Just turn around, head back to campus and crawl into bed. No one will know. You can start back in tomorrow and it'll be fine. Don't worry about speed – take it easy. Your main competitor is yourself. Who cares? No one besides Mom and Dad is about to watch you anyway…"

Shut up, Lily thinks. *Just shut up.*

Except for her, the pool is empty. Lily considers waiting for Coach Robert and her teammates, but that's a slippery slope. If she doesn't jump right in, it means she'll have to sit around, overthink things, and find reasons for blowing off practice. It's far too easy to forget it and head to breakfast... those homemade cronuts are about to come out of the oven at the school store...

Lily's suit is damp, snapping against the chilled skin of her shoulders - her own fault, since she was too tired to hang it up to dry the night before. And now she's about to spend the next 90 minutes following the black lines on the pool floor as she pushes her body to the end of practice. The actual swim isn't that bad, although as the first swimmer in the lane, she'll the other swimmers drafting off her strokes and creating pull.

Even without Coach Robert, she knows what to do. Start with a four hundred, free IM. Then four 50's descend. Each 50 has to be faster than the one she just did. Next she will scale back with a bunch of 25's sprint.

As she repeats the memorized practice, someone else enters the pool area. It's Tyler with his slow smile, long arms, and perfect swimmer's body – the guy who's been haunting Lily's dreams for months. Not only is he the best-looking senior at Prescot, Tyler is a rising star in the swimming world.

She pretends to ignore him and checks her goggles as he climbs onto the block next to hers. "Bet I'll beat you to the other end," he grins.

His challenge startles her. Usually the swimmers are far too exhausted to talk to each other. Lily swallows and retorts, "It's practice, not a race."

"It's always a race." Tyler dives in a split second before her.

Her lips tightening, Lily snaps into the air. As soon as she enters her lane, she forgets everything else. It's just her and the water.

In swimming there's a split second when kinetic energy takes over and everything becomes weightless. Lily is surrounded by bubbles in a cold and quiet place, one beautiful instant when the water is all hers and anything could happen.

It disappears as Lily resurfaces into the stroke she's trained to do since preschool. Her legs and arms weave a sinuous trail, more eel-like than fish. Three dolphin kicks propel her forward so she can cut through back to the surface to find her rhythm of arms, movement, and breath. Just as she gets it right, her turn comes up in one moment of controlled disorientation before she heads back to the other end.

Back and forth, back and forth, back and forth. Each stroke has a thousand variations. She has to control each muscle with precision, including her lungs since one misplaced arm or badly timed breath could knock her out of finals. With hundredths of seconds at stake, Lily relies on all of her hard work to get her to the top.

As in chess, Lily has to make a series of split-second decisions: two dolphin kicks, not three, good breakout. Don't breathe too much. Keep going without air. Get ready for the turn, snap your legs, that's it…

A quick flip as the universe swirls around her, and she's on her way back. One stolen gasp for air, just enough to feed her starving lungs.

Don't fall behind, she tells herself, but don't die at the same time. Ahead of her she can see the bubbly torpedo shape of Tyler as he slices through the water.

Water has been Lily's element since she was four. It represents constant physical pain as well as a kind of freedom that non-swimmers will never understand. Lily fights to carve milliseconds off her times as she heads into her second turn and kicks off from the wall. Her body can feel the slightest deviation from perfect form.

The polyester straps of Lily's suit chafe her shoulder, her thigh muscles ache, and her right shoulder is on fire. The Prescot swimmer's cap squeezes her skull like a medieval torture device. If she wants to hit the goal practice time Coach Robert has set and keep up with Tyler, she won't be able to take another breath for another ten seconds. Already her lungs protest, burning from the lack of oxygen.

Lily pushes through the pain until all she knows is speed, water, and triumph over gravity. Everyone on Prescot's swim team races the clock for a spot on the Championship team. Her own struggle has paid off, and already Lily's been picked to represent Prescot in four individual events at Prep School National Championships. Haddigan, another prep swimmer and Lily's teammate, will swim the 100 backstroke.

And Tyler. Of course Tyler will also represent Prescot at Nationals.

Arms piston through the water. Legs kick in perfect balance. Lily's core controls all motion, her back and abs padded with muscle. It's an ongoing war against time, water, and herself.

Her eyes burn from chlorine. She's only eaten half a power bar, so her body's about to cannibalize its own fat and muscle tissue.

On Lily's final lap her swimmer's high kicks in. She's about to break the 54-second barrier – a lifetime practice goal. It's there in front of her, a sunken treasure she can just brush with pruned fingertips.

It's always a race, Tyler said. Well, she's about to show him exactly what she can do.

She reaches the final turn. The moment her feet push off against the back wall, Lily's stomach cramps up so violently she nearly sucks in water. It's a punch to the gut, a swimmer's sudden agony, and she struggles to finish. For one perilous minute she feels she might drown.

Injuries are part of any sport, but the pain in her belly is impossible to fight. She's just able to make it to the edge where she hauls herself out of the pool and flounders to a bleacher seat. Its metal bars dig into her wet skin, and she shivers despite the heated atmosphere in the huge pool area, built by a former Prescot student who went on to medal at the 1964 Olympics.

Across the enclosure, Tyler has also climbed out of the water. He and Coach Robert, who has entered during the impromptu race, face each other like determined bookends. Although she can't hear them, it looks like they're in the middle of an argument. Lily gropes for a water bottle in her swim bag, ignoring the usual ache in her biceps and the velvet feel of chlorinated water as it drips down her skin. The nausea slowly eases, and she's able to relax.

Tyler frowns at the coach and crosses his powerful arms, head tipped back in a cocky attitude. Other than their shared New Jersey, roots Lily has no other connection with him. By a trick of fate they've both wound up here at Prescot, the top-rated private school on the east coast.

Lily could try to start a conversation or ask him how practice went.

"Hey, gonna visit your family? I'm heading to Jersey this weekend," or "Hey, Tyler. What did you think of the new weight machines?"

She could say that, but she won't. She's in ninth grade and Tyler's on the brink of graduation with a scholarship offer from a D1 college. It's easier and less embarrassing to ignore him.

He approaches her after Coach Robert dismisses the team. Lily pretends to search for something in her swim bag, not looking up until he clears his throat. Tyler stands in front of her, all powerful shoulders and wide chest. "Looked like that last lap hurt."

Lily doesn't want to admit how much pain she was in. "Yeah, but don't they always?"

What if Tyler wants to hook up? His eyes have the intense look of a guy who's interested.

She's meeting up with James after practice. Should she text him an excuse? They're going to the library for extra study time before class, so she can't use homework to get out of it.

"Not me." Tyler's chin tilts up so he can look down at her from an impossible height. "They don't hurt me. If you're a real swimmer you don't feel pain."

He's crossed the line into asshole territory. Despite his athletic beauty, it turns out he's kind of a dick. "Thanks for the tip," Lily blurts.

"Are you going to finish early?" Tyler's eyes are so dark she can see her reflection in them, her face tipped up to his. "Winners don't quit, you know."

"Your wisdom is amazing. You should print that on a t-shirt." Lily's protesting stomach swoops when he laughs, and she stalks back to the pool to finish practice.

"Where's your head, Batista?" Robert shouts. "From where I'm standing it isn't in the water."

"Sure it is." Lily jumps in and surfaces to grin at him.

Robert kneels down and smacks the surface to send a wave into her face. "Belly all better? Good. Get back in the game and start over." He stands up, and starts to slap the day's practice printouts onto a line of kickboards at the poolside.

Lily swims over and looks at one of the papers, held onto the kickboard by water tension. Eight 200's on 2:30. With a dramatic groan for the coach's benefit, Lily swims to the end of the lane and gets ready to start in on the main set.

A few other swimmers have arrived, making the pool water swirl with their strokes. Haddigan waves a silent "Hello" to Lily. "You're late," Robert screams. Haddigan makes a face, plunges in, and catches up with the others.

Staci wanders over to ask if she can leave early, a plea Robert waves off in scorn. "No, you can't leave early. I tell you what you are gonna do, you're gonna get your butt in the pool and finish the set."

"What, are these on the interval?" Staci asks, right on cue.

Lily giggles and climbs back onto her block. She snaps into the air, executes three dolphin kicks, and manages to swim with enough concentration to make Robert shut up. He's a rarity in swimming, a black guy who swam for his high school and made it into the Olympics before his decision to retire and coach. The swim team's lucky to have him.

Back and forth. Lily, Staci, Haddigan, and the other swimmers follow the lane lines, breathe, turn, and when they finish, climb out for the next 200. Lily shakes with hunger by the time they finish the set, and she gulps down most of her sports drink.

"I have to meet up with my tutor," Haddigan tells Robert when she reaches the starting block.

"You said the same thing yesterday." He doesn't even look up from his time sheets. "And the day before. And I just went through this early dismissal nonsense with your little friend over there. Don't even start."

Haddigan expels a long, aggrieved sigh and gets ready for the next 200.

• • •

Lily swims through the rest of the main set, struggling through the 200's since she's better at sprints. With a sigh of relief, she makes it to the 100's.

• • •

Robert never stops blowing his whistle to get their attention, calling out sloppy turns and lazy strokes. He mimes the motions he wants at the poolside, his arms bent into a dancer's pose. It's the only way he can communicate, since the swimmers can't hear underwater.

When it's time to haul her body out of the pool and change into sweats, Lily's knees are shaking with exhaustion. She hasn't even started the dry land stuff yet. Her feet slap the cement, splattering little rainbows and bubbles of pool water. It's a huge relief to change into clothes and hit the warm gym, even though it stinks of rubber and sweat.

Lily starts on the weights and tries not to think about food. The effort blows up with Tyler sits next to her on one of the machines, clanks slabs of steel onto the weight pile, and lies down to start his chest and shoulder workout.

"I'm starving," he pants. The muscles slide under his skin with each rep. His dark body is so sculpted it's crossed the line from human to art.

Lily forces her gaze onto her own machine and her mind onto the task. "Me too," she says. "And guess what? I've got time for either a shower or food. Not both."

"The struggle is real." Tyler tilts his head to wink at her and laughs when she grins at him. His good humor is infectious, brightening the dark morning routine. "You like Tribeck's?"

"Are you kidding? I love Tribeck's." It's the only deli in the little town next to Prescot, famous for homemade soup and gourmet sandwiches. When Lily swims well at a meet, she treats herself to the bacon and pesto special. "Don't even talk about it now, though. You're so mean!"

"We'll go later, like this weekend. Or next, whenever." He doesn't wait for her answer. "But right now, power bars just aren't gonna cut it."

Lily sees the other swimmers are listening in. Nothing gets their attention like food, but she's concentrating on his implied invitation. "You got that right," she says. "Cronuts at the school store?"

Tyler lets down his stack of weights. Lily's poisonous little temptation kicks in immediately: You could go right now. Just blow off the rest of the workout and go and eat. Bet if you asked, Tyler would be up for it.

But Nationals are around the corner. "We should eat egg whites and kale," Lily says mock-seriously.

"Oh, hell no," Tyler gasps around a massive stack of ten-pound slabs. "Cronuts."

Any talk of food always makes the other swimmers join the conversation. "Eggs Benedict," Staci offers from her perch on a reverse gravity machine. "With bacon and those crispy potatoes cooked in butter."

"Pancakes," Haddigan adds, "with strawberries and a buttload of whipped cream."

"Chocolate first though," Lily insists."

"Nah." Staci shakes her upside-down head. "Bacon comes before sweet stuff."

Tyler nods. "Absolutely." Lily looks at the toes of her sneakers and concentrates on her lats.

When her circuits are complete, Lily dashes into the locker room and pulls off her stinky workout gear. Sweatpants and t-shirt hit the floor with a slap as she steps into the shower to sluice away pool chemicals with soap and dechlorinating shampoo. Legacy of a German grandmother, the blond ends of her streaked brown hair will turn green by the end of the season.

Hot water eases the tightness in Lily's back. She's had too many worries about practice and the upcoming meet. Lately she finds herself lying awake from the nerves until she passes out from exhaustion. Yasmin, her roommate, has developed a habit of throwing a pillow across the room when Lily dolphin-kicks in the middle of the night. The combination of sore muscles and competition worries make it difficult to sleep and give her strange nightmares.

Lily also obsesses about Tyler, something she doesn't like to admit to anyone – even herself. Other girls talk about his body, that chest, those long eyelashes. She notices the way he tilts up his chin when he talks, like a young prince who expects Lily to be flattered when he pays attention to her.

If she's honest with herself, being around him makes her nervous – totally unlike James.

If Tyler is an arrogant prince, James is the classic nice guy. Everyone at Prescot says so. Lily met him in her American Lit seminar in September, and he offered to help her with the first project. They've hung out a few times in the dining hall, and once he took her out for yogurt. His kisses are as nice as he is – soft, undemanding. He's polite and comes from what Lily's mom would call 'a good family.'

Ugh. No time to think about it. Lily turns off the shower and emerges into the steamy locker-room.

"Someone's got an admirer," a sly voice says in her ear. Staci stands next to her by the mirror, taming her chestnut curls with a wide-toothed comb. "You should see the way he looks at you."

"Tyler?" Too late Lily realizes she's given herself away. "I mean, we're just grabbing breakfast."

"Yeah, sure." Staci nudges her with one elbow. "Be careful, though. I mean, not to be a bitch, but he just seems a little shady. And maybe I've heard a few things."

Yeah, like he's hot as hell and the best swimmer in the school? Lily wants to say. And he seems to want to hang out with me, not you? For a minute she's pissed at Staci, as though the girl might try to interfere with – whatever this is with Tyler.

Her locker is at the end of the row, near the single full-length mirror. When another athlete yells from the showers to ask for conditioner, Staci shouts there's an extra bottle on the windowsill. Then silence descends on the locker-room. It's far too early for jokes and team solidarity.

There's no time to blow out Lily's long wavy hair, and after double practices all week it's pretty fried anyway. Lily puts on clean sweats before she follows Haddigan out of the humid locker room into the cool dark of a Massachusetts morning.

Prescot is huge, a far-flung campus curling like a possessive lover around the shores of Stoddard Lake. Although spring has started in Lily's hometown, snow still clumps along the sanded track. Lily digs her hands into the pockets of her hoodie to reach for elusive warmth.

Instead she finds her phone, feels it vibrate with an incoming text. The screen lights up at her touch and reveals four sentences:

You're such a bitch. I can't believe how mean you are and what you did. Don't call me anymore.

We're done.

2.

Lily sucks in her breath as she reads. The text comes from Erica, her best friend since elementary school. She thought things were better than ever between them after their last conversation over the weekend - when Erica complained she had no friends left in New Jersey, and Lily called to invite her to Prescot. "Please, girl," she begged. "I miss you. Just find some time and drive up here for the weekend."

Why is Erica so mad? The two of them had a blazing fight back in August before Lily left for Prescot, but they made up again by Christmas – or at least Lily thought they had.

"What's up?" Tyler appears on the sidewalk right behind her, where Lily still stares at her phone. Erica's words, she realizes, hurt worse than the earlier bout of stomach cramp.

"Oh, nothing. Just a weird text." Together they cross Keene Road, dotted with Range Rovers and smart cars. Lily's hands shake as she examines the phone, waiting to see some sort of explanation.

There's nothing, just the four sentences blinking like little grenades on the screen.

"My friends were jealous too when I got my scholarship," Tyler says softly. "You have to let it go or you'll drive yourself nuts worrying about other people's feelings."

Her thumb hovers over the X to delete Erica's text. Maybe if she erases the evidence, it won't be real. "It's nothing."

"No?" His palm ghosts over her waist. He's not actually touching her, but Lily can sense his fingertips near her skin. "Damn, I'm starving."

The text's sting fades from the warmth in his broad hands. "Me too," she admits. Her stomachache is now completely gone, banished by hunger.

"Yeah. I'm always starving. Hope they have hash browns. Even Prescott can't fuck up a hash brown. And I could kill about three of those cheese and bacon sandwiches. And didn't someone mention cronuts?"

"Ugh." She remembers she's about to taper and can't pig out as much as usual. For a swimmer, tapering is an essential part of competition. A few days before her big meet, Lily will reduce her practice to reduce stress on her body. Since the 1960s, the Taper is one of the most important parts of swim training. It means more energy, but it also means she won't be able to eat as much as she usually does.

"Ugh what? Don't even tell me you don't like bacon."

"Of course I love bacon. I'm about to taper, though."

"Riiiight." His voice drips with sarcasm. "Don't even. Like you didn't just burn a ton of calories just from dry land, never mind all those laps in the pool."

They reach the light and noise of the dining hall and walk inside together. Even at this early hour there's nowhere to sit, but Lily's used to Prescot's cramped quarters. The students talk, text, and eat at the same time, palms cupped over the glowing rectangles of their phones. Some of them are soccer stars, others concentrate on track. It's like living in a foreign country where all the citizens are beautiful and athletic.

Lily gets a tray and follows Tyler to the line. He grabs two plates loads them with double scoops of eggs, potatoes, sausage, a few rolls. As she helps herself to eggs and fruit, Lily sees her reflection on the sneeze guard: flat face and slanted blue eyes framed with streaky blonde hair. She's not stunning like Haddigan, with those long auburn braids, or Staci, with her perfect complexion, but guys seem interested enough.

Tyler selects a few final pastries and jerks his head for her to follow him. When he's not smiling, his face is dark and intense. Like Lily, he doesn't fit into Prescot's 'old money' atmosphere.

He leads them to a windowsill at the back of the food hall. His tall body swims through the crowd as easily as he cuts through the water, and he never turns to see if she's behind him.

James calls out her name as they walk past his table, but Lily pretends not to hear. She'll talk to him later.

Tyler pats the wide windowsill where he's planted himself and his huge tray of food. His legs take up half the seat, forcing Lily to squish herself into the corner.

Like Tyler, she doesn't bother with conversation before she starts wolfing down her eggs. Their bodies are starved for protein. Lily can't remember the last time she wasn't desperately hungry. "It's the swimmer's family curse," her mother says. "Everyone wants a meal, then a snack, then another meal. And then dessert."

When her plate is empty, Lily eyes the extra rolls on his tray. "Uh, you mind?" she asks.

"Here." He shoves the bread over just as her phone beeps. Tyler raises one eyebrow but doesn't ask.

You can't even talk to me now, bitch?

Lily bends closer to the screen as though she could reach through the glass and touch Erica's face. What the hell has happened to her friend to cause such acidic bitterness?

Quickly she types in a response:

Erica, what's wrong? What happened? Did Courtney tell lies about me? Something I said or did? I'll call you when we can talk. Whatever you heard, it's not true.

Determined not to let the text ruin her day or get into her head before Nationals, Lily shoves the phone in the back pocket of her jeans and takes another bite of Tyler's roll.

"What was that all about?" Tyler raises one eyebrow and bites into a croissant.

"Friend from home."

"Didn't look too friendly. Same one who sent the bitchy comment before?"

Lily raises her head. "Did you read my texts?"

He drops his fork and raises both hands. "Sorry," she adds. "I don't know what her problem is. Trying not to let it get to me, you know?"

It's just her luck. Erica has lost her mind, and of course it's happening at the exact moment when Lily finally gets to hang out with the guy she's been crushing on all year.

Tyler puts down his Danish. With careful, deliberate motions he picks up their plates and stacks them on one side so he can move closer to her on the wide windowsill. "People get jealous, right? They have no idea what we go through every day, how hard it is just to get out of bed when it's still dark outside."

He's wrong. Erica does get it since she's just one step below the national level. "She swims in the gold group," Lily explains, but he's too intent on his own thoughts.

"And it's not like we head off to a glorious, heated gym to sweat our butts off. No, we jump into a freezing pool and swim back and forth for hours."

His thigh is close to her shin. Lily has to admit his lean, muscled body is the sexiest thing she's ever seen.

Tyler leans back against the window, head tilted back in his arrogant way. Is it arrogance? Maybe it's just his own brand of confidence, the way he knows his body and what he can make those long limbs do.

His eyes are painted with shadow so she can't see where he's looking. Conversely, that angle means her face is in the light and he can see every movement in her face, can watch her look at his broad chest and thick neck.

Around them the bright crowd chatters over breakfast and phone screens. Lily knows the students' lives aren't all perfect. Dave, at the next table, lives in two time zones, lobbed back and forth like a tennis ball between divorced parents. Annika, the redhead who listens and nods as Dave talks, has been raised by three nannies.

"You know you're not like them." Tyler leans forward so she can see his eyes, intent on her. "We're different, you and me."

"I was just thinking the same thing," she begins.

"Lily?" James arrives at an exquisitely timed wrong moment. "I just finished breakfast." He glances at Tyler. "Hey. Hope I didn't interrupt anything important."

Tyler doesn't respond, just gets up, lifts the trays with athletic ease, and heads towards the carousel for dirty dishes. As he passes, his shoulder brushes James's arm. "What's with him?" James asks. Such a display of marked territory is unusual at Prescot.

"Who knows? Anyway, sorry." She'll have to hang out with James after all. Lily picks up her swim bag, makes sure her phone is still on her back pocket. "Probably he's trying to get into race-mode. Nationals are around the corner, like I told you already." She stops and forces a wide smile. "Meet you at the library later, around 8?"

James grins. The dirty blonde curls on the side of his undercut bounce as he falls into step beside her. "Yeah, sounds good. I'll bring our group notes plus a series of slides Will and I worked on earlier."

This is good, Lily tells herself. A study date is much better than some random hook-up with a guy she just talked to for the first time, no matter how deep that instant connection was. Going to the library with James is way better than anything stupid she'd end up doing later with Tyler..

• • •

Physics is taught, like all classes at Prescot, through whole group discovery. They're given a problem and have to develop the equations behind it without books or lectures. After the usual argument over the best seats, Lily and the other students get down to work on a puzzle about shopping carts and a 19° slope. The students discuss different solutions and the 'squeaky wheel' concept Phan put forward with a few days earlier as Dr. Rhys-Jones, the teacher, heads to her desk. "Get right to work," she directs. "Joachim, you're in charge. Laptop charger #2 is on the fritz, so take turns at the other stations."

Lily tries to follow the discussion as her classmates produce earnest theories, but she longs for a simple lesson with notes, worksheets, and pop quizzes. How many times at her middle school in New Jersey did she complain about homework and exams? After all the seminar and group learning at Prescot, Lily would love to be faced with a simple pop quiz.

Sunlight streams in through lead-paned windows over the orange-gold of wood floors and shades the muscles under Joachim's shirt as he writes the newest theory at the board and touches the calm faces of Lily's friends. There's a breakthrough in the problem when Phan produces a scribbled diagram. The squeaky wheel problem is solved, thanks to a chart of stickiness / slowed speed ratios Joachim has designed.

When she has a break, Lily checks her phone. However, the screen is still blank. Erica, if she has received Lily's message, hasn't responded.

In Lit, the group discusses the stories of Katherine Mansfield. Lily gets paired with two guys to research Mansfield's relationships with women and the impact on her writing. Other micro-groups search for other clues and quotes to support their theses. By the end of class they have a cohesive outline for a research paper, one each student will need to write by next Monday.

Lily stifles her dismay, since literature isn't her strong point. Like her mom, she's more of a math and science person.

By lunchtime, she's got the shakes from hunger. Lily grabs her backpack, yells to her study group she'll text them later, and dashes down to the dining hall. Already the tables have filled up, so she grabs the same seat she shared with Tyler the night before. The bread of her sandwich is dry and the lettuce limp, but she chows her meal in huge bites, complete with chips and Orangina.

Erica's text, when it arrives, falls like a dead bird onto her lap. *Do NOT text me anymore, bitch. I already told you we're done.*

Lily puts down the crust of her sandwich. The mellow lines of the large room blur, and she wipes her eyes with the back of her wrist. Breath rattles in her throat as she rereads the words on the screen.

She can't just sit there and do nothing. Lily wipes her fingers on a napkin and types, willing Erica to read it and understand how much this silent series of accusations hurt.

Erica, I have no idea what I did to make you write to me like this. Just tell me so we can talk about it. Maybe someone out there is spreading rumors. It's the only thing I can think of. But if I hurt you, just explain what happened so we can figure it out and I can apologize.

Please.

Lily considers what she written, words ripped straight from her heart. With a shuddering sigh she hits send. The pingback is instantaneous. Lily's phone number has been blocked on the other end.

Her balled-up napkin goes back on the tray, cup on the side. Lily climbs out of the window seat, heads to the drop-off, and delivers her dirty dishes to the staff. She passes Staci, who waves for Lily to join them.

She forces herself to smile, shakes her head, and mouths "Later."

Outside the campus basks under the weak sunshine of April in Massachusetts. Lily finds an empty patch of grass, sits on the ground, and takes out her phone to punch in a contact.

There are two rings before the voice answers. "Lily?"

"Hey, mom," Lily says. "Can you talk?"

"Not really." It's office hours in New Jersey at the clinic where her mom works. "What's up?"

The words explode out of her. "Mom, Erica keeps sending me all these hate texts. She's called me a bitch at least three times. She says I'm a slut and says I know what I did. But I have no clue!"

"What?" Mom echoes Lily's confusion. "Impossible. You've been best friends for years. What happened?"

"I have no idea." Lily hears the stress in her mom's voice but plunges ahead. "And she blocked my number so I can't even call her. Can you believe that? Can you call her mom? Please? It's – the whole thing is so weird."

"Lily, I don't know. I don't want to involve the Winslow family in your little argument…"

"It's not my argument!" Lily huffs. "I have no clue why she sent all those nasty messages. They're so mean. Could you just call her mom and kind of feel her out?"

"Okay, of course I will. Calm down." Mom's support is colored, as usual, by the spiky, exasperated love between mother and daughter. "How are you otherwise? Want me to come up this weekend? We could go shopping, or out to dinner…"

Lily's about to say yes when she remembers Tyler. Would her mother approve if she met him? He's older, and already he's giving off a bit of an attitude. It's scary and edgy and pretty damn sexy, but her mom would probably warn Lily against dating a senior.

"No, I'm fine. Maybe in a couple of weeks."

They say good-bye, and Lily hangs up. At least she's made a move and gotten in touch, a first step. Maybe her mom can find out if Erica's phone has been stolen or, if not, what Erica thinks Lily's done.

Although the wind is a sharp blade on her neck, the sun feels good. Lily tips her head back, closes her eyes, and watches the red of her inner eyelids.

A soft thump next to her wakes her up. Although she expects Tyler, James is the one who's arrived. He lies on the ground next to her with one corner of his mouth pulled up. "Didn't want to wake you." Lily has to admit he's a good-looking kid, golden hair tousled over one eyebrow. His sport is lacrosse, but he's always threatened to switch to ice hockey.

"Wasn't asleep." Lily forces her thoughts away from Erica. "What's up?"

"Just wanted to tell you the history test wasn't too terrible. The notes I went over last night helped. Plus, I found more research this morning." James hands over a stapled sheaf of papers.

Lily takes the papers and tells him thanks. He's a great guy, even if he looks like a magazine ad for shirts: clean-cut but slightly edgy. However, conversation with James feels like trudging through a swamp, all slow and careful, and she has to search for a new topic. "How did practice go?"

"It's this afternoon."

So they can't even talk about sports. "Uh, thanks again for this." Lily rolls up the papers and puts them in her backpack. "Seriously, you went above and beyond. I owe you a coffee."

"Yeah?" His eyes sparkle. "Meet up later?"

"Oh." Lily can't bear the thought of more questions and answers over coffee with this guy – plus there's the half-promise she gave Tyler to go into town before afternoon practice. "Sorry, I have double practice today." She rolls her eyes, tips her head back and forth. "Gets a little crazy before

Nationals, you know?"

"Thought you were about to taper?"

"I thought so too. Tell my coach, okay?"

Her meager attempt at a joke doesn't make him laugh or even smile. James pats her arm and gets to his feet, an awkward process for such an athletic kid. She squints up where he's outlined blue against the sun, and he stares back. "Guess I get it," he says in a soft voice. "See you later, Lily." The damp blades of grass stay flattened under his Nikes as he walks toward Bryce Hall.

"Damn," Lily whispers. Later, she promises herself, she'll call him and make it right. She'll buy him cookies or offer to take him out for a sandwich at Tribeck's.

It'll be fine.

3.

Propped up on her narrow dorm-room bed, Lily scrolls through the pictures of Erica on her phone. A selfie at a birthday party: Lily sits on Erica's lap, Erica sticks out her tongue. Their faces are smooshed together in a fierce hug.

Pictures after their practice when they were still on the same team. Later, Erica at one of Lily's events – her first club Nationals.

More selfies at parties, the mall, and concerts. Their faces are lit by green light from the cheap glow sticks Lily's dad bought them from a street vendor.

The high-contrast Compton meme Erica made for them: Straight Outta Swim Practice. Most recently are a few pictures Erica's mom took at their beach house, silhouettes of their skinny frames pressed side by side on the sand surrounded by the final red and orange of a perfect summer day.

• • •

"Got laundry?" Staci slouches against the doorframe of Lily's room, swinging her own bag from an index finger.

Lily looks at the floor. Clothes are piled up in wrinkled heaps, discarded as soon as she gets back from class. There's a pile in the corner of jeans, underwear, and socks, all in a wrinkled pyramid where she pushed them off her legs and left the garments on the floor. At the time she was too exhausted to put them away. She had just enough energy to fall on her bed and pass out.

"My roommate's a slob," Yasmin comments from the corner of the room. She wrinkles her nose and snorts.

"Shut up." Lily grins. "Bet half of this stuff is yours." Yasmin extends one long arm to point at her own laundry bag, limp on the door hook. "Guess I'll have to catch the next one," Lily adds.

Staci disappears, and Lily slumps into the hard chair by her desk. She should read European History. The wind swirls around the top floor even in spring and batters the window. Outside the leaves toss against the glass panes.

A light touch rouses her, and Lily looks up. "I'll help you clean up if you want," Yasmin offers. "Maybe you just need a new start, you know? Has to be tough to getting up and running off at the crack of dawn each day."

"Yeah, okay. Thanks." Lily gets up and helps Yasmin pick up the piles of denim, cotton, and silk. A few shirts cover a forgotten bathing suit, musty and still damp. It smells like chlorinated hot dogs. Yasmin claps her hands over her nose and backs through the door Staci left open, eyes wet as she retches.

With a long line of embarrassed apologies, Lily scoops up the disgusting suit. She throws it into the trash and sprays the container with Lysol from the stash her mom buys her each semester.

The suit has left a Rorschach mark of mold on the floorboards. How did her life get to be such a mess?

"It's okay." Yasmin cautiously enters, grabs her laptop, and retreats to the hallway. "Mold makes me gag, though. Sorry."

Lily's been a swimmer for so long she doesn't register chlorine any longer. Her sense of smell has narrowed to food and Tyler's aftershave.

She slumps onto the desk chair. If she gives up swimming, she could keep her room neat enough for Yasmin. There'd be more time to study, to play other sports, to just be a girl. No more 5AM wake-up calls, no more scrambling in the dark as she searches for her athletics bag. No more homework under the sheets with her phone as a study lamp. No more impossibly long laps, 200's on an empty stomach with a low-grade headache from hunger and oxygen deprivation.

Swimming is what she does – it defines her in ways Yasmin and even Erica could never understand. Ever since she was four, Lily's been trolling the black line to chase a stronger, brighter version of herself – one who can swim the 50 freestyle in under 24 seconds.

The thought of breaking the 24-second barrier makes her turn back to the huge pile of work beside her laptop. When her phone chimes, Lily shoves it under a legal pad without a glance at the text. If it's from James, she'll have to turn down another coffee date. If it's another hate-text from Erica, she'll worry about her friend instead of studying. Erica, Lily's best friend. Her homegirl. Her bff, who helps herself to snacks in multiples of nine, who can't enter a room unless it's been swiffered and cleaned with bleach wipes.

Erica has a dry wit no one else seemed to notice. "Got your holy water?" she used to murmur whenever they saw the mean girls in middle school. "I brought extra wooden stakes. Here, have a silver bullet."

Lily turns away from the phone, pulls her hair back, and secures it with the elastic around her wrist into a messy bun on top of her head before she opens her laptop and dives into physics. Lips firm, she attacks the shopping cart problem until the equation yields itself with lovely simplicity.

The text waits until she puts a dent in her pile of project work. Lily picks up the phone and reads the message, coming from a phone number she doesn't recognize.

Fuck you. We're done.

• • •

"Hi, Mrs. Winslow. Is Erica there?" Lily tries to speak calmly. Inside her stomach flutters with anger, cold rage at the line of insults held in talk bubbles under Erica's name on her phone.

"Well, hello! Is this Lily? How are you?" Mrs. Winslow's voice is warm, low-pitched and husky. "We miss you so much. When will you come back to New Jersey for a visit?"

Lily picks one toenail with her thumb as she explains the swim schedule, how preparing Nationals eats up all her free time. "I hardly have time to get my homework finished," she adds.

"Get it done, Tigerlily," the husky voice says. "Your grades are still good, right?"

"Oh, yeah. Sure. I'm able to schedule my time to make sure I keep on top of everything." Lily switches into polite mode, her auto-response to Erica's mom. The woman is friendly – affectionate, even – but the Winslow family's wealth is a stone obstacle, a massive pyramid made of stocks and buyouts and corporate bonds.

"Good luck. Now, what did you want?"

Lily repeats her request. She can't wait any longer to talk to her friend.

There's a pause before Mrs. Winslow says to hold on while she sees if Erica's at home. Lily jiggles one knee and resists biting her thumbnail.

After what seems like hours, Erica's mom picks up the phone again. "I'm so sorry, sweetie. Erica's gone out – it slipped my mind. Life is so crazy lately, you know? I mean, Rory just started travel soccer, plus we've got swim practice and another round of private school applications. You know how tough it is."

Unable to listen to more news from a world where she's no longer welcome, Lily interrupts. "Could you please tell Erica I called? And ask her to call me back?"

"Absolutely. You'd better go and study, right? Keep those A's for your fancy school."

Mrs. Winslow adds a goodbye and hangs up. Lily taps her phone against her chin and stares out the window. There's nothing else she can do except dig back into physics. Get the schoolwork done, she tells herself, and prep for Nationals. Otherwise I'll be in deep shit.

In seventh grade she and Erica made a pillow fort in Lily's room and watched Pretty Little Liars under the blankets. After Hannah and Caleb broke up for the twentieth time, Lily realized Erica had fallen asleep with Ham, one of Lily's guinea pigs, on her chest. Lily covered them with her warmest duvet, wriggled close, and drowsed on Erica's shoulder.

The memory of how warm it was under the blankets with her best friend makes Lily shiver in the shadowy dorm room, even though she's wearing her warmest sweatshirt.

• • •

Practice after a late night of studying make it feel as though Lily swims through molasses instead of water. Her arms make short, choppy strokes instead of the long reach Robert insists on.

In order to hit the 51, Lily has to work like a lost soul escaping a demon. As she pulls her body through water, it's impossible to turn off her mind. Wisps from the night before float back through the bubbles, a horrifying dream about her and Erica pushed off of a ship in middle of the ocean. Heavy chains padlocked them together so they slid beneath the waves, screaming until saltwater filled their lungs.

By the time she hits the end of the pool, Robert's already in the middle of a lecture about timing and control. She nods. There's nothing to say in her defense, because he's right. Her strokes are crap.

Lily turns back to the water and forces her thoughts off Erica to concentrate onto the directions Robert gives her, the way he mimes the arm positions he wants from the side of the pool. She catches glimpses of his face, intent on her movement through the lane.

Halfway back her stomach cramps. Lily tries to push through, but it happens again. Her throat closes with the horrifying certainty that she's about to get sick.

Lily flails to the wall, climbs out, and runs to the trashcan. There she vomits what little she has in her stomach with huge heaves that rack her entire core. The stuff splatters on empty Gatorade bottles and power bar wrappers.

When Lily's sure she's done, she wipes her mouth with the back of her hand. Robert crosses his arms and widens his stance. He doesn't say anything, since words aren't necessary.

You know what you need to do.

Lily takes a deep breath. She goes back to the pool, slides into the water, and finishes her practice.

4.

"Anything else happen with the hate text you got last night?" Tyler talks around a huge bite of cronut. If it were anyone else Lily would find it annoying, but with him it's cute. They eat as they walk across campus to their first class, since there's no time to sit.

"I tried to text her all last night and this morning. Couldn't get through. Got nothing in return."

He swallows and reaches for another pastry. "I hate to tell you this, but it sounds like your little friend blocked you." Lily's about to protest – there's no way Erica would ever block her – when he interrupts. "So you were texting her the whole time you were with that guy?"

"Who, James? No, we were in the library. Studying." She sneaks a peek at him, finds his gaze on her face. It's intense enough to make her drop her eyes to the ground.

"Studying, is that what they call it nowadays?"

"Yeah, since it was actually studying." The conversation's gotten weird, and Lily remembers Staci's warning. "Is there a problem?" she adds.

Tyler tosses the rest of his cronut to a squirrel and shrugs. "No. Whatever."

She should try to escape from the way his green eyes bore into hers, but she likes the way he leans closer as he talks. Tyler touches her without hesitation, long fingers wrapped around her bicep.

If he just wants sex, he'll find out soon enough she's not into it. Lily can't deny his looks: straight nose, sun kissed skin, full under lip, white teeth, athletic build. He's the cutest guy she's ever met.

James, with his dirty blond hair and ready smile, can't compete.

I'm a little freaked out by how quickly you've come on to me is what Lily really wants to tell him, although she stops herself in the fear that Tyler would think she's uncool. But it must show on her face.

His smile fades. "Don't think I'm a player. This isn't a game to me. I'm not one of those guys out for a body count, and if you think that's what I'm after here, you're wrong. All kinds of girls come at me at parties, you know? And I'm not into it. I want a real girl, a girlfriend who understands me." He runs his hand down her arm, firm fingertips painting swirls of electricity onto smooth flesh.

"Whoa." Lily holds up both hands and laughs. "How about we take it down a notch? Maybe stick with coffee for a while and see where it goes."

He seems to consider. "Hm. How about the guy you met last night, though? Is he going to be a problem?"

"I already told you his name. James." Lily chews the corner of her lip. "And he's just a friend."

Tyler beckons for her phone. She hands it over, and he types in his number. As he's about to give it back, it jangles with an incoming text message. Lily closes her eyes. "Oh, no. Not again."

"You need me to take care of it?"

Lily shakes her head and reads the new text, coming from the same unknown number. *Hope everyone finds out what a slut you are, bitch.* For a moment shame pours over her, as though somehow she's done something wrong.

Please, Erica. Please call me. We have to talk. Lily sends her text to the new, anonymous contact and hopes Erica will explain what the hell has happened.

"Maybe her iPhone got stolen. Bet your friend didn't even write this stuff, nope, it's probably just some fat dude sitting in his mom's basement." The warmth of his skin where their arms touch makes Lily feel light, as though she just sucked in a huge bubble of early sunlight.

She drops her napkin and faces him. "Of course! Why didn't I think of that? Some lowlife has Erica's phone, maybe stole it at a party or swim practice. Although she doesn't usually go to parties, but, whatever. I've been trying to talk myself down from a ledge since she first started sending those rage texts, but you just made me feel so much better."

He looks down at her with his characteristic arrogance. "Okay." His left cheek folds into a crease, an elongated dimple: a secret smile. "But it's weird your friend didn't get her phone shut off if it went missing."

The idea makes her deflate. "Oh. Right. Duh."

"But I'm also sure there's a rational explanation. I want to hear what happens. Keep me posted."

It's a dismissal if she's ever heard one. Lily looks at her watch – ten more minutes until class starts. "Yup. So – see you later?" She can't keep the inquiry out of her voice, and his dimple deepens.

Tyler doesn't answer. He stands and crosses his arms over the breadth of his chest, a confusing gesture that could mean anything.

Lily turns away from him and heads towards Walker, the building where physics meets.

Even though she's determined to be a strong, independent woman, at the last moment she looks back to see if he's still watching her.

He isn't. Tyler has already disappeared into the crowd.

• • •

Her mom's navy Volvo waits outside the dormitory building, packed with suitcases, athletic stuff, and some plastic bags marked with the red Target logo. Lily heads out to the mom's car but runs back when she remembers the Out-of-Town/Overnight forms she has to file in order to leave the school for a long weekend.

She pushes the pink and yellow sheets get into the dorm faculty's inbox on the wall beside the communal hangout room. Staci and Yasmin are in there, side by side on a tweed couch, Staci with her feet up on the butcher's block coffee table.

Staci looks up to see Lily by the doorway. "You're gonna kill it!" she says.

"Kill what?" Yasmin frowns at the laptop screen.

"Finals. National championships. In Connecticut," Staci explains. "Wish I could go. Say hi to everyone."

"Oh." Yasmin purses her lips. "Good luck, or break a fin, or whatever they say."

"Bye, guys. Don't have too much fun without me." Lily waves goodbye to them and heads out to the car.

"We had to be on the road an hour ago." Her mom's voice is filled with dismay as Lily buckles up.

"Did you get my new tech suit?"

The car shifts into traffic. "Yes, I did, for 400 dollars. Can't believe those things only last for 15 swims." Competition tech suits shed water instead of absorbing it and allows for faster swims. Despite Mom's complaint, there's no other choice.

"I really need two," Lily complains. "Did you get me two?"

"You did hear the part about 400 bucks, right?"

"How do you expect me to get a 23 in the 50, then? Thanks a lot."

"You're welcome, since I picked you up and gassed up the car and bought all the gear. And packed your stuff. And got you this." Mom hands Lily a bag, grease-stained and still warm from the ovens: her favorite grilled cheese from Tribeck's.

"Awesome." Lily tears open the bag and sinks her teeth into buttery sourdough.

"You're welcome."

"Mm-hm." It's their usual snippy conversation, filled with insults and demands to mask Lily's fear of the upcoming Nationals meet. "Did you talk to Erica's mom yet?"

"Yeah, it was weird. She blew me off, but in a nice way."

"Right? The whole thing is so weird." Lily puts down the rest of the sandwich. Already the nerves have started to kick in, and the conversation about Erica isn't helping.

"It really is. We've all been friends forever." Mom flicks her a sidelong look. "Going to eat your sandwich or not?"

"I don't feel good."

"Oh, please, not this again. Every meet, I swear to God. I'm not listening to you complain about another stomach ache before you go and swim." The car winds through lanes of stubborn traffic, and Mom sniffs to punctuate her disapproval. "I did buy you another tech suit, by the way."

"Oh my God. You're the best." Lily balls up the bag in one greasy palm. "Got wipes?"

Without a word, her mother points to the glove box, and Lily finds a plastic brick of damp cloths. She cleans her hands, leans back, and resists the urge to check her phone. Instead, Lily stares out the window and thinks about the cronuts she finally had in town with Tyler a few days earlier, his handsome face bright as he described new warm ups Coach Robert had made for the meet.

She has to concentrate on her own life and forget the texts, the weird conversation with Erica's mom, and the disappointed look James has on his face whenever he sees Lily and Tyler together on campus. According to the psych sheets, it looks like Lily will have a sweet spot for the event, an inside lane away from the slow water on the sides of the pool. She owes it to Robert, and to herself, to break the 24-second mark in her freestyle 50.

The car hits a pothole, since there's always construction on the highways in New England. Lily grunts as her stomach cramps. She throws what's left of the melted cheese and grilled bread into the greasy white bag marked Tribeck's – Sandwiches With Style!

• • •

At the meet, Prescot is assigned a perfectly timed warm-up. It's not too early so Lily will still be loose for her event, and not late enough to tire her out. She jumps into the pool behind the other swimmers in the lane and tries not to swim on their feet. There's nothing worse than a try-hard who swims too fast and, as a result, slaps the leading swimmer's feet on every other stroke.

Her taper seems to have come together pretty well. By the time her first event rolls around, her head's in the right place and, as usual, the nerves have turned to excitement.

She knows exactly what she has to do.

Things head downhill after she steps up on the blocks: a swimmer's nightmare. The competitors are all ready to go and someone false starts. It means Lily and the other swimmers have to step down from the blocks and wait for the officials' decisions.

She tries not to look at the girl who did it, but when a lady with a clipboard approaches, Lily's eyes irresistibly follow. The conversation between official and swimmer is short and too quiet to hear, but everyone knows what's going to happen.

A false start means elimination from the race. The wide-eyed girl is led away from the blocks, her shoulders shaking. She's probably trying not to break down in front of the crowd.

Inside the pool area, the atmosphere grows electric with tension. False starts put everyone on edge, including the spectators. Don't miss the beep, Lily prays. She's certain the other swimmers are thinking the same thing.

Finally, the rest of the swimmers are asked to mount the blocks. Lily gets back into position and wills her stomach to stop flopping around. She rolls her neck, heart racing and concentrates on the lane in front of her. It's her best event, and she's determined to race the hell out of the 50, even with the false start distraction. "Take your mark," the official's monotone voice blares over the system, followed by the usual beep to start.

There's a moment of flight followed by cold, bubbles, and silence. It's Lily's moment, her own split-second when nothing else exists, not the crowd nor the other competitors. With the velocity of her dive, she's already hit the fastest speed she'll achieve in the race. As an athlete, her job is to translate that velocity into a perfectly executed race.

Lily's muscle memory takes over. Everything else disappears as she whips one, two, three dolphin kicks.

Almost all conscious thought is gone. Lily propels into freestyle. She looks for the "T" on the black line on the bottom of the pool, the signal for her turn, just as her body begins to demand more oxygen. There's no time to breathe, and she has to deny her lungs as she prepares to flip off the wall.

More bubbles, a moment of disorientation into the turn. Lily's feet springboard off the wall. She steals a sideways gasp of air and propels into the second half of the race. Her arms are lead, there's a cramp in her side, and she's starving for calories and oxygen.

When her fingertips touch the wall, Lily feels she's swum a good race. Her eyes go instinctively up to the huge scoreboard, expecting to see her name in the top slot.

Her number is blank. After driving her body to the utmost, her touch-pad has malfunctioned. The wall, sensitive to milliseconds, has failed to register her time.

Lily blinks away hot tears. She waves to an official, an older woman with a deep tan and French braid. "Excuse me. What was my time?"

The woman checks her clipboard and raises one eyebrow. "Wow. 24.5, honey. Good race."

It can't be true. Lily knows in her bones she beat almost all the other racers. However, according to the scoreboard, the other competitors have finished under 24 seconds.

That time knocks her out of finals and the top 24. Numb, Lily listens to the swimmers in other lanes shout and jump into the arms of their teammates. Everything has gone wrong – there's no way she could be so low in the results, not with the way she just performed.

"Sorry, kid," the official says. Lily just nods. Swimmers must be professional, polite, gracious at all times. Even though it hurts like hell, Lily forces herself to smile at the lady and pretend her best event hasn't just been snatched out of her grip.

• • •

"Maybe I should talk to the coaches." Mom rummages in a huge bag to dig out another towel, which she hands to Lily over the railing from the spectators' section.

"And tell them what?" Fury and disappointment make Lily's voice crack. "We all have to swim the race again?" She buries her face in dry terrycloth. Half a year of early practices and puking up her guts beside the pool have just been pissed away by a faulty touch pad. Around them the excited voices of other swimmers and coaches echo in the huge space. The air is warm, but Lily shivers. "Got any food? I feel like I need food, but I'm not hungry."

Mom tosses a power bar at Lily. "You need calories. Start with this."

The bleachers creak under the solid weight of a large body. Lily looks around her crinkled foil wrapper and sees the bright new moon of Tyler's smile, teeth white against his tanned skin. "Sucks," he declares.

"You still have your 100." Lily's mom talks louder than usual, probably trying to make certain Tyler knows about her presence.

Lily clears her throat. "Yeah. Have to concentrate on the next swim, not worry about the last one."

"It's not your best event, right? Just gotta get through it, I guess." Tyler steps to the top of the bleachers and extends a hand to Lily's mother. "Mrs. Batista, right?"

Lily manages to swallow her power bar. "This is Tyler."

"Oh, hello." Mom flicks her gaze over him, too quickly for anyone but Lily to notice. "What are you swimming?"

"Butterfly." Lily's used to cut guys in tiny male racing suits, but Tyler's body is ridiculous. His large shoulders and tiny waist make him look like a flesh Dorito.

"I kind of guessed." There's a dimple in her mother's cheek, as though she's amused by something.

Lily clears her throat. "Got another event today?" she asks Tyler.

"Yeah." She gets the feeling he's about to say more, when they're interrupted.

A short man with slicked-back hair and big ears hangs over the railing next to Mom. "Hey, Birthday Boy!"

"Ugh, I'm old. Don't remind me." Tyler retorts.

Lily hitches up her towel, and her mother holds out a t-shirt. Lily mutters her thanks and puts it on to keep her muscles warm.

"Dad, stop." Tyler's crescent smile is gone, replaced with his father's intensity. It's weird to see the similarities between them: a short, pudgy Italian guy with his tall, athletic son.

"So!" Mom pulls out power bars and offers them to Lily and Tyler. "Birthday today, huh?"

Even under the industrial fluorescents, Tyler's smile brightens the pool area. "18. Finally legal."

Her mom doesn't bat an eyelash. Felicity is the perfect swim mom, pleasant and ready to schmooze at any opportunity. Lily's annoyed by her mom's social ability except for moments like this one, when Mom hides awkward situations under a flow of bright chatter. "Well, many happy returns. Get any good gifts?"

Tyler's dad pushes forward and offers a hand dusted with black curls over his knuckles. "The usual loot. Right, Ty? Half year's worth of MRE's for our underground shelter – although you need to forget I said that or I'd have to kill you." He brays with laughter, although it doesn't sounds like a joke.

Tyler nods. His dad – Eddie, as he introduces himself – grins. It's a sweet, happy smile, as though he just bought his son a car for turning 18 instead of six months of survival food in the case of an apocalypse.

The rest of the swim events crawl by. Lily's 100 is coming up. She's not slated as a top seed and most likely will get an outside lane. Still, after the touch-pad fiasco, she has to try her best so she can prove to her teachers four days of missed school is worth it.

Haddigan is also at the meet, up next for her 100-backstroke event. Lily puts away the power bar when Haddigan's race starts. She stands, claps and cheers for the first lap of Haddigan's race on the bleachers. On the flimsy white chair next to her, Tyler jigs one knee and checks his phone.

At the turn, Haddigan seems to lose focus and over-rotates. Lily can see the extra splash as soon as it happens, a mistimed reach putting her behind the front of the field.

"Hey," Lily says when Haddigan returns from the pool slumps

beside her, a pile of misery wrapped in a wet towel. "Your time was better than mine."

"Thanks, but everyone knows you should have finaled in your first event. That hand time was so off-base." Haddigan trains her bright green eyes on Tyler. "Right, Tyler? Don't you think?"

He shrugs. "It happens. You just have to deal as an athlete and shake it off even when the touch pads screw you."

Lily opens her mouth to argue but closes it after a second. He's not wrong. After all, she knows she swam her best. Each inch of the race from her dolphin kicks to her finish was done with precise muscle memory. Even if the damn touch pad worked against her, Lily has to keep focused on the next event.

So when her 100 freestyle comes up, Lily is ready. Tyler jerks his chin up at her before she makes her way to the starting blocks.

Lily is placed in an inside lane. Her dive is timed perfectly with the buzzer so it's not a false start, but she still gets an extra hundredth of a second.

Entrance splash.

Body at the perfect angle for speed.

Cold.

Chlorine.

Bubbles.

Lily becomes an underwater flying fish, the constant black line on the pool floor guiding her to glory. It all feels good, feels just right. The high-pressure training she's gone through for years streams her into her race, makes her propel forward with three perfect dolphin kicks. Her muscles pull against the pool water, and she takes a moment to breathe. The quick burst of oxygen takes her into the turn, keeps her going.

Lily can't see anyone in front of her as her body tires. This is what she's used to, the daily fight against her exhaustion and the determination to keep going. Even when her arms feel like they're made out of iron and her legs won't move, Lily steals more air and kicks harder into her second turn.

The 100 yard race is double that of the race of the 50, so she has to keep fighting and swim it all again. Lily forces her mind onto what she's doing. Stroke, kick, stroke, stroke. Reach out farther just like Robert always yells at her to do. Steal a breath. Streamline and kill the last turn. Make it count. Reach farther. Kick harder. Do it. Just do it.

And when her fingertips touch the wall, Lily turns and sees her time. After all the drama, she's placed first in her heat and has made it into finals.

• • •

Lunch is the usual soggy sub served on a too-small plate. Lily wolfs down the limp sandwich anyway, chases it with Gatorade and a bag of chips. Next to her Tyler eats two large helpings. His sharp teeth snap off huge bites of food. They stare at the pool while they chew, watching the hypnotic vista of the first male warm-ups before it's his turn. It's an unsynchronized dance of arms and swim caps as the competitors follow each other up and down the lanes.

"Sure you want all those carbs in your system?" Robert appears next to them and jabs one index finger at Tyler's plate.

Tyler wolfs his chips, licks salted grease off his hands, and crumples the plate. "It's all good," he says.

"Yeah. 'Cause you already got your scholarship, except I still have a team to run."

Lily sneaks a look at Tyler. His face is smooth, but she notices a tiny crease between his eyebrows. "When do we come back for finals tonight?" Maybe she can distract Robert from jumping down Tyler's throat.

"Five-thirty. Make sure you rest and stretch after the boys swim." Robert sniffs as Tyler extends long arms, one hand holding out the paper plate. Without a word, Eddie appears over the railing and takes the trash in one furry-knuckled fist. His left hand is folded around a book called "The Terrorists Next Door."

"Your dad's really into survival, huh?"

"Aren't we all?" Tyler's grin is slow, lazy. She's about to ask him more about MRE's and his dad's shelter, but he pulls out his phone and starts to scroll through his Instagram feed.

Lily pulls out her phone and does the same thing. The flesh on the back of her neck grows cold when she sees there's another text from an anonymous number.

You fat bitch. You're going to lose your race. The only reason you made it this far is people are sorry for you and your slow ass.

Lily leans forward so her hair covers the screen. It doesn't work. She feels blunt fingertips tuck the damp strands back behind her ear, and Tyler peers at the words. "Damn," he states. "Shady as hell."

She closes her eyes. The constant floating sensation she has from swimming so often makes the bench underneath her bare thighs sway. It's not real, she reminds herself. The building is tons of concrete poured into a huge foundation, and the world doesn't swirl around her. "Why," she whispers.

"Bet your friend's jealous." Lily picks up her head and stares at him, his chin tilted up at the usual angle. "People are weird. Want to suck the life outta you. To be honest, girls are worse. I hate to say it, but it's true. They get ideas in their heads, think they're better than anyone else, want to keep you down in the dirt. We claw our way up every morning, right? Out of the darkness."

For Tyler, this is an unusually passionate speech. Behind him swimmers slice through the pool, water splashing into muggy air.

"Yeah, I guess." Lily tilts her head to consider him.

"Let me see that message again." She hands Tyler her phone, and he bends over it. The drops from his skin spangle the screen like gems. "Kind of formal, right? 'You're going to lose your race,'" he mocks. "Who talks like that?"

"Oh." Lily cups his hand with hers to reread the message. "Not Erica, that's for sure. Remember when you told me her phone must have been stolen? Bet that's what happened." He doesn't answer, just slides his fingers until they curl around hers.

"Hey girl what's up!" Haddigan bounces up between them, and Lily jerks back with surprise. For a moment, before Haddigan's arrival, she existed in a pocket universe alone with Tyler and his ideas. "Ooh, sorry. Did I step on a moment?"

"Nah." Tyler stands up and lets the towel around his shoulders fall to the bench. "Time for my warm-up anyway."

Lily watches him climb down and walk to the blocks. As he gets into line to wait for his turn to jump into the pool and join the pattern of circling arms and kicking legs, the light catches his skin from above. Tyler looks like a young god, his long neck thick with muscle.

"Lily," Haddigan sings in her ear. "You with me?"

"What?" Lily frowns. "I'm right here."

"Mm-hm." Haddigan crosses her arms, and a dimple pops out in one cheek. "Girl, you are in so much trouble."

• • •

The wait for prelims to be over is pure torture. Lily and her mother have been up since dawn for their final day of competing, and there's no time for a nap. She dozes on Haddigan's shoulder as the male swimmers race. At least the butterfly event keeps her mind off Erica and the hate-texts. When it's Tyler's turn to swim, Lily sits up, wipes her cheek, and blinks herself awake.

"Gross," Haddigan comments. "You're drooling over him."

Lily ignores her friend and sits forward to watch Tyler's event. True to his word, he breaks a meet record and is seeded first for finals in the evening events. When he passes Robert, Lily catches Tyler's smile and the raised middle finger he gives the coach behind his towel.

It's mild enough behavior, but the gesture could get him onto probation at Prescot. The school demands perfection from all athletes, especially at off-campus events. Telling a coach to fuck off doesn't fit in with the school's squeaky-clean image. "I can't believe you!" she hisses when he returns from the pool.

Tyler's lips part in a snarl. He looks like a wolf ready to tear out her heart before the corners of his mouth quirk upwards. "Just playing," he grins. "No one saw. Except you. And you're not telling, right?"

"Of course not."

He tilts up his chin again, his usual unspoken reply. Seconds tick by as they stare at each other. Lily feels he already knew what she was about to say before he even asked. Around them the other athletes chat and the coaches yell at their teams. It's all outside their little world, as though she and Tyler are back to being enclosed in a tiny bubble. She feels like he's already inside her body.

His full lips part, and she shudders, afraid of a demand she won't be able to decline. But all he asks is if she wants to go get a slice of pizza, and it turns into the typical swimmer's *Well, yeah, of course I'm hungry* conversation.

Except Lily isn't hungry. But she doesn't tell Tyler.

They get into line at the concession stand behind a group of other swimmers. A couple of the athletes wear towels around their shoulders. Others stand in nothing more than what amounts to glorified underwear. Lily's used to it, she's seen it all her life, but it strikes her how strange her sport is and how blasé she's become about skin and nudity.

There's no body hair in sight. The athletes are all on taper. Most of them shaved the night before to shed extra drag in the water. Lily loves the sensation when it all goes right: energy and smooth skin working like a new car engine so her body shoots through the pool. Combined with muscle memory, it's a win.

"What are you thinking about?" Tyler demands.

Lily hesitates. "Hope I'll swim fast tonight," she admits. "What are you thinking about?"

He snorts. "Pepperoni. It's the way to go."

The soggy slice of pizza leaks orange grease, soaked up by the paper plate. Lily realizes she's not going to be able to eat it, and she pushes the food away.

"Are you really not going to eat that?" Tyler doesn't wait for her answer before he folds her pizza into his mouth. She mutters her stomach hurts, has been killing her all day. "Oh," he responds. "My last swim will land me straight onto the A relay when I get to Rosemont College. Can't wait. They won't know what hit 'em when I finally arrive."

• • •

The snap of the silicone cap against her forehead drags Lily back into the present. She forgets pepperoni pizza, the word bitch on her phone screen, and even Tyler. It's time to go through the race in her mind, picture her dolphin kicks, the usual pull through the water, and the snap of her feet on fiberglass as she goes into her turn.

Two shrill whistles. Lily suctions her goggles onto her eyes and steps up on the damp block, one foot behind the other. She's hunched over, almost touching her toes. It's a completely vulnerable position.

Lungs burn as Lily sucks in air. Her thighs tingle from the tech suit where its elastic cuts off circulation.

The loud Beep echoes throughout the large pool arena, and Lily dives into her element. After a full day of competition, the final swim is torture. Lily uses the hurt to forget her stomach and the way her head aches. She pushes through the pain and feels her body take over. As though she's separate, watching from above as muscles and bones pull through the water, Lily's conditioning takes her to the start, to the turn, to the final heat. Already she can feel the gag reflex in her throat, and she forces it back.

No. Not happening. Not here, not now, after all those mornings and swims and hard work.

Through sheer determination she makes it to the end of the pool. When she looks at the scoreboard and sees her time among the leaders, Lily's nausea fades. Still, it's difficult to climb out of the pool, and she nearly falls onto the scarred concrete around the water.

"Whoa," the girl next to her says. Her hand claps onto Lily's elbow to steady her. "You okay?"

"Yeah. Just been a long day of competition."

"I hear you. Come on, I'll help you over to your coach."

"I'll be fine," Lily insists. She doesn't want to ask for help, wants to stay strong. Beside her the pool wavers in splotches of blue and purple, and her vision grays out from the edges. "Just a tough race. Tough, tough race. Got to get onto the road, you know? Get back to school, right? Can't stop. Gotta keep going." Lily knows she's not making any sense, and it's not just from oxygen deprivation or nerves.

Something is seriously wrong.

5.

Lily wakes up in a place she doesn't recognize. The room is dark, but muted light struggles in through what look like heavy curtains over a large window. A boxy table stands between two hotel beds. She lies in one, and a fuzzy lump snores softly in the other.

The room whirls as she struggles to get out of bed. Blankets seem to knot around her ankles, and Lily nearly cries with frustration. It feels like she has a poker speared through her skull, and she knows she's about to throw up.

There's a thump from the other bed, followed by soft, purposeful footsteps. Her mother stands in front of Lily and holds out a plastic bin. There's no time to process her mom's presence before Lily loses the contents of her stomach.

Lily's face is sponged off with what feels like a wad of damp tissue. She hears the tinny clink of a ginger ale can on the table near the bed. "Just in case," Mom shouts. No, she's not shouting, but the noise sears through Lily's ears like red-hot wires.

"Hurts," she moans. The pillow under Lily's neck is warm, too warm. She grumbles and tugs at the hot lump until Mom supports her head and flips the pillow. "Race," Lily whispers.

Mom kneels next to her bed. "Ow, my knee popped," she complains. "It sucks getting old. Nine out of ten would not recommend."

"Race," Lily repeats. "Wha-?" It's impossible to talk more. Her mouth feels like cotton batting, but she knows if she drinks the ginger ale she'll have to upchuck again.

"…Your personal best… a solid third… Robert says…" Mom's voice wavers out as the room begins to expand and contract. Lily feels like she's imprisoned inside a beating heart.

The lamp by the side of the bed is turned on to its lowest setting.

Even that dim light hurts her eyes.

Somewhere a shrill voice demands Strawberry, a stuffed lion Lily owned when she was in pre-school. The girl asks for Strawberry, over and over again, and the words go through her brain like hot wires. Water runs down her cheeks. "They won't shut up," she hiccups.

"Oh, Lily." Mom's voice is thick and bracketed by an undignified sob. "I think we have to... your fever... I can't..."

The room wheels around, and an unknown force pulls a sweatshirt over her head. Lily feels her mother drag her outside, where the cool air on her cheeks makes her moan. The plastic slide of the SUV seat under her butt, the trashcan between her legs. Throughout the ordeal the voice keeps up its tirade. "Don't want to go outside, want to lie down, don't want to go in the car, No mom no no no no no. Strawberry. Strawberry. Now."

With a burst of shame, Lily realizes the annoying voice belongs to her. She's the one who demands Strawberry.

And she can't make herself stop.

She's hot, plucking at the sweatshirt. She's cold, shivering so violently her teeth clack together and bite her tongue. The darkness outside the window explodes with fireworks, huge blazing wheels of green and red and yellow. They make her so dizzy her stomach protests, and she spits into the trashcan held between her weak thighs.

The darkness is gone, replaced by too-bright lights and the sensation of movement. Lily feels herself being pushed into a chair and wheeled inside a room where hunched figures wait. The air is cool there, blown out of a noisy unit along the floor. She shivers again, but the AC brings her back to herself and she's able to understand where she is.

They're inside the emergency room at an unknown hospital.

Mom's gone, and her absence leaves a perilous hole in space. No, she's talking to a person wearing scrubs. A nurse. Or maybe a doctor?

A long episode follows, filled with pokes and prods on Lily's fiery skin. Her mother's voice answers the doctor's questions and jolts with what sounds like panic. There's the pinch of a needle on Lily's arm. The artificial taste of grape on her tongue: disgusting. The liver-shape of a bedpan in her arms. Nothing comes up. Lily is empty, and yet her body refuses to stop those painful heaves. Maybe her stomach is trying to push the illness out of her veins through her throat and mouth. The sound she makes is deep, almost alien, a series of hawking retches Lily's never heard come from a human.

"Just have to let her system…work through it…nothing we can do… keep her hydrated…" The figure in blue scrubs is talking, although his words make no sense.

More movement. Lily lies back on a crunchy hospital mattress. She watches white tiles wheel past overhead, interspersed with Mom's face and the cool pressure of her fingers. Lily clings to her mom's hand, afraid her mother will abandon her in this bright space.

"Strawberry," Lily moans.

Her body plunges into water. She swims through submerged tunnels, a maze where she has to find her way out so she can suck in oxygen. There's a mask on her face and a man's voice. "Breathe," he says. "Just breathe, Lily."

The sheets under her hips are slippery with cold. A tube leads out of her arm to a plastic IV on a metal stand. Mom's in the hospital room, chin slipping off her fist as she dozes in a chair.

Lily blinks and feels a small, fuzzy object get tucked into the crook of her arm. What the hell? The cubicle, compartmented off by a blue screen, is lit with a soft glow, and she's able to see there's a stuffed red lion in her arms.

None of it makes any sense, and Lily closes her eyes so she can float away from the cold, white world.

• • •

If the bed could stop changing size Lily would feel better. The mattress grows until it's huge, an endless field of chilled cotton. She's lost in its folds, unsure of how to return.

Before she can protest, the mattress shrinks until there's no room for anything, not pillows or a body sweating out sickness. Only the needle in her arm keeps Lily rooted to the present. A young man with curly, chestnut hair comes into the space and changes the bag. Lily watches from her unstable bed as he unscrews the port and hangs a full bag of clear liquid from the IV stand. The guy never says a word - maybe he's not even real. Perhaps none of it is real. Time and space have come unstuck, and Lily has no idea if she's inside a dream.

He finally stops fiddling with the tube in Lily's arm and leaves. "Mom, mom, mom." She hates the whine in her voice. "Mother."

"What?" Her mom scrubs at one cheek, sits up, and blinks hair out of her clumped eyelashes. "What is it?"

The tears burn Lily's skin. "I don't know where I am."

"Oh, sweetie." There's a loud scrape as Mom drags the chair closer to the bed. "We're in Massachusetts, in the hospital. You started to act – um. Different. Well, crazy actually. Can you imagine? On the road of all places. I had no idea what was… You frightened me, baby."

Her mom never talks like this. Lily flops onto her back and looks up at the pitted ceiling. "Everything's fuzzy. It makes me feel sick."

Mom flashes into her vision with another of those kidney-shaped pans. "Think you need to throw up again?" Lily's arms feel like overcooked noodles as she pushes away the pan, and Mom puts it on the tiny table beside the narrow bed. "You had a bad fever. Talked about all kinds of weird stuff. It started after Nationals and just got worse…" Her mother's voice tails off, and she bends to tuck her face into Lily's neck. "I was so scared," she mumbles. "So, so, so scared."

After a few moments Lily nudges Mom away. "Hot," she grumbles. Her mother nods and returns to the chair. The smudge of dawn outside the window highlights stained posters on the wall: "Una mujer embarazada nunca toma sola" and "Don't forget your self-exam!" Mom glances around the room before she digs in the leather purse Lily's dad bought several birthdays ago and pulls out her phone. "Daddy must've messaged me a dozen times since we got here." She types rapidly.

"Tell him I'm fine." Lily blows out a long breath. "Guess I can't have food, right?"

"Are you hungry? It's a good sign." Her mom continues to squint at her phone. "Lily," she begins.

"What."

"You talked about Erica. A lot."

"So?" But Lily knows what her mother doesn't ask – how bad has it become? Is there any return from the dark space between two former friends? "I didn't know what I was talking about. It's no big deal."

• • •

In bright, cold light of morning, Lily's fever has reduced enough for her to leave the hospital. Her mom insists on taking her back to the hotel room so she won't spread infection around the dorms. The plan is to stay there for a few days so Lily can recuperate and catch up on class work. Prescot, in its constant chase for high school rank, doesn't allow students to fall behind in their studies no matter how sick they get.

Even though Lily still shakes with chills, her mother stops by the campus for a list of make-up work. When Mom returns to the car, her lips are compressed. "I got a couple of your assignments. Some of the teachers were not very cooperative." She clips off the words like a trainer who has to harness a young, overly energetic puppy on a leash.

Lily's tired from the night. She launches into a long list of complaints, how she doesn't want to do the work anyway, and even if she did it wouldn't make a difference because there's no way she'll catch up now, not with getting sick right after Finals.

"Jesus, Lily," Mom interrupts after they've pulled into the hotel parking lot. "Enough. Let's just do what we can when you feel a bit better. Once you're settled, I'll head back over to school to catch up with the other teachers."

Instead of calming Lily down the idea makes her go off again. By the time Mom shepherds her into the room, cleaned of germs and puke by the hotel staff, Lily has only enough energy to fall onto the stiff mattress.

She wakes up to the smell of soup and a knock on the hotel door. Through her lashes Lily sees her mom pull a mug out of the tiny microwave, curse as she wrings her hand, and cross the room with quick, annoyed steps. She grasps the handle and yanks the door open.

Lily catches a glimpse of Tyler, dark and perfect in the hall beyond the room. "Hey, Mrs. Batista," he begins. "Thought Lily might need…"

Mom interrupts. Lily can't hear what her mom says as she pushes the visitor out into the hallway. The door closes to a slit and shuts Lily out of their conversation.

Lily grunts, pushes back the sheets, and tries to get out of bed. The room whirls, and tiny stars crowd her vision. She's determined to stand and walk so she can yell at her mom. Unfortunately, her body disagrees. Suck it up, Lily thinks, and forces her legs to stay straight.

Before she can say anything, her mother comes back inside with a pile of books. "Thanks again!" she calls before closing the door firmly.

Lily launches into loud complaint. "Why'd you him out like that? Just so rude. I didn't even get to say Hi!"

Mom puts down the books, holds up her phone and presses the camera icon. The image is reversed so Lily can see her own face in the screen. Yellow skin, matted hair, bags under her eyes… "Oh," she mutters. "Okay."

"You're welcome." Mom puts down the books. "He brought some of the schoolwork I couldn't get earlier, so you can start tonight if you feel up to it."

"I don't…"

"No, ignore what I just said. Let's start with soup. You haven't eaten since your last race."

The mug, filled with powdery broth and dried parsley, smells good. Lily blows on it and spoons warm yellow liquid into her mouth, but her eyelids droop after a few bites. Mom takes the spoon just as Lily falls asleep.

A great worry haunts her dreams, chases her through freezing pool water and stifling caverns filled with steam. She's back inside the enormous maze, the one linked with underwater tunnels. Faraway voices echo through the strange, nightmarish place.

Lily's forgotten to bring something important. If she doesn't find out what it is, she'll be forced to drown under the metal pylons holding the maze together. The walls are studded with brass rivets and huge flywheels. Her hands slip as she tries to turn one, maybe find a way out of the watery prison, but palms slide on slippery metal and she submerges. It's a dream, Lily thinks. It's just a dream.

Her body won't work right, and slowly Lily's fingers slip off the wet brass. The water covers her mouth and nose. She's about to breathe it in.

Just as Lily's about to drown, her body jerks wildly and she wakes up with a gasp.

• • •

Her mom makes Lily take a bath. Although she doesn't want to move from the hotel bed, Lily has to admit it feels good to lie in warm water. It's the light version of her dark, wet nightmare.

She's tempted to hold her nose, go under, and see how long she can hold her breath, just as she used to when she was five. Her dad freaked out when he found her like that the first time. But her lungs feel like limp newspaper, and she knows she won't last for long.

When Lily emerges from the bathroom, Mom argues on the clunky hotel phone. "I understand she's responsible for all work missed, but can we at least get make-up work?" Her voice rises. "How can she complete the assignments if we can't get the material? No, of course I can't leave her. My daughter has a serious fever, do you understand? And she can't keep anything down. Yes, I was there this morning. No, I wasn't able to find all the professors."

The litany goes on and on. Lily realizes she's terribly thirsty and chugs the plastic cup of soda beside the bed. She pokes the pile Tyler has sent over. Her mom doesn't stop talking as she waves at Lily and winks.

He's brought physics and American Lit, and a few of the books she needs to do the catch-up work. With the hotel's complimentary Wi-Fi and more soup, Lily is able to lean back among the pillows and reads through some of the assignments until her fever spikes. When the numbers and letters begin to crawl on the laptop screen like insects, her mom reaches over to hit Save and shut the laptop.

• • •

Each day a maid comes to change the sweaty sheets for clean, smooth cotton. Lily has to go and sit on a slippery chair in the hallway while the room is cleaned. It's hard to stay upright and not puddle onto the rug with exhaustion. All she wants to do is sleep.

Prescot's pool seems like a bright jewel locked inside a far-off treasure chest. "You'll be fine," Mom insists when Lily complains about missing practice. "Of course it'll take time to get back up to speed, but Robert says you have to rest. If you attempt to work out now we'll be set back even longer, so don't even think about it."

The hotel pool is a tiny kidney. It smells like chemicals and new tile grout. Lily sneaks down there while her mom talks to her dad on the phone and stares at the water. A few kids splash each other in the shallow end. She could cross the entire length in three dolphin kicks and five strokes. Still... her body longs for exercise, even though deep down she knows she can't hack it so soon after her illness.

"Don't even think about it," her mom warns. How did she know where Lily would be? And how did Felicity sneak up behind her?

Her perfectly manicured hand folds over Lily's shoulder and pulls them back to the elevator. "Are you kidding me? You could get sick again and be here for another week, is that what you want?"

Lily can look over the top of her mom's head by now. Did she shrink? Or did Lily grow during the time in the hotel?

Together they trail through miles of carpeted hallways back to their room. Her throat closes along with the door, and she feels as if they've lived in the tiny space with its large television and small beds for months instead of days. "I want to go to the grocery store, get you real food instead of ramen or powdered soup," Mom says. "Maybe rotisserie chicken and a bowl of pasta, but you have to promise me not to jump into the hotel pool while I'm gone. You hear me?"

"Jesus," Lily snaps. Her bones ache, and she falls back into the newly made bed. "Enough. I just want to take a nap."

"You can't." Mom pushes a pile of papers into Lily's hands. "Just downloaded and printed these. We'll need to finish them over the weekend to catch up."

It seems like her mom hangs over Lily for hours, stripping off the hotel comforter and sets up pillows behind her head. There's a clutter of pens on the bedside table beside the clunky old phone and a glass of water. Mom hovers over the pile of books and papers, fussing with the assignments.

"Can you just go get me food already?" Lily is exasperated with her mom's presence.

At last Mom picks up her red leather purse and leaves. Lily's alone inside the room for the first time in what feels like forever.

She takes a deep breath. Already her lungs have lost capacity, shrunk from days of inactivity and weakness – another thing she'll have to work on when she gets back to school. Lily picks up a pen, shuffles the papers together, and writes her name on the top one. It's a series of logic problems, typical Prescot stuff, but without a group of students to field ideas and discuss solutions, the assignment seems impossible.

Forcing herself to concentrate, Lily sets up a messy chart. Her brain feels filled with static, fussy and uncoordinated. She's delighted – and shocked – when she works out the first answer.

With slow deliberation, she fills in the sheet and slides it under the pile, a tiny victory. I am not a moron, Lily scrawls on the margin of her scratch paper.

A heavy object thumps on the wall of the room next to hers. The dull sound is followed by a crash and the quick sound of a cry, cut off by another thump.

Lily freezes, pen poised over her notebook. She hears the door open and shut with a click, followed by a series of muffled sobs.

Is it a married couple? Maybe the wife is being abused. Lily should call 911 or get help, knock on the door, ask if everything's okay. But what if one of them gets violent, has a gun?

Or she could call the front desk and say there's a situation on her floor and they should send a manager up to check. She might be wrong, though, and the staff would just end up wasting their time.

Although she holds her breath, the sobs stop. Lily goes back to her work, telling herself it was just a movie. Or a misunderstanding.

Besides, someone else will go and help.

She scratches her way through half a calculus assignment before the door opens. Filled with questions about the guests next door, Lily thinks for a moment it's a guy from next-door brandishing a pistol. Instead Mom stands there with a bag in each hand, the key card balanced between two fingers. "Your face is all flushed," she says as soon as she comes in and puts down the food on a table. "Time for a break."

The chicken, misted with steam and butter, smells divine. Lily eats a few bites, but she can't keep her eyes open. Is Tyler is on the campus, eating cronuts or those Tribeck's sandwiches? Maybe he talks to another girl and tells her about his win at Nationals.

"Want to go back to school," she mutters. "Sick of this room, this hotel, this bed. Sick of being sick."

Mom snorts and smooths the pillow. Maybe she feels how hot it under Lily's skin and flips it to the cool side. "Robert sent you a get-well card. He wants to display your medal from Nationals in the gym."

Lily thinks of those cabinets in the hall filled with black and white photos of young athletes in weird little wool swimsuits, their hair parted in vicious, straight lines, dates written in white ink. Tri-State Champs, 1951. Eastern Tourney, 1963. There are players with pale legs in tiny shorts kneeling in front of a basketball court, barrel-chested wrestlers and determined women in cats' eyeglasses, all immortalized for one shining moment of fame.

Panic spears her, and she sits up. "Do we still have my medal from Nationals? Did I lose it?" Lily doesn't remember the trip home.

"Still got it. It's in my backpack."

The pillow is cool under Lily's neck. Her mom has the medal for Robert. Nationals have been completed, and Lily is catching up on her work. Soon she'll be back at Prescot with Tyler and her friends. Everything's fine.

As Mom goes to pull the little zip around the pocket of her pack, maybe so she can show Lily how organized she is, there's a flat buzz from the bedside table.

A text.

Nice job on third place. How does it feel to be insignificant? No one likes you, not in Prescot or Jersey either. Why didn't you just die while you were sick, bitch?

6.

"Lily's back!

"Hey, baby girl."

"Oh my God get your ass over here right now!"

Staci and Haddigan bombard Lily from either side so she's bracketed between two warm bodies. Staci, as usual, forgets she's right next to Lily's ear. "I missed you so much, oh my god, never get sick again." She gets even louder when she's excited.

"Ow." Lily rubs her ear and hugs them, one after the other. "So what's up?"

"Are you kidding?" Haddigan loops her arm through Lily's elbow and drags her across the mossy sidewalks of the campus towards Prescot's class buildings. "How're you feeling?" Before Lily can answer, Haddigan bubbles about the recent meet. "You got third in finals. Nationals. Finals. Third. You placed. Like, how are you even real? Are you kidding me right now? Your name's popped up on coaches' laptops all over the country. Bet you start to get calls next year from colleges."

Lily tries to protest it was only third place and she doesn't remember much anyway, but Haddigan's right. In fact, Mom's told her Glasbury University has already reached out and wants to set up a meeting next summer. She'll be a junior, a cloudy version of herself who doesn't exist yet. "How behind am I in all my classes?" she asks. It's easier to change the subject.

"Depends." Staci launches into a long description of an essay for American Literature and the calculus quiz. Lily realizes she's managed to keep up and will even pull decent grades if she does extra homework for the next few weeks. It'll depend on sneaking in more homework after lights' out and hoping she doesn't keep Yasmin awake.

Lily asks if anyone's seen her roommate. Staci shrugs, says they haven't ran into Yasmin too much lately. "I think she went on a ski trip with her parents over break," Haddigan adds.

"A ski trip? It's April!"

"They flew to Chile. The Andes. Her family's filthy rich, you know. Oil money," Staci explains.

"Oh. Huh." There's just enough time to go and get a snack before class. Food is far more important than her roommate's social status. "I'm starving. Still have to catch up after a week of no food. See you guys at evening practice, okay?"

After another round of hugs she breaks free and joins the long line in the café. She's able to snag a bag of cronuts and head over to class.

"I know one of those is for me."

Tyler's voice is rich and low. It buzzes in Lily's ear to reach a hidden layer she is just discovering: a trembling, breathless spot no one's ever accessed before him.

"Sure." She has to keep it simple, friendly. It's easy to hold out the bag and turn away as he takes a cronut and bites into it.

"Your mom tell you I stopped by?" Tyler's tongue swipes over his lips.

Lily nearly trips, and she feels hot blood flush her cheeks. "Yeah, I meant to tell you thanks for doing that. No, seriously, you were a lifesaver. I talked to Staci and Haddigan – you know them, right? They're both on the team – and I realized I'm not too far behind in class. Thanks to you. And those books you brought." Lily bites into her cronut to stop more dumb words spilling out of her mouth.

"Well, you know. I try." Tyler goes off on a tangent and explains how he stood up for a buddy when no one else would talk to him. It's a long story about a girl passed out a party, and a guy who posted pictures of her on Instagram. "He just kissed her," he insists.

Lily should argue with him, since it sounds pretty shady, but she doesn't know the people involved. By this point they're inside Dawson. The strap on her backpack slips, and she hitches it up. "Uh, see you later," she says.

"Yeah." But he doesn't move. Lily senses he expects her to do something, but she doesn't know what it is. It's like an imminent failure, and she can't do anything to stop it.

"Ty? Is everything okay?" Lily hears the uncertainty in her voice, and she flushes.

He closes his eyes and shakes his head – a brief, alien motion. "You're not meeting him anymore, right?"

For a second she has no idea what he means. "James? Is that what you mean?"

Tyler steps closer. "Forget about him. You and me," he insists. "We're gonna eat dinner and hang out before you catch up on homework. I don't want you spending your time with anyone else."

He isn't asking. It's a demand. Lily's about to protest when he turns on one heel and walks off, chin up and shoulders tilted back. She's never met anyone so confident.

• • •

"Look at this." James slides his laptop over to Lily, and she cranes her neck to see it. They're in the library to prep for the quiz.

Tyler doesn't know about the study group. After his demands she figures it's probably better not to mention it. Lily tells herself he's too busy to care as he prepares for graduation and college.

Instead of the War of 1812 research they're supposed to read, James has found an Instagram account of a girl she doesn't recognize. "What?" Lily reads through the updates, frowning. Tracy is the name on the account. "She's a swimmer from New Jersey. Uh, okay, but why are you showing me this?"

"Look." James scrolls on the touchpad and points at the screen.

Last night with TyTy! So sweet.

At dinner with Tyler #MyMan

Planning for the future #engagementring #wedding

Okay, I'm sorry I posted those pictures. I had no idea you'd get so upset. Please forgive me, baby. I didn't mean to make you mad. Please take me back.

The pictures are typical: a girl with dark blond hair in swim gear, big smile on her face. Tyler stands behind her, long fingers spanning her hips. It's followed by clip art of brides and diamond rings. The last image, though, shows Tracy in close up, face scarred with tears. The girl holds up a small, deadly object in one hand – a razor blade.

Lily closes her eyes. "What does this have to do with me? So Tyler had a deranged girlfriend. We all have a past. Nothing I can do about it, although of course I hope the poor thing is okay and didn't hurt herself."

She's babbling. It's like her brain has stopped working but her mouth hasn't received the message.

James sits back in the chair. "I know. It's the final update, though. There's nothing else from her. And - this." He clicks on the picture and points to Tyler's comment.

Tracy - we are done. You're a loser. Go kill yourself. Leave me the fuck alone.

Lily's forehead is slicked with sweat. "He might not have posted that message himself. Maybe he was hacked."

Her voice wobbles with indecision. What the hell should she do? After all, she's also the victim of online bullying. Still, there's no way to help this Tracy person.

It's all ancient history by this point, or so she tells herself.

• • •

"Can't believe you gave Prescot your medal." Tyler shakes his head, leans back against the wall, and pushes a few fries into his mouth.

They sit in their usual window ledge. Lily has no idea when it became 'theirs,' but no one tries to join them anymore when they're together. It's as though she and Tyler are in their own bubble, invisible to the crowd of sleek, beautiful students around them.

She nods. Of course the medal goes to Prescot. It's expected all sports triumphs should bedazzle the halls of the gym, like estate diamonds on the wrinkled neck of a feisty old lady. "Is yours there too?" Lily asks around mouthfuls of chicken Alfredo.

"No way. Mine's in my room at home. What? Don't look at me like that. I'm the one who swam the heat, busted my ass to get gold. Nobody's gonna touch my medal except me and my dad."

"But Robert said…"

"Robert can fuck off." Tyler leans back and props one bent elbow on his knee. "The guy can't touch me. Besides, I already got my scholarship."

"I know, but don't you want to go down in school history?" Lily remembers the black and white photos, the players in their old-fashioned uniforms.

"No one pays attention to that stuff. You know what I see in those cases? A bunch of sad, old memories no one even bothers to dust anymore. The only people who look at them are the athletes or their families, and one day they'll die out. Then it's all going to turn into junk behind glass."

Lily puts her loaded fork onto the tray and pushes the slice of apple pie towards him. "Here. You have it."

Tyler scoops up a large spoonful while Lily finds a napkin and wipes her mouth. She pulls out her phone and swipes through the latest slew of texts while he eats: Yasmin wants to know when Lily will come back to their dorm room and if she intends to unpack the luggage all over the floor and bed. Vincent, Lily's little brother, says HELLO in all caps, surrounded with exclamation points and smiley emoticons. The single word brings Vincent to mind as though he stands in front of her, all whipcord energy and eager motion. She texts him back: *Hi, I miss your silly face.*

"What's up?" Tyler has abandoned the pie, and he cranes his neck to see her phone.

Lily holds out the phone to show him. "Vincent. My brother. Wish he could have come to Nationals with us."

"Huh. I'm an only child. Means I get all the attention." He raises and lowers his eyebrows. She's intrigued by the tiny gesture and leans forward to get her phone back, but he scrolls through her apps. "No, wait! I want to see what games you have. What, no Fallout 4? No Zombie Highway?"

"Give me my phone." Lily grabs for it, unable to hide the laughter in her voice.

He holds it up over her head and keeps scrolling. "Flat Pigs! You kidding me? I beat it months ago."

"But I'm so close to getting a full side of bacon."

"Do you even hear yourself? Bacon!" He snorts. "Actually, bacon is always pretty good." Tyler still checks out her phone. As she reaches out for it again, he taps on the screen and tosses it to her. "There. If you want it so badly."

The phone nearly slips through her hands to drop on the marble floor. Lily's blood boils. "Hey! You wanna be careful with my damn phone?"

Tyler jumps down from the windowsill and picks up their trays of food. "Let's take a walk." It's like he hasn't even heard her or, if he has, he's refused to acknowledge her words.

She can't think clearly. Blood pounds in her ears. Around them the students laugh and talk. Their lives are stabilized by stocks, bonds, and trust funds. It's tempting to escape Tyler and join them, but her knees shake and her eyes can't focus. Evening practice has been almost impossible after days spent in bed. Maybe her temperature isn't back to normal after her fever, because she doesn't seem to have control over herself. Lily follows Tyler out of the dining hall and out into the night, splintered with cold even though it's May. Her stomach bubbles, still slightly queasy.

Tyler doesn't look back to see if she's behind him. He heads towards the campus ringed with academic buildings and dormitories. Yasmin is up there in their bedroom, waiting for Lily to come and clean up the mess.

Not happening. Instead, Lily's about to create an even bigger one.

It's no surprise when she walks right into Tyler's long arms where he waits in the shadow of one of the campus oaks. He's a warm island in the chill of the night, and she tips up her head to look at the smooth skin of his neck. At the same moment he looks down, and their noses bump. The kiss seems so natural – short and lovely.

Tyler hums when his tongue brushes hers. There's soft breath on Lily's cheek, and she can smell his masculine, clean scent. For the rest of her life, spring nights will evoke this particular smell, of soap and warm, athletic male.

It lasts for a few heartbeats. Their lips part, and Lily's lashes flutter open. Tyler stares down at her, one brow raised, eyes dark and intense on hers.

He raises his hand to brush one knuckle against her jaw. At the touch, Lily feels she has to step away before her mind spins off into the leaves and branches.

If not, she'll end up doing a walk of shame. In her fifteen years, no other kiss has been so gentle or, she thinks, so memorable.

"Huh," she says. "Nice."

"Yeah, well. No more dates with James or Jimbo or whatever his name is. I heard about your little library interlude the other night. Don't do it again." With a quick wave good-bye, Tyler grins and lopes off into the darkness.

Lily steals a few minutes for herself to breathe in the night and taste Tyler on her mouth. There's a bunch of stuff she has to get to. She has to read a short story for Am Lit and go over the latest physics homework, unpack, talk to Yasmin and make sure everything's okay between them.

She trails up to the dorm room, a shadow swallowed by cool, fragrant night. Staci calls her name from the students' common room where she and Haddigan sit on the couch, their legs pressed together as they read. Or talk. Or whatever they're doing. Although Lily would love to stop and catch up with all the Nationals gossip, she still has to drag herself up at 5 am.

Swimmers have strong legs and lungs from hours of exercise and dry land workouts, but Lily finds herself gasping for breath as she reaches the top floor. Although Mom and the doctors at the hospital say she's better, Lily still gets shivery at odd moments. Her forehead aches when she's in class; she staggers with dizziness when she's about to dive into the pool. Her recent fever still makes her lungs ache.

When Lily unlocks the door, Yasmin's just climbing into bed. Her pajamas have little dolphins all over them, a present from her brother who's a Miami fan. She flops back on the pillow and doubles it under her neck.

Everyone in the dorm is well aware of how much Prescot pillows suck.

"Hi," Lily says. She knows it's late and, worse, she still has a few hours of homework.

"Don't tell me you're going to start studying now!" Yasmin screeches.

"I'm so sorry." Lily throws down her backpack and looks around the room. Yasmin has shoved all of Lily's clothes to her side of the dorm so it looks worse than ever. "As soon as I catch up with schoolwork, I'll clean up my crap. I promise."

"You keep saying that and it never happens." Her pillow muffles Yasmin's words.

"I know, but I didn't plan on getting sick." Lily finds a garbage bag and piles the clothes into it before she slams the slippery black mass into their tiny closet to deal with it later. "Besides, some of us didn't get to go skiing in the Andes, you know."

"What does that have to do with your mess?" Yasmin yawns and rolls over. After a few minutes her breathing evens out.

Lily angles the desk lamp so the light won't fall on Yasmin's face. There's nothing she can do about her laptop except dim it as much as possible. Several pages into the story, Lily's phone pings. Ignoring Yasmin's sleepy grumble, Lily turns it to vibrate and reads the text: *Can't concentrate.* It's from Tyler.

Me either, she writes back. A second later she adds a smiley emoticon.

You're so dumb. What are you doing?

Homework, she answers.

Haha. I'm graduating soon, so I'm done with that mess.

Yeah, well I'm a lowly freshman so I have to keep working.

Okay. Lily is about to return to her story when he adds, *Bye kid.*

Good night. Lily turns back to the Lit story, one cheek smooshed up under her fist as she props herself up. It's been a long time since texts have filled her with such brilliant balloons of happiness. As she takes notes for class discussion and researches the writer's bio, Tyler continues to text with updates, how he's brushing his teeth, climbing into bed, lying on his left side. *What side do you sleep on?*

I don't know, she answers. It's like having him in the room with her. *Gonna steal my roommate's pillow. He's out cold.*

Lily finishes, gets ready for bed, and turns out the light. Throughout the night she wakes several times to a soft ping and another text. *Derek snores – threw his own pillow at his head.*

And - *Thinking about you, Lily.*

• • •

It's cold, and it's early, and Lily's stomach already aches. Please don't hurl, she begs herself as she swims up to look at Robert's practice sheet on the board. The last set consists of four 100's descend, six 50's descend 1 to 4, hold 5-6, then twelve 25's easy/fast. As practice sheets go, it's not too bad.

Lily launches off the wall and loses herself after a few laps. Sometimes her body seems to become part of the water, like being a fish or a mermaid. She once described it to Erica, who just laughed and shook her head. "You already are one. Look at you, with your long hair and perfect swimmer's body. No wonder you've had more boyfriends than I've had haircuts."

"Yeah, not hardly," Lily argued, but she has to admit attention from guys has never been a problem.

At parties, at school, brothers of friends and guys she works with... She's seen enough double takes and interested stares to know guys like her. Whatever. It's never meant anything, or at least not until last night.

By the time she finishes the 50's, Robert has arrived by the edge of the water. "Here's our champion!" he announces as she climbs out to get a drink.

"So sweet! Haddigan told me all about it." Staci grabs her from one side, and Haddigan from the other so Lily's encased in a girlfriend sandwich.

"Celebration breakfast?" Haddigan says. "My treat."

"Aw, you guys are so nice. Can't think about food right now though."

"Still feeling out of it?" Staci asks. "Haddigan told me you were sick."

"Oh my God. It's like I had the plague. You have no idea – fever, not to mention my stomach…" Lily's voice trails off. Tyler stands by the pool. Water drips off his wide shoulders. His arms are crossed. As soon as their eyes meet, he turns on one heel and grabs his bag. Still drenched, he punches the door and leaves the pool.

"What's the matter with him?" Staci shakes her head.

"He medaled too," Lily says. "Maybe he feels we should have congratulated him."

"If he donated his medal to Prescot, I would have." Robert's deep voice rumbles out of his chest.

Although the coach is intent on his clipboard, Lily sees the way his bottom lip pushes out, how his jaw pops. He doesn't like Tyler, she realizes.

"All right. No breakfast sandwiches until you finish those 25's and dry land." Robert makes shooing motions at the three girls.

Lily caps her water bottle with her palm. "I've got school work to catch up on," she says. "Gotta leave early."

"Don't even start with your nonsense," Robert warns her. "I understand you just swam at Nationals, but your future competitors are eyeing to take you down next year. Do not give them the chance."

Lily tells mutters she'll be on time for afternoon practice and will catch up then. Staci and Haddigan don't answer. They just watch as she picks up her bag and runs after Tyler. Do they know what she's doing? No matter – Lily will do it anyway, even if it's a bad career move.

In the hallway, Lily pulls on sweatpants and drags a t-shirt over her head. Like Tyler, she's still soaked. Trying not to think about what the chlorine will do to her hair and skin, she runs up the hall and is just in time to catch him as he leaves the gym. "Hey," she says breathlessly.

"Guess you're celebrating." The stark comment is accompanied by a quick twitch of his neck. There's a dent between those thick eyebrows, and she wants to smooth it out with her fingers. "Guess your friends want to take you out, since you're so wonderful and talented and filled with school spirit."

"Don't be like that," Lily begs. "I told them you medaled too, but the coach said you didn't donate…"

Tyler stops. She gasps and nearly walks into him. "It's mine," he says. "The medal is mine."

"Okay." Lily's heart beats so hard it hurts her ribs. "Just … calm down. I'm just trying to explain why Robert didn't mention you." They're on the path that leads to Keene Road. She can feel the new twigs of the laurel bushes along the path press into her back.

"Well, don't." Tyler stops, closes his eyes, and shakes his head. "Those girls are all fake, trying to pretend they know you. I know you."

"Yeah, you do." Lily breathes out and cups the damp flesh of his neck with her hand. He pulls her in for a hug, sudden and fierce.

"I wanna keep you all to myself," Tyler murmurs in her ear. "All the time."

"The world's not like that." Sure of herself again, Lily smiles up at him. "And you know I only want to celebrate with you. Cronuts?"

"Hell, yeah."

His good mood seems to be restored. Lily will have to talk to him later about her friends, since she's not the kind of girl who ditches her buddies just because she's got a boyfriend. Even though I just did, she thinks.

Oh well. She'll make it up to Staci later. The list of catch-up items has just expanded, but Lily refuses to think about it. Tyler's arm is warm around her shoulders. The water was cold and perfect this morning. She has a medal in the 100, and she's caught up with her schoolwork.

"…Notice?" Tyler asks.

"I'm sorry, notice what?"

His hand slides down and taps her phone where it rests in the back pocket of her sweats, just over her butt. "No more mean texts."

Lily shakes her head. "I don't know what you're – what?"

His laugh rings out, and he cuddles her under his shoulder. "You won't get any more nasty junk from your frenemy. The chick from Jersey. See? I blocked that anon on your phone last night while we were at dinner.

Well, you call it anon, but we both know it's your former best friend. Point is - you won't hear from her anymore."

7.

"Dad calls the guinea pigs turd machines." Vincent, Lily's little brother, sprawls across the carpet in her room. Ham ignores him while Lettuce chews the cord of Lily's sweatpants.

"He's not wrong. Get her butt on the towel, Vin." Lily pokes the ancient beach towel over to Ham with her toe, and Vincent shoves the guinea pig onto it. "So what's been going on?"

It's Friday, the second-to-last full day of the long weekend before she has to drive back to Massachusetts with her mom. Normally Lily would spend most of her time at Erica's house, but she doesn't even know if Erica realizes she's home for the long weekend. She could unblock the anon contact, but it seems disrespectful to Tyler after all his support throughout the entire texting debacle.

"The usual," Vincent yawns. "Practice, more practice, and oh yeah, lotsa practice after that."

Lily gives up on Ham and prods Vincent with her bare foot. She's missed her baby brother, although there's a chance they'll end up in a brawl by the end of the night. He is twelve, after all, which in Lily's opinion is the Age of Annoyance. "Still splashing all the spectators with your butterfly?"

He slumps and tells her to shut up. Lily snorts, flops onto her back, and scoops up Lettuce. The pig purrs on her chest, tilts up its chin for tickles. "How's it feel to be a Nationals finalist?" Vincent asks.

"You know. Surreal, like it happened to someone else. I got sick right after the meet, so I can't even remember much."

He grunts, rolls over into the crook of her arm so his face is hidden. "So you're dating that guy Mom told me about?"

"Tyler?" Lily knows there's a smile in her voice. "Yeah, I am."

"Why?" Vincent asks the carpet. "What's so great about him?"

There. Lily knew he would start to be annoying. She plops Lettuce beside Ham on the towel and sits up. "Why do you ask?"

"Mom doesn't like him."

"No, Mom doesn't like Tyler's dad. And I can't blame her. He's a weirdo."

Vincent humphs, pulls Ham into his chest, and stands up. "Guess we've got practice this evening."

"I guess we do, Captain Obvious." Lily shrugs and goes for a Kleenex to clean up a few stray guinea pig turds on the carpet. "Gonna get ready now?"

"Yup." Vincent heads to the door. She's intent on tying the cord of her sweatpants. When he speaks, the crack in his voice surprises her. "Don't you think people are kinda like their parents, though?"

He doesn't even give her a chance to argue, just disappears before Lily can say a word.

So annoying.

• • •

Practice is long, cold, and wet. Lily swims with her former teammates, too busy to talk about anything but the evening's practice. Erica isn't there, of course, since she's in the gold group at the Y, where she started her career. Still, it's disappointing.

When she finally finishes, Lily showers, gets changed, and hugs a few of the girls in the locker room. She puts on Chapstick and scowls into the mirror. The overhead lights at the Y make everyone look washed out.

Maria, her former coach in New Jersey, waves them out of the locker room. "Practice is done, girls!" the woman shouts. "You can go anywhere you like, but you can't stay here!"

Lily heads out to the parking lot to sit on the cement steps and wait for her mom. The bright flash of headlights, parents who wait to pick up the athletes, makes her shield her eyes with one hand. When an unfamiliar car pulls up she considers running back inside until her mom arrives.

The rough concrete snags her sweats as she gets up to head back into the Y. A loud beep from the car makes Lily's heart race as she freezes on the step. A creep, she thinks. I really don't need this.

"Lily?"

Erica.

Lily forces herself to breathe slowly. She doesn't scream or launch right into a bitchfest. "Hi," she says as she turns around, fascinated by how calm her voice is.

"What the hell?" Erica demands out the window. "You blocked me? I've been trying to text you all month, and I finally figured out I'd been blocked. Why? What did I ever…"

"Are you kidding me?" Lily throws down her bag and strides over to the car. Erica sits in the passenger seat, a bottle of hand sanitizer in one fist. "You're the one who blocked me! You texted me shit for weeks – called me a bitch – said all kinds of mean stuff – how can you even ask me that?"

Erica frowns as her jaw drops. "I have no idea what you're talking about," she says.

"Look." Lily swipes her phone. She's saved most of the texts to a Notes app, just so she could confront Erica with the evidence. "See? Look at this – and this. What did I ever do to deserve such nasty shit, Erica? You're so mean!"

"Oh, my God." Slowly, Erica hands the phone back to Lily. "I swear to you I never wrote any of those texts. No, listen," Erica presses when Lily blows out an angry breath. "You know me, Lily. I don't do stuff like that."

"No, you don't." Lily agrees. "But at the time it was really hurtful." She blinks and stuffs her fists into the pockets of her hoodie. The two girls stare at each other until Lily asks, "Whose car is this?"

Erica waves her fisted bottle of sanitizer at a fuzzy, dark figure behind the wheel. "Remember Nolan? My cousin?"

Lily sticks her head in the window. Nolan, the lenses of his glasses obscured by the light streaming out of the Y, reveals thick braces in a tentative smile. "Hi, Lily," he splutters. "Sorry, I didn't…" Whatever he's about to say is lost in a prolonged fit of coughing.

Erica laughs, a wet gasping sound, and pats Nolan on the back. "I begged him to bring me here to see you. He has to get back before midnight, though. DMV rules and all that."

Lily feels as though her blood had been frozen and now is starting to break up, like a river after a hard winter. "I'm happy you came." Dumb words, a ridiculous attempt to mirror what a relief it is to have Erica back.

"Me too." Erica scrapes back her limp hair with both hands and winds a ponytail holder from her wrist around it. "But who do you think sent all those nasty messages?"

Lily shakes her head. "I have no idea. Maybe a kid from school got your phone? I don't know."

"But you said you got a bunch of texts, all on different dates. It doesn't make sense."

Nolan stops coughing, picks up a bottle of Fiji water from the console, and takes a long swig. "All cleared up?" he manages to say. "You all good?"

"We're good?" Lily echoes softly, leaning in Erica's open window. The boy's face flushes – Nolan, according to Erica, has always had a thing for Lily. "Can you call me? I'll unblock you, but…"

With a flourish, Erica squirts a dollop of hand sanitizer on one palm. "Exchange numbers with Nolan since my phone was obviously hacked. I'm going to shut it down tomorrow but we can stay in touch through him."

"Oh. Hey. I…I don't know…" Nolan's eyes bug out.

"Good idea." Lily doesn't have time to listen to Nolan's awkward attempts at conversation. "Here – text yourself on my phone, and I'll set you up as a contact." He clears his throat as he takes it, but Lily focuses on Erica. "How are you, anyway? God, I've missed you."

"Me too. You have no idea how much. Can we meet up for lunch tomorrow? Gold group doesn't have practice, thank the Lord." Erica finishes her ritual and stows the sanitizer in her purse.

Lily's stomach clenches. Tyler's supposed to Skype her later, but she'll have to make it work. "Yeah, awesome. We'll figure it out."

Lily moves back to the steps and waves goodbye. She'll be able to figure out what happened with those texts now that she's back in communication with Erica. Finally.

Someone has been sending hatemail on her friend's phone and Lily intends to find out who it was.

• • •

After seeing Erica, Lily's able to sleep through the night for once. Even Tyler's constant messages and pokes don't keep her awake.

When her eyes open, the morning light in her bedroom seems brighter than usual, more hopeful. She watches shadows from the trees wave over the ceiling until she doesn't want to lie in the crumpled sheets and nested blankets any longer.

She wriggles into workout clothes and heads downstairs. From the foyer, she can hear her parents in the kitchen. Their muted chatter seems more intense than usual, and she pauses in the hallway.

"I just don't like the thought of a freshman dating a senior," her dad says.

"I know, but what can we do? Lock her in her room or make her wear a chastity belt?"

Lily walks into the kitchen, where Mom and Dad sit over coffee. "I'm right here, you know." She goes to the fridge and pulls out a Gatorade. "Going for a run."

Her dad looks up. "Need company?"

He sometimes heads out with Lily on the trails when she's home, but this morning she's not feeling it. Besides, it's time to check in with Tyler – he'll wonder what she's up to. Plus, she needs to let him know about the lunch date with Erica.

"Next time, Dad." After a long swig of Gatorade Lily heads outside. The weather is warmer in New Jersey, and as she slaps her way onto the quiet, tree-lined street, sweat trickles down her back. It's nice to sleep late during vacation, but her body grows sluggish, a reaction to the loss of pool time. Already she's twitchy, filled with energy to burn off.

It feels good to push her body to the limit, to watch the houses pass by, smell fresh air instead of chlorine. Lily feels an ecstasy of endorphins, the athlete's natural buzz, as she continues beyond the boundaries of her neighborhood and heads out to the sports park near her house.

There are softball and soccer games going on. Some of the players laugh, others look grimly determined to play hard. On the sidelines, parents and siblings chat on phones or yell encouragement at the players. One red-faced woman shouts at the coach, and as Lily jogs past she hears, "Put her back in the game, ya frigging asshole! Where the hell d'ya think your damn salary comes from? That's right – my taxes!"

Lily speeds up to leave the angry mom behind. Perspiration trickles down her back, but it feels good – swimmers never get to sweat it out in the pool. By the time the soccer players fade in the distance, her crumpled t-shirt marked with the dumb phrase So That Happened! is soaked. Lily shuffles from one foot to the other. She doesn't want to lose the great momentum she's built up along the run. When she unlocks her phone, there's a long line of texts from Tyler.

Hey girl

Whassup

Lily

Where are u?

The final one is in capitals.

ANSWER ME NOW OR WE R DONE.

Her triumphant burn from the run fades instantly. Lily stops, pushes his contact button, and waits as his phone rings. An electronic voice picks up – Tyler never bothered to personalize his message.

With a long breath, Lily stretches her left Achilles. Her muscles and skin feel too tight, wound up to the point of snapping, and she feels like she might hurl. Her thumb ring flashes in a stray line of sunlight.

Hi! I'm here. Just went for a run. Sorry, bby – didn't mean to ignore you. Just felt so good to get out. Plus slept in with no morning practice, for once, felt really good, so I decided to get out there and hit the pavement for a few miles...

She stops vomiting words and hits Send.

The screen stays gray, a crystal ball without a future. Lily knows if she stands there any longer she'll lose it, so she drinks half her Gatorade bottle and heads back to the soccer fields. The mom who cursed out the coach has disappeared, maybe forced off the field. Lily keeps going, but the earlier ease of movement has disappeared.

By the time she makes it home she's completely soaked. Her hair is plastered to her scalp, and her shirt sticks to her. She longs for a shower but first checks for a response.

Nothing.

Ty, I am SO sorry, she thumbs onto the screen. *Forgive me? I'll make it better soon, promise.*

Lily adds a winking emoji, hits send, and strips for a shower.

When she climbs out, there's a text waiting. Lily's chest contracts as she opens it, but the message comes from Nolan's number.

This is Erica, remember? Still want to meet later? Lunch, maybe sushi? We haven't talked in forever.

After a quick reply to accept and set up a time with Erica, Lily wraps up in a towel and heads to her room to get dressed. As she steps into underwear, clips on a faded sports bra, and picks out a shirt, she sneaks several looks at the phone.

Nothing.

The bedroom is a whirlwind of discarded clothes and books. What would Yasmin say about the mess? Lily decides to clean up. She figures it'll make the time pass until Tyler returns her call or texts. Clothes, both dirty and clean, go into the laundry basket since she can't bother sorting or refolding them.

Mom peeks around the corner just as Lily puts the final book, Ready Player One, on the shelf. "Hey, you cleaned up!"

"You don't have to sound so surprised about it."

"No, I..." Mom sniffs and pokes at the laundry basket. "Please tell me you didn't just throw all the clothes in here. I washed those jeans, you know."

"But they were all creased and dusty and stuff. Gross." Lily's phone buzzes with an incoming alert, and she decides to use humility as a Get-Mom-Out-of Bedroom strategy so she can read the text. Please, please, please let it be Tyler. "No, you know what? You're right. I'll sort them out. Maybe I'll even iron if I get motivated."

Mom's eyebrows shoot up to her hairline, but she withdraws. Lily pushes the door shut with one socked foot as she checks her phone. It's a selfie from Staci, eyes crossed and tongue out. Next to her, Haddigan blows out her cheeks and distends her nostrils.

You guys are a shoe-in for the Senate. Got my vote in ten years. Lily sends her fake-happy, dumb-joke reply. She dumps out the contents of her laundry basket, but she can't remember what was clean. In the end she piles the clothes back in along with the wet towels from her recent shower and makes a plan to sneak them all into the washing machine when her mother isn't looking.

• • •

"The whole thing was weird." Lily scoops up a tuna roll with her chopsticks to dunk it in the wasabi-soy mix. "All these mean texts came from your number, and I couldn't get through. The last one was the worst. You told me I should die. Called me a bitch, too."

Erica looks up from her noodles and reaches for Lily's hand. "No way. Now you know it wasn't me. Right? Tell me you never thought I'd send you anything so awful. I'm so sorry you had to read that. You must have felt so alone."

Lily moves her chair so she can hug Erica. "Yeah, it was pretty bad. And of course we knew all along it wasn't you."

"We?" Erica sets her chopsticks on her plate, fussing with them until they're in a perfect 90-degree angle.

"Tyler and me. I. Tyler and I."

"Right, you and Tyler." Erica takes a drink of water from the bottle in her backpack. Lily waits as her friend digs into the front pocket, pulls out a small container of hand sanitizer, and rubs the stuff into her palms.

"So the anonymous douche bag said you should die? That's just so creepy. Can I see?"

"Yeah, sure." Lily pops another spicy tuna into her mouth before swiping the screen. Too late she remembers the anon number was blocked after Tyler's attempt at protecting her. "Damn it. The texts are gone, except for what I saved in Notes. I forgot Tyler blocked you. Well, not you. Whoever sent the nasty messages. You know, Hater or Waste of Space. We have to come up with a name for this anonymous person."

"Creep." Erica laughs, her sharp cheekbones pushing the purple, shadowed crescents under her eyes. "Let's just call him Creep."

"Or her."

"Right, or her."

"And you blocked me on your phone," Lily adds. "Did you realize that?"

"I did?" Erica frowns. "Nolan already returned it, so we can't check the history. Guess it doesn't matter though, since we can communicate through his number for now."

Lily stabs Erica's noodles with her chopstick. "You gonna eat that?" Erica pulls a face, which Lily ignores. Already her body demands more calories, and she slurps down her friend's leftover noodles. "Any idea who did it? Who sent the texts?"

"It's kinda hard to tell, since I never saw them," Erica replies. "You said they started out by calling you a bitch, right? And it sounds like they escalated from there."

Chewing the last of the noodles, Lily looks for a menu. "Green tea ice cream," she muses. "You ever try it?" Erica shakes her head, and Lily motions to the waitress. "We're gonna try it."

"You and your food."

"Don't even!" Lily knocks her elbow against Erica's. "Sometimes I can't believe you're a swimmer. Food is good. Food is the best."

"I can't..." Erica shakes her head, as though she's unwilling to finish her thought. "Anyway. Back to the texts. Do you have any ideas?"

"Honestly, I guess it could be anybody. Second-graders are hacking into companies these days."

"Yeah, true. Guess it will stay a mystery." Erica holds up a thick oblong phone, two evolutionary steps up from a Nokia. "My mom got me this burner thing so we can text. Nolan programmed it to go to his number while we wait for a new account. He says no one ever calls him, so it's okay."

Lily sits back and laughs at her. "Awesome machine, my friend. Wish I had one of those things. Catapults are cool too - plus there's this nifty invention called the wheel."

"Haha." Erica reaches out and grabs Lily's hand. "I missed you. God, school sucks so bad without you there. Remember Sonya? She's even nastier than usual. And Courtney! Oh. My. God."

"Really?" Lily's distracted from the measly dessert menu. "How about Toni? She was such a supreme witch when we were in …Oh. Wait."

Tyler's picture, the one she got of him after Nationals, flashes on her screen. Lily hides a sigh of relief, and she shoots Erica an apologetic glance. "So sorry. I have to take this call."

She turns in her seat so Erica won't overhear. "Hi." Tyler's voice is colder than a morning plunge into Prescot pool. "What, I text you ten times this morning, and all night, and all I get are three back from you? Did you meet an old boyfriend in New Jersey or something? Are we done now?" He pauses to draw in a breath. Lily can hear it shudder over the connection, and she opens her mouth to tell him No, he's the only one in her life. Of course he is.

Too late. Already he plunges back into his accusation. "Did you fuck him?"

Although he's not there, Lily feels her head rock back as though he's slapped her across the face. She stands up and walks to the alcove where the restrooms lurk in the back. The argument might be worse than she anticipated, and she doesn't want Erica to overhear. It seems shameful, the way Tyler talks. It's all her fault, though, since she never should have slept so heavily or worked out before getting back to him.

"Of course not," Lily pleads. "Tyler, please don't. Like I told you, I was out for a run. No swim practice this morning, and I just had to exercise…"

"Uh huh." His voice drips with suspicion and distrust.

She can't believe the direction the conversation has taken. "Please," Lily repeats. "I've put up with enough from that bad fever and all those hate-texts."

"I…" She can almost hear the gears whirling in his brain. "Don't put this on me. It's your fault. Okay? I wanted to go to New Jersey with you, but my dad said no. Said we had enough expenses with college right around the corner. And when I move there we won't see each other, so excuse me for wanting to spend as much time as possible with you now while we have the chance."

His voice has become breathy, and Lily feels the sharp flame of anger in her chest recede. "But I feel the same way!" She holds one palm out as though he stood right in front of her. For a moment she can picture it, how his eyes would half-close in characteristic derision. He likes to look down at me, she realizes. "Look, I'm just visiting my family, sneaking in as much practice as I can get. Oh, and reconnecting with Erica."

"Erica? The bitch who wrote you those texts? Are you kidding me right now?"

"But she didn't write them… look, can I take you out to Tribeck's when I get back? Tell you the whole story?"

She hears his sharp inhale. "Maybe."

"Maybe?"

"If you're good."

"Good!" Her heart leaps as his tone slides from anger to desire. "I'm always good."

"Is that so? Gonna hold you to your word. And maybe I have a present for you."

Lily grins, relief coursing through her heart. "Oh yeah? What is it?"

"You'll have to wait until you get back to find out."

She says goodbye and clicks off the phone. It's time to return to Erica.

At the sushi bar, workers in white shirts and caps slice octopus and salmon with quick, even strokes of their cleavers. Erica spins her stool, watching the fish being sliced. When Lily approaches, she stops herself with one fingertip on the bar. "Well, hello there Miss Thing. Care to tell me his name?"

The phone goes into her back pocket as Lily tries not to smile. "I don't know what you mean."

"Yeah, riiiiight."

The hell with it. "His name's Tyler," Lily admits.

"Cute, very cute. So, is this serious? Like a real relationship, not the thing you had with Nolan in first grade? When you wrote each other notes every day?"

Lily giggles. She's friends again with Erica, and she and Tyler have made up from the morning weirdness. He got her a gift. Life is good, even if her boyfriend soon has to move to another state for college.

"Yeah," she admits. "It's serious."

8.

The days are warm enough in Massachusetts for Prescot's outdoor pool to open. Lily and Tyler run there after late practice to rinse off the sweat from their dry land workouts. Tyler launches into a loose cannonball, long limbs and graceful muscles pulled towards his body, and plunges under the surface. She can see him curl and twist, a graceful merman. Lily follows down the ladder into the circle of his arms. She floats closer and leans her ear against the broad plain of his chest to hear the drum of his heart. The beat is always slow and strong, even when they're making out.

"Those 150 butterflies nearly killed me," he says into her hair. "Damn. Gotta schedule a PT appointment for my shoulder."

Lily trails water over his arm, silver liquid on brown flesh. "You should," she agrees. "Don't want to strain your rotator cuff before you hit summer meets and college."

"Yeah, just what I said. Are you deaf?" He pulls her close by her waist to nuzzle her neck. Lily hums and treads water lazily next to him. It's a golden moment, one she wants to hide in a locket or a beautiful little box with a golden key. If only she could keep this memory forever.

"Where's your ring?" he asks suddenly. The slim band is the present he hinted at over the phone, a promise ring with their names engraved inside.

Her finger is empty, naked. Lily surges out of his arms, flies up the ladder, and rushes over to her swim bag. She dumps the contents on the ground and breathes out when the ring Tyler gave her drops to the concrete perilously close to a drain.

"Don't lose it. You're so irresponsible sometimes." Tyler throws a towel at her and begins to dry off with quick, vigorous strokes.

The ring safely back on her finger, Lily towels off and pulls on sweats. "Gonna get changed?" she asks.

He shakes his head. It's warm enough now to eat on the campus. They can grab a sandwich and find a spot to sit. All the benches will be taken, but Lily doesn't care. She and Tyler can spread out a towel to eat while she looks over her history homework. If she studies for her Spanish essay test and manages to read a few chapters for American Lit, she won't have to keep Yasmin awake for too long after light's out.

• • •

They walk over to the grill for sandwiches, bags of chips, and drinks. He orders soda, and she buys unsweetened iced tea. A few girls say hi to Lily as she settles down on the grass and tries to get comfortable, but it's hard to ignore the wet stretch of Lycra against her butt. Next time, she promises herself, I'll change out of my suit before lunch.

Staci wanders by with two guys Lily doesn't recognize. Prescot is huge for a New England private boarding school, and she still encounters new people after two semesters. The three of them wave, and Staci tells Lily there's a dance coming up on the weekend. Message delivered, she heads off with the guys behind her like a couple of ducklings.

"I have to go visit Rosemont campus this weekend." Tyler bites into a meatball sub and stares into the distance.

Lily's hardly surprised. With college right around the corner, it's surprising he's had time to hang out with her at all. "Looking forward to it?"

His eyelids sweep down and up in a slow blink like an old-world movie star. "Whatever. I mean, I connected with some of the freshman class, you know? Don't want to go in like a loser, right? So I'll have some friends. Oh, and did I tell you Ben's my roommate?"

She's heard about Ben a few times, another swimmer on the Y team back in New Jersey. "Oh yeah? Awesome. So your social life is taken care of already."

"'Taken care of?'" Tyler gestures with his sub. "Jealous already?"

"No! What?" Lily puts down her chicken salad sandwich. Her stomach hurts, and sometimes she still loses her appetite. "I really don't care who you hang out with in college. You've got to meet people, like you said. Besides, I trust you."

He snorts but picks up his sub again and takes another huge bite. A few tense moments pass before he mumbles a few words around his food. It sounds like he just said, "You better."

Better what? Trust him? Of course she does – she just said it. Why has he turned her statement around and dumped it back in her lap?

Lily doesn't know what to do. Swimming is a series of split-second decisions, so she's used to working in the moment. Should I start my turn? Take a breath? Go for another dolphin kick? In the middle of each lap she analyzes real-time data and reacts instantly.

If she responds to him in the same tone he just used, the situation will go south. Arguments with Tyler are slippery things, filled with pitfalls she never expects. Somehow she always seems to come off badly. The whole situation back home when she was out running, for example, erupted out of nowhere. Lily still has no idea what she did wrong.

Since Lily doesn't know what her mistake is, how can she stop herself from doing it again in the future? Does he want her to be in touch with him 24/7?

Talking to her boyfriend is like a cliff dive into a deep lake. Lily doesn't understand him – he's a mystery. He's not an open page, like James.

However, Lily begins to see they need to have a talk about their relationship before he goes off to college.

She looks at him, wrists hung over bent knees like an American Eagle model. If she launches into a discussion about Rosemont and her girlfriend status, he'd blow up in her face. Lily senses the tension simmering under Tyler's skin. He would freeze her out and destroy their golden moment in the pool. In the end Tyler would make it all seem like her fault.

So it's easier to talk about New Jersey instead. "Never got the chance to tell you about Erica," she begins, but Tyler interrupts.

"See, this whole thing is messed up. This girl sent you nasty texts, made you all depressed, you can't tell me you weren't because I know you were, and now you're just friends again. Simple as that. It's like you're happy to trust her again. You know what happens to people like you? Bad shit, that's what. "

"But it wasn't her after all. I told you already."

"She could have lied." He emphasizes the final word with extra syllables: Lye-ee-duh. "Don't you see? You're clueless, no offence."

It's not the first time his 'no offence' means 'what I just said is really offensive, so just suck it up.' Tyler doesn't understand, and Lily scrambles for words to make him see the truth. "Erica's been my friend since first grade. I don't know what happened with the weird texts – we have to figure it all out. She uses a different phone now, anyway."

"Sure, since I blocked her from yours." Tyler holds up the end of his sub roll and throws it at one of the fat campus squirrels. "I just don't like the thought of you hanging out with her, but whatever. You gotta make your own mistakes. Don't blame me if it all gets fucked up and you get fucked over in the process."

The entire conversation has gone like a car sliding off a wet road, like a bad freestyle event, like an argument. What he's said bugs Lily, but she can't quite put her finger on it to call him out. Instead, she tries for another distraction. "I have to read Pale Horse, Pale Rider for Lit."

"Say what now?"

Lily laughs. "My book for Lit class." She fishes it out from her swim bag and waves it under Tyler's nose.

"You're gonna sit there and read while we're together? C'mon, that's lame. Throw away the book. Burn the book. Tear up the book."

Tyler reaches for the volume, and she snatches Pale Horse, Pale Rider from his outstretched fingers. "Cut it out!" Lily laughs. "I have to finish it tonight, and Yasmin's already mad at me from last night."

"Oh yeah, last night." He props his head on the book and bares those sharp, white teeth in an exaggerated grin. "Go ahead. I won't stop you."

But his hair, still damp from the pool, makes Pale Horse, Pale Rider's pages frill on the edges like romaine lettuce. Lily sucks her teeth and gives up after a few paragraphs.

"Good," Tyler purrs. "You're done. Now we can go get ice cream."

• • •

The room is dark when Lily sneaks back into the dorm. It's a relief to strip out of the wet suit and damp sweats and get into dry pajamas. Her gym clothes, as usual, flop onto the floor. I'll pick them up before practice, she promises.

Exhaustion makes her arms shake as Lily gets ready to catch up on homework. Her flashlight is under the pillow, the sheet a thin, cotton shell over her head. She feels like a fragile snail in the grass, as though she tries to escape a descending Doc Martin boot before it crushes her.

Lily flicks Pale Horse to the right page and starts to read. She reads a few pages before the phone vibrates: *Hey. Asleep?*

Homework, she texts back. *You wouldn't let me do it earlier, remember?*

His only response is *I'm bored. Entertain me.*

Lily knows he'll bug her until she throws him a bone, so she pulls up her pajama shirt with one fist to reveal her chest, smiles, and snaps a quick selfie. From under her sheet-cave Lily hears an aggressive pillow thump followed by an aggrieved turnover from Yasmin's bed. *Got to go – roomie's pissed.* She adds several x's and o's and gets back to her book.

When the work's finished, her eyelids are heavy and itchy with sleep. Already midnight has come and gone. The morning alarm will be dreadful, but Lily sets it anyway and lies down.

Sleep waves over her, silent and immediate. Her dreams are filled with worry and the threat of danger. Lily squeezes her eyes shut and drowns in the darkness.

• • •

The edges of the morning are already streaked pink and gold when the phone alarm blares in her ear. Lily drags on her last dry bathing suit, kicks the wet stuff from the night before under the bed, and tiptoes to the door. Yasmin is a motionless lump in the other bed.

Lily closes the door as quietly as she can on the peaceful sound of her roommate's soft snores and sneaks down the stairs. Outside the air is soft with dawn and pollen. She takes in great gulps of oxygen untainted with chlorine and reaches for her phone in the front of her bag.

Nothing. The phone is missing.

Lily curses, sets down her swim bag, and pulls out all her gear. She's got shampoo, goggles, swim cap, towels, extra clothes – but no phone. It must still be in her bed from the midnight conversations with Tyler, maybe under her pillow or tucked in the blankets. He likes her to leave the screen on Facetime, says he wants to watch her sleep.

If she runs back, she'll wake Yasmin and be late for practice. With a growl of disgust at her own forgetfulness, Lily slams the stuff back into the bag and jogs to practice. She ignores her empty stomach. As usual, power bars will just have to be her breakfast.

Staci's in the water when Lily walks into the pool, and Haddigan hangs on the wall to push stubborn strands of brown hair beneath her cap. Tyler is nowhere to be seen. The girls wave at Lily and tell her their practice is almost ready. Even though the coach still writes on his omnipresent clipboard, Lily knows the first line will be a 400 warm-up. There's no reason not to step in and get started.

Tyler will understand. People leave their phones behind all the time. Her thoughts dart like minnows, trying to figure out a covert way out of the pool and back to the dorm. Deep down, she knows the opposite is true – if she doesn't call him, he won't understand, and she'll have to spend days making up for it.

Staci would ask her where she's going if Lily sneaks off. Yasmin would wake up and be pissed. Robert would make her pay in push-ups.

Lily's stuck at the pool with no way of reaching Tyler.

The water slicks her thighs, an embrace from a cold lover. In the lane next to hers, Staci turns in a tight underwater flip and heads back down the pool. Her strokes chop up the surface for Lily and Haddigan. The laps are always rough for the first swimmer in the pool, and the three of them try to draft off the first swimmer.

By the time Lily nears the end of the warm-up, Robert's got their practice sheets on the kickboards. A few other team members join the group at the edge to check the practice.

"5 100's on 110?" Staci says in dismay. "Did I mention I have to leave early?"

"Did I mention I don't care? Get your butt back in the pool." Robert glares at his clipboard and marks a line item in red sharpie. Staci dunks her head underwater before she pushes the wall.

Practice proceeds as usual. Time speeds by when they swim 50's, yet slows to a glacial pace when they have to swim 300's. Lily's worked her way down most of the practice sheet when Tyler enters the pool area.

"I know he's your boyfriend," Haddigan mutters into Lily's ear, "but holy shit. He's like a Greek statue."

Robert's obviously about to launch into his 'Nice of you to show up' speech. Tyler doesn't look at Lily or the coach, before he climbs on the block, launches into the air, and hurtles through the water with powerful dolphin kicks. When he comes up, he starts his freestyle stroke.

Lily's jaw drops, and Staci gasps. "What the hell is he doing? He didn't even warm up yet! He's gonna to blow out his shoulder..."

"Hey!" Robert yells. "Hey!" When Tyler doesn't respond, the coach blasts his whistle several times. Staci claps her hands over her ears.

Tyler reaches the end and rests one broad palm on the edge of the pool. "Whaaaat?" It's like he wants to annoy the coach.

Robert runs to the end of the pool, squats next to Tyler's wet-otter head. The girls can't hear what they're saying to each other.

"Guess these laps won't swim themselves." Lily turns away, knowing if she watches any longer she'll go out of her mind. Is Tyler annoyed again because she didn't answer his morning texts? He knew she was going to practice. Maybe he's just sick of getting up early.

Still, she should have remembered her phone. It's all her fault.

Only her fierce concentration on the black line below her and the warning stripe for the turn keep Lily's mind off Tyler and his obvious anger. Wind up, shoot forward. Reach your limit, and push past it. Quick break of air. Lily sucks in chlorine-tinged oxygen, feels the endorphins flood her brain and body as she breaks the laws of gravity and physics.

Robert's by the end as she finishes her laps, tapping the red pen on his chin. She shields her eyes to look up at his silhouette against the overhead lights. "Your last lap didn't suck, Batista," he comments. "Keep this up and you just might become a real swimmer."

• • •

"I texted you all night." Tyler's voice is low. He doesn't look at Lily where she sits next to him on a campus bench. No one's out this early besides swimmers and a few hell-bent track stars. "You didn't answer. So I thought you'd text me before practice. Obviously I was wrong."

It explains the buzz she heard all night. "I left my phone in my room this morning. There was no time to run back for it or I'd have been late to practice, you know? And last night I was asleep. I finished the book you wouldn't let me read yesterday and passed out. Plus Yasmin isn't too thrilled about our midnight conversations." Lily waves away the cronut he holds out. She's eaten too many of the fat-and-sugar-laden sweets, and it's time to stick to egg whites and protein for a while.

"Why should I care what she thinks? She's nothing to me. Should be nothing to you, too. And how dumb is that to leave your phone behind? What, are you an idiot? How did you even get into this school in the first place?"

"Yasmin's my roommate. I have to care what she thinks. It's unfair to just expect her to put up with my shit. Bad enough my clothes are all over the floor, not to mention the wet swim stuff and my early hours." Lily finishes her egg sandwich and tosses the crust to one of Prescot's enormous squirrels. It catches the food, darts up a tree, and disappears among young leaves and arrows of sunshine.

The golden morning light touches Tyler's scowl, and Lily tries again. "Look, you're about to graduate. You've got everything you wanted – a secure spot on a great swim team and a scholarship. I've still gotta make it for three more years."

"See, this is my point. We don't even have a summer together." Tyler wads up the grease-stained bag and throws it into a nearby trashcan with a clang. "I wanna max out each minute, or whatever. But if you don't want to, hey. Just tell me. I'm out, no problem."

Lily stops him with one hand on his arm and feels the muscles tense under the thin fabric of his shirt. "Of course I want to be with you all the time! But it doesn't mean I can skip homework or get bad grades. We – we just have to find a balance?" Her anxiety turns it into a question.

"You have to. I've gotta do nothing but slide through graduation." Lily's about to argue, but he pulls her close with one palm at the small of her back and bends over her mouth with parted lips.

His breath is sweet with sugar, edged with coffee and warm male scent. "Just a joke," he mutters between kisses. "Don't you see? You'll lose me if you don't wake up and get a sense of humor. Anyway." Kisses and more kisses in between each whisper, down her jaw to the sensitive flesh on her neck. "Make sure you text me back tonight when I text you." The whisper is intense, right in Lily's ear.

"But if I'm already asleep…"

"Figure it out." One last biting, sucking kiss, and Tyler pulls back to touch the side of her neck with a satisfied grin. "Nice. You're marked. Now everyone knows you're mine."

• • •

Through the rest of the day, Lily feels as though she swims a mile-long pool lane. There's no time for rest and a gulp of oxygen, no wall for a turn to give her aching body a burst of speed. The day will be scheduled with nothing but chores, school, and practice. Lily wades through classes and takes time for a quick lunch with Staci and Haddigan. When school is done, Lily bolts to the library to meet with a tutor before she heads to the pool. Each time she checks her phone she gasps at the time and how quickly the day slides past.

Practice is a rush of dry land in the same clothes she stuffed into her bag in the morning. "You're marked," a voice says in her ear, and Lily whimpers before her head jerks up. She's fallen asleep against the shower wall. Under the pulse of hot water she misses Erica so fiercely it makes her stomach ache.

When she's done, Lily runs out of the gym and eats a few power bars on her way back to the dorm. She has to get back and clean up the room so Yasmin won't be mad.

As Lily runs up the stairs, she hears lowered voices from her doorway. "I've tried to get along with her," Yasmin says. "I really have. But..."

The other person shushes her as Lily walks into the double room with its low ceiling and blue curtains framing the tiny, dormer window. Ms. Haskins, the teacher who lives downstairs with her partner and two adopted kids, leans against the beige painted wall. "Hello, Lily," she says. "We were just talking about you."

The frustration of trying to catch up, not enough sleep, and Tyler's possessive attitude spills over. "Nice," Lily spits out. "Talking about me? Behind my back? What the hell? Whatever Yasmin accused me of isn't true. I've worked my butt off to catch up on grades, and now I'll get punished for it."

Yasmin starts to speak, but Ms. Haskins interrupts. "No one will be punished. However, it does seem the school has paired you with the wrong roommate, and we accept the blame. You have to understand Yasmin's concern – grades are very important to her and to her family..."

Lily slings her filthy workout bag on the rumpled bed, plops onto the mattress, and pulls one knee into her chest. "They're important to me too."

"Could I just explain for a second?" Yasmin spreads out her arms. "I know you've had to catch up on your work, Lily, but when you stay up late it keeps me awake. If I can't sleep I won't do well on exams. I just – it makes me panic just to think about it." The girl's chest rises and falls rapidly. Either Yasmin's a great actress or she's genuinely upset. "Not to mention the mess on the floor and the desk, chairs heaped with dirty clothes, and the smell of chlorine. It makes me sick."

With a great effort, Lily manages not to shout, "You make me sick!" It would get them nowhere. Control, she thinks. Instead she ignores Yasmin and looks at Ms. Haskins. "So what happens now?"

"Actually, we're in luck." The dorm advisor stands and adjusts her Oxford shirt so it sits neatly over slim stomach and wiry arms. "I've got an empty room on this floor, so Yasmin can move out tonight. You'll have this double all to yourself."

Lily looks around. The chipped, beige walls are already bare. "Did you start the process already? All your stuff's already gone, right?"

"Look." There's a pleading note in Yasmin's voice. "You don't understand. My father gets furious when I don't get perfect grades. My grades slipped last week, and he … well. I have to do this. There's no other choice."

"Can you give us a minute?" Lily asks Ms. Hankins. The woman frowns, tells Yasmin to be quick, and slips out of the room.

When the door closes, Lily explodes. "Really, Yasmin? Do you think you could have talked to me first? You have no idea how terrible this term has been."

"No, I do! First you were sick, and then you got involved with Tyler..."

"Wait, what?" Lily's confused. "He's the only good thing that's happened to me lately."

Yasmin looks at her for a second and closes her mouth. "Okay. It's your business, and this is all beside the point. Uh, not to make it all about me, but like I said, my dad pitches a fit at the least thing. I'm not even talking about straight A's. If I don't get every single question on every test right, he takes it out on me, on my brothers, on my mom as well."

Lily slumps onto the bed, unable to think of a response. Yasmin's brown eyes seem about to overflow with tears.

"There's no other option," the girl says softly. She turns away to swipe her face in one sleeve of her sweatshirt and pick up the last of her books.

"Maybe you need to talk to, I don't know, a counselor about what he puts your family through." Lily's words slip out.

"Really? You're the last person who should give me advice. Start with yourself before you tell me to look for help." Yasmin's eyes narrow as she spits out the words.

Before Lily can ask what she means Yasmin leaves the room and closes the door with a firm click.

9.

With Yasmin gone Lily has the largest room in the dorm and the most flexible schedule. She can stay up until midnight if she wants with no one to yell at her or be disappointed. "I'm so jealous!" Staci declares from the next shower stall as they stand under the stream of scalding water and scrub chlorine out of their hair. "I mean, my roomie is understanding, you know?" she adds. "But no one's happy about the 5 am alarm."

"Plus they just don't get it." Haddigan pops her head in around the tiled wall to talk. "They're all 'Just sleep in for once,' and I'm all 'No way. Not an option.'"

Suds sluice over Lily's body as she yells back, "Exactly!"

But between the Yasmin debacle and texting Tyler a thousand times a day, Lily's swim times have gotten slower. She wants to carve at least two seconds off her 50 freestyle, and instead the numbers keep inching over the 25-second mark.

Robert tells Lily she has to break down her stroke for a longer, less choppy reach in the water. The thought is terrifying, since it will mean slower times for months, maybe a year. Better now than later, he says, but she can't force herself to try it out. Lily's limbs seem to be filled with sand lately. Swimming, once a joyful act of freedom, has become a wrestling match with herself.

The teachers are piling on the homework. Exams and projects breed like rabbits as the weather gets warmer. Maybe the thought of Tyler going to Rosemont makes her sad, less likely to push herself. His graduation hurtles towards them, with only a few days before until his departure for college in early June. Tyler plans to spend the summer training with his new team.

Lily leaves the shower, towels off quickly, and joins her friends at the full-length mirror. She twists her hair into a thick braid, adds athletic wrap to keep stray ends out of her face. "How was your practice?" she asks Haddigan.

The girl brushes mascara on her sandy lashes with quick, expert strokes. "Not bad. Feel like I need a new dry land circuit though, you know?"

"Right?" Lily abandons her makeup and pulls on her sweatshirt. "Seems like I'm caught in a rut."

"Maybe over the summer we can meet up and exercise for real, run a few 5K's or whatever." Haddigan caps the mascara with a flourish.

"I heard beach runs give you a great workout," Lily says.

Staci wedges herself between them. "I want in on that. We can text each other every day, right? Facetime and stuff to keep on track together?"

They head out of the gym, filled with ideas for the summer. Lily feels a flash of hope. A different routine might propel her back into the top ranked times, and maybe she won't have to start over on her stroke.

Tyler's voice breaks into their plans. Lily looks up and sees him, one arm raised to beckon her over.

Haddigan bumps Lily with her hip. "Looks like it's time for me and Staci to head out."

Lily tries to protest it's not necessary and they can all walk to breakfast together, but her friends have already crossed Keene Road. By the time Tyler catches up with her, Staci and Haddigan have disappeared among the crowd of students who head over to pick up breakfast before class.

"Hey, you," she starts.

His smile has disappeared. "Why didn't you wait for me?"

"What?" She shrugs. "I didn't – I mean, I was just talking to Staci and Haddy about summer plans. You know, workouts and stuff…"

"I thought I was your summer plans."

Even as he glowers at her, Lily thinks how handsome he is, jaw mulish with temper and black eyebrows low over his eyes. Still, he can't call her out for talking to her friends. "You'll be in college!" she protests. "Besides, we were talking about 5K's, not bars or clubs."

"Forget it," he blasts. "Sorry I ever brought it up. You have fun with

those 5K's and your friends or whatever while I work my ass off in college."
He sprints between two cars on the avenue, making one driver break with
a squeal and lean on the horn.

Lily stares after him, her mouth open. What the hell was that all about?

• • •

Hey bby I'm so sorry I didn't mean to make you mad
Please Tyler just answer me
Just let me apologize
There are two days left together and you've made me sad. Pls call or
text me
Don't shut me out like this Ty please
Please bby call me. You weren't at our windowsill at lunch and I miss u

• • •

The last part of physics class might as well be in Ancient Sumerian.
Lily's words to Tyler float on the tiny screen, hopeful bait in an empty sea.
She knows if she stops sending texts one after the other Tyler will make
her pay by ignoring her for days. That idea is unthinkable, like falling into
a hole in the space-time continuum.

When the class ends, Lily rushes out of the room to see if she
can catch Tyler as he comes out of his World Lit course, but the hall is
deserted except for a guy and girl making out on a wooden bench. Lily
stops, unsure what to do. She's just about to head back downstairs when
the girl looks up and sees her. "Looking for Ty?" she asks.

"Yeah," Lily admits.

The guy kisses the girl's neck, but she seems to ignore him and smiles
at Lily. "The seniors have a graduation meeting. Bet he's there."

The two start to lick each other's tonsils again, and Lily turns away. It
she can just find Tyler, the whole fight will blow over.

It's not like she even knows what she's done to him, anyway.

You in a meeting? she texts. *It's a big campus! Just tell me where you*
are and I'll bring you French fries.

There's a minute before she gets a response: *French fries would be good.*

She blows out a long breath. *Where are u?*

Just come downstairs.

Lily stashes her phone and clatters down the steps. Tyler waits for her on the ground floor, his backpack hitched off one shoulder, dark sunglasses on. "What took you so long?"

She nearly misses a step. "Uh, can you tell me what I did to get you so mad?" He folds his arms, doesn't respond. "So, what, it's a kind of weird guessing game now? You're gonna jet off to college soon and leave me here at Prescot. Is this how you want to spend our time together?"

Tyler shrugs. "If you say so. You were the one who took off with your friends after practice, though."

The sheer absurdity of the accusation nearly makes Lily laugh. "You're mad because I headed out of the gym with Staci and Haddigan? Listen, you're the one who gets me. Who understands me on every level. Who else knows about my sport and my state, who sees the real me? The one no one else can even understand?"

She leans forward as she talks, willing the beautiful boy in front of her to listen and understand. He's incredibly important to her, and he should know it before he heads off to college, before it's too late.

But his eyes are hard and won't let her in. "You failed my test," Tyler says. Without another word, he walks out of the building into the soft green of Prescot's campus.

• • •

Lily studies for her physics exam, an essay the students will have to write together in class. She scrawls quotes from their text sources and her own notes on the back of cards, contributions she can add to the discussion of light waves and velocity. Since it's a group project, the essay could go in any of several different ways. Lily will have to prep for each possibility.

Her desk sits near the dormer window with a lamp on one side. She pictures what it must look like from below, if a late-night creep on campus looked up at the desk and saw her writing in the dim glow of the desk light.

She finishes another card and sits back in the chair with a sigh. A glance at her phone shows her zero texts.

Does this mean she and Tyler done? The mere thought gives her a warm rush followed by absolute panic. Who will she talk to when he's gone? Where will she sit for lunch and dinner? Who'll share a bag of forbidden pastries with her after practice?

Just thinking about u, she writes.

Her stomach eases when she sees the responding three dots come up. *Thought you had to work on your exams,* he answers.

I do, but I can still think about u. About us. At least - is there still us?

A few seconds pass, and Lily wonders if she's pressed too much. His text, when it pops up, is almost cheerful: *U r so dumb. Of course there's still us. U got my ring remember?*

Apparently he hasn't finished. *We can have guests at Rosemont in a couple weeks. When u r done school, I dunno. Come and see the campus. Hit a few parties. Whatever, I don't care. If u feel like it.*

The invitation is a long message for Tyler, and Lily's heart swells. She actually feels the organ press behind her ribs. Still, she doesn't want to go overboard with enthusiasm and scare Tyler off. *Yeah, sounds good,* she writes. *Let's forget all the weirdness from today and make up for it tomorrow. OK?*

Yeah. She waits, but he seems to be done.

Lily scrolls back to reread the conversation. After all the angst of their argument, his acceptance and implied approval makes her smile among the books and papers on the physics of light waves.

One phrase from their conversation catches her eye: 'hit a few parties.' Has he already met other students? Team members? Girls? Lily knows she won't be able to concentrate until she stalks his accounts. Minimizing the physics information, she brings up Twitter and Instagram. Tyler has created profiles there, complete with pictures of his swimming career and a few selfies.

He's already got several hundred followers on Twitter, and the number of Instagram followers approaches a thousand. Lily isn't one of them.

She scrolls through the posts and sees one from a girl with a long ponytail called Bree wearing a Rosemont sweatshirt and waving at the camera. *Hey Ty!* is written under the picture. *Thanks for following back! Can't wait to meet up in a few days!*

Lily pushes the laptop back and presses her fingertips into her eye sockets as she considers what a stupid decision it was to look at his profiles. Of course, she could just call him and ask who Bree is, but would it start another cold war with Tyler? She can't stand another shut-out.

Instead she forces herself to finish her physics note cards, look over the material for Lit class again, and write a sample outline for her calc exam (also an essay.) Since Yasmin no longer lives in the room, Lily shoves the books to one side, grabs a baggie with her stuff, and heads to the communal bathroom to scrub her face and brush her teeth. A few other late-nighters stare into the mirrors with bleary eyes. Lily flaps a tired hand at their reflections.

Ms. Hankins pops her head around the door. "You're late, girls. Finish up and get into bed before I write you all up for breaking the lights-out rule. Lily, you're still in street clothes. Go and get ready for bed this instant."

"Sorry," Lily mutters and dries her face. She scurries back to her room, yanks off her t-shirt, and pulls off undies, jeans, and socks with one violent motion, leaving the stack of garments in the middle of the floor. Why did the body disappear, Mulder? I'm not saying it was aliens, but it was aliens.

She shakes her head. Yasmin's gone. Messy piles of clothes no longer matter. Lily can trash the entire room if she wants.

Once the lights across the campus wink out like fireflies in the dark window. Lily grabs her phone, plugs it into the charger by the bed, and gets under the messy covers. In bed, she texts a Hi, a heart, a kiss. A moment later, Tyler's Facetime call rings through. "Tired?" he asks with a yawn.

"Yeah. You are too, obviously."

"Yeah." They look at each other onscreen for a minute before he closes his eyes. "Don't have too many nightmares."

"Okay." Even though she's exhausted, Lily wants to ask him a few questions. Why did he friend the Bree chick? What does 'can't wait to meet up' mean? Will they survive the long-distance?

"'S pretty cool," Tyler slurs.

"What? What is?"

"Well, you know. Even though I'm gonna be far away, we're gonna fall asleep together like this every night."

"Oh." Lily feels her heart melt again, and she smiles at the screen. "Yeah, we can."

"Yup, until it's official and we don't need Facetime anymore. Just be together."

"What's official?" she whispers.

"C'mon, you big dummy." Tyler waggles his third finger at her. "Til I can put a ring on it. A real one."

"Oh." Lily swipes her hand over his face on the screen, a soft gesture. "Can't wait."

"Of course you can't." He holds out the phone and shows her his shirtless chest. "Betcha can't handle all this."

Lily laughs. "Get over yourself." Her blood races, and she can't hold back a giggle as he lies back down and gets comfortable. Take that, Bree, Lily thinks.

"I can always see you. All the time. You're never alone." Tyler whisper fades into a soft snore.

Wired to the wall by the phone in her hand, Lily closes her eyes and dives into oblivion.

10.

Exams don't start until after lunch, so Lily takes a few minutes to hang with Staci poolside. One lone swimmer is left in the water after practice, a junior working on his turn. Robert squats at the far end and glares at the kid's shark shadow underwater. When the boy breaks at the end and hangs on the cement lip, Lily can hear his gasps for air across the huge enclosure. The coach gives a few instructions in a low voice, and the swimmer's hair flings out silver teardrops as he nods.

There are other sounds in the pool – the usual squeaks from the equipment next door, muffled shouts from the ice-hockey rink, the mournful whistle of an exasperated trainer. They're punctuated by wet slaps of feet on the floor: Haddigan, wrapped in a towel, approaches Lily and Staci with a broad grin on her freckled face. She sinks onto the end of the bench and twists her towel into a cone so she can screw it into her ear. "This is awesome," she comments. "Don't have to rush off to Advanced Calc in my wet suit. We can even go get breakfast! Like real food, not just bagel bites in a bag."

"Bagel bites are the ultimate supreme," Staci says. "Hey Lily, ya missing Tyler yet?"

"Oh." Lily considers. Tyler's at Rosemont already, since the swim team has to spend the summer there. "Yeah, of course, but I'm happy for him as well. You know? He got such a great scholarship, and the Rosemont team is amazing. Well, so I hear, anyway."

It's what they all want, the shining star of college acceptance with an athletic letter and admission into a good sports program. Tyler has accomplished what Lily dreams about for her future. Each sports activity she does, every volunteer program the team goes to – they're all steps on the ladder to make it into college and, for a few talented athletes, the Olympics.

Staci shakes out her towel, grimaces, and lets it fall on the wet floor. "Ugh. Time for laundry. How's he doing, anyway?"

The waves break against the edge of the pool as Robert stands and his swimmer launches into another succession of swim turns. "Busy," Lily says. "I mean he has to get settled in, meet the team, a bunch of college start-up stuff." She doesn't add that he hasn't contacted her yet.

She's sent out her hourly updates: *Now I'm in physics, about to head out of physics to Lit, gonna go grab a turkey wrap, time for history, getting ready for practice...* It's become a habit to detail each movement she makes with a text.

Tyler knows her schedule, and if she doesn't follow up as soon as a class ends, he'll get angry. Her stomach churns when she recalls just how angry he can get. Tyler is a complicated riddle with a constantly changing answer. Or, more likely, he's a maze with walls that shift as she tries to follow her way to the end.

"Paperwork," Haddigan supplies. "Got to be tons of paperwork when you first get on campus. And don't they start class early?"

"Oh yeah," Staci chimes in. "I bet there's a ton of stuff you have to handle as an incoming freshman athlete."

Lily feels a rush of affection for both of them. Staci and Haddigan are golden girls who will sail through life with serene flair. Haddigan's mom invented a special keyboard for physically challenged students, and Staci was born into a family of wine barons. They act like anyone else at Prescot, though – friendly and supportive.

Of course, they have their own hidden problems. Haddigan never sees her parents because her mom travels ten months out of the year on speaking tours or delivers TED talks. Staci never talks about the years her father spent as a state senator and was implicated in a junk bond scandal. Even with all of that weird history, they steal shampoo in the locker room and drive Robert crazy by begging for early release from practice, just like everyone else.

"Want to get food and cram over breakfast? Get crumbs all over our laptops?"

"Ew." Lily laughs and chucks her towel at Staci's head. "Sounds vile and repulsive – of course I'm in."

• • •

The campus is filled with students, normal for any sunny day at Prescot. Most of the kids recline on towels or blankets. A couple of lucky students hog the last bench space. Lily, Haddigan, and Staci dump their swim bags on a damp pool towel, and Staci rips off her t-shirt to reveal a bikini top. "What?" she says when Lily pretends to choke with horror. "I came prepared. Jealous much?"

"Go die," Haddigan replies without rancor. "No one forwarded the bikini memo."

Lily snorts and gets out her tablet. "Anyone start on the Flannery O'Connor final?"

"Yeah, me." The voice is masculine, comes from a few towels over. Lily looks up. James lies on his stomachs as he flips through a thick textbook. "We've got the test this afternoon. You?"

"Right after lunch." She scowls at the screen and flips through the pages. "I just don't get it, though. Who would let their daughter go off with a stranger? And give him their car, too? Especially if she's deaf!"

James gets up, steps over a few of his friends, and plunks down next to her. "I've read the story. There's all kinds of good stuff in it, about hearts and souls and how to be more than the sum of your parts."

"Yeah." Lily concentrates on the last few pages of The Life You Save May Be Your Own. "The guy, Shiftlet, says you can pull a man's heart out of his chest and dissect it, and you still won't know any more about him. I mean, obviously! What do you expect, to read "I'm an asshole" engraved on my left ventricle?"

The students around them snicker, but James edges closer. "Exactly," he says. "Everyone's a mystery. There's no way anyone can tell if you're good, or, you know, evil. Just by looking, I mean. Even if I carved your heart out of your chest."

"But, still. You can tell what someone's like by the way they act. If you're a good person, you'll do nice things. Volunteer in a charity or help your friends."

"Like James is doing right now," Staci laughs. She nudges Lily with one toe and leans back on her elbows to squint at the sun.

"But maybe not." He leans forward, eyes intense with sincerity. "Maybe someone seems to be a good person, but underneath they're not. It happens all the time – politicians get caught in affairs, the nice neighbor turns out to have a few bodies buried in the backyard. Interesting, don't you think? Everyone has so many more levels than you see on the surface."

"Jesus." Lily feels winded by the thought. It's a revelation, the thought that she's an enigma to everyone else - just as Tyler is to her. She pats the towel for a pencil and sits up to write furiously on the receipt for bagel bites. "You just gave me an idea for the essay today. Damn, James, I owe you."

"Lucky. I still need a topic," Staci says idly. She plops a rolled-up sweatshirt over her eyes.

"Don't suppose you'd let me take you out as a reward? Just as a friend?" James asks. Lily glances over the rim of her sunglasses. The smile on his face doesn't quite reach his eyes. "No, don't answer. I know you're all taken and stuff." He emphasizes the word 'taken' with jazz hands. "Sorry I asked."

Lily smiles, tells him it's fine. She doesn't want to make a big deal of it. She and James never had much between them – a few kisses, one semi-intense make-out session in the Biotech section of the library. He seems to cheer up, digs in his bag for chips, and hands them around to the clusters of studying students on towels. Swimmers aren't the only athletes who are constantly famished.

By the time they've finished the chips, the four of them have to run to their first exams. Lily feels sweat run down her back as she heads into the room. Haddigan's in the class with her, so Staci and James yell good luck and head to their own exam.

She's ready to go, extra pens on one side and thick pad of paper open to the first page, when the phone vibrates. Lily looks around, but the other students check a few last-minute notes or peer at their laptops.

Wht up 2 pops up on her phone.

Just about to take Lit exam, Lily writes back. *How are r you? Can't wait to hear all the stories! Have to take an exam right now tho.*

Wate wut I wnna tlk

Lily feels a thread of panic in her gut. From his spelling she gets the idea Tyler's been drinking. Maybe there's a party on-campus or he's snuck a few Natty Ices into his room. However, Lily can't worry about it. The professor breezes in and prepares to start the 90-minute clock on their essays.

Bye bby I love you, she dashes off and powers down her phone. He's got to understand her grades are important. After all, the process of graduation and college selection still lies ahead of her.

Tyler's text is a distraction, but luckily the ideas she and James talked about on the campus yield a strong outline for her essay. The quotes she researched earlier fit into the idea of the mystery in other people's hearts, and Lily writes easily with only a few glances at the notes she brought. Next to her Kyrie, a girl from a nearby town in Massachusetts, groans and stabs the Delete button on her laptop. Lily gives her a sympathetic grimace and returns to her own work.

Am Lit isn't her favorite subject by a long shot, but Lily's outline (prepped over several nights while she waited for Tyler's call) makes the test seamless. She finishes ten minutes early, enough time to turn in her paper and check her phone.

Lily's heart sinks. One text floats on the screen. *How u gonna get out of this Lily how long will u work 4 it bout to find out.*

Her hands shake as she responds. *So sorry, Tyler. I had to take my test. Couldn't just blo it off – it's the final.* She sends the text, misspelled word and all.

There's no response.

• • •

111

Once exams are done, Lily rushes to her dorm room and tries to call Tyler. He's actually recorded a voicemail greeting: his voice screams, "What?" followed by a blast of loud music. After the beep Lily gabbles long strings of pathetic words. She's sorry, so sorry, she had to take a test, there was no way to text in class…

Another heartless beep cuts her off. Lily forces herself to put down the phone and turn her attention to the piles of clothes on the floor. She heaps them into a large dirty pile and a tiny clean one. Of course she's missed the weekly laundry run, but the dorm stocks several clunky machines downstairs. Lily sorts the clothes, grabs a handful of quarters, and hauls her nasty sweats to the basement.

When she gets back, Tyler still hasn't responded. Lily sends him X's and O's and a smiling selfie.

The clean clothes go in drawers, ready to be stashed in her suitcase. With the floor cleared, Lily can see how dirty the room is. There's a dark stain in one corner of the rug, and papers litter the place. Her desk is a stew of books. The bed looks like a hurricane swept through earlier. T-shirts and bras poke out from the drawers of her dresser as though they're waving a cheerful hello.

Lily stares at the unresponsive screen of her phone, plugs it in, and sends a few more messages. Tyler had asked how long would she work for it. She could just let it go…

But the thought is impossible. His anger would boil over, and they'd be done. No more late nights on Facetime, no voice in her ear as they fall asleep together. It's not an option.

Please, bby, just talk to me.

Lily presses Send and goes to get her laundry. If I walk down the steps and don't see anyone I know, she thinks, there'll be a text when I get back. She's regressed to the seventh-grade version of herself, when she believed magic spells were the only way to get a guy to notice her.

She makes it down without running into anyone, loads up the dryer, and runs back up. Just as she opens her door, Yasmin pops out of the bathroom in a silk robe. "Hey there," she says, tapping one fingernail on the door.

Lily mutters Hello and slams the door. Just as she thought, there's no response on her phone. For a moment she hates Yasmin. Even though it's illogical, she feels the interaction has ruined her mojo so Tyler won't text her back.

Old papers go into the trash. Lily wipes up the stain on the floor with a torn sweatshirt and throws it away on top of the discarded tests and essays. Maybe her mom will bring spray bleach next week when it's time to move out for the summer. With extra cleaning supplies she can…

"Hell with this." Lily checks again, her stomach in a knot. She ejects a dry sob when there's no response.

The room is clean, and the clothes will take half an hour to dry downstairs. There's nothing else to do but wait, unless she checks in on his Instagram and Twitter. Once the idea sprouts, Lily can't rest until she brings up the apps and has a look.

Tyler has a long list of new followers, the majority female. *Hi cutie!* one girl called Mia Sofia writes. *Wish all freshmen looked like you!*

Even though she knows she's being stupid, Lily scrolls through the other comments. There's one post buried among all the girls, a brief check-in from a sports bar. *Out with the team,* Tyler writes. He doesn't specify any names.

Twitter yields the same results. Lily recognizes a few names: Ben, his roommate, plus a couple of the guys Tyler trained with in New Jersey.

Lily closes out of social media hell and glances at her phone wallpaper, a quick shot of her and Tyler together at Nationals. She catches her lip between her teeth at the sight of her smile and his wide grin. They look so happy and in the moment.

She's about to turn off the phone and go check on her laundry, when she sees the time. It's already half-past, which means swim practice is nearly over. Lily gasps, throws down her phone, and pulls off her clothes in a pile on the clean floor. Her breath whistles as she yanks on her swimsuit, drags on her last pair of sweats, and runs for the door.

When she reaches the ground floor, Lily remembers the laundry. It's a house offense to leave stuff in the dryer for too long, but she'll just have to chance it.

Her ponytail whips her neck as she runs across campus and Keene road to the gym. It feels as though every slow walker is out for a leisurely stroll, and several times she has to push her way around teachers and students with a quick apology.

When she slams into the gym, Robert is cleaning up the practice sheets. Lily runs up to him and launches into a long explanation. "So sorry," she says. "I'm so sorry, coach."

"Hi there!" Haddigan pops out of the pool, and Staci hands her a towel. "Where were you, slacker?"

"I'm so sorry," Lily repeats. She feels like she has apologized all day. "Got caught up with exams, and had to meet with an advisor…" It feels like an electric shot to her intestines when she realizes she's just lied to her friends and her coach. "Plus my room was super messy," she mumbles.

"It's okay, these things happen, take a breath. You don't need to be sorry." Robert claps her on the shoulder. His grin fades as he adds, "Just remember there's a competitor out there who made it to both practices today. Now hit the gym, and give me double the effort."

"Yeah, okay." Lily sucks in air and limps over to the weight room.

• • •

Ms. Haskins waits for her when Lily returns from the gym. Her gut rolls, maybe with hunger or nerves, as the dorm adviser shows her the pile of clean, crumpled clothes balled up on top of the dryer. "I know this time of year is hectic," the woman says, "but you still need to consider the other girls. Communal life is difficult enough without all this mess."

"I'm sorry." More apologies.

Ms. Haskins folds her arms and watches as Lily picks up the clothes, carries them up to her room, and dumps them on the floor next to the garments she left before her rush to the gym. The static holds the clump together before it subsides under its own weight and settles in a gray and maroon heap. She might as well have never bothered to tidy the place.

Ignoring her belly, Lily picks up her phone. Tyler still hasn't responded, but there's a friend request from a guy called Ben. She's about to delete it when she sees his residence is listed as Rosemont. Ben – the name's familiar.

Lily plops onto her crumpled sheets and accepts his request. An instant later a message pops into her inbox on Facebook: *What's up hey Tyler says you need 2 keep texting if u want him 2 talk 2 u just thought u should no.*

Hi, she sends back. *Uh, who are u?*

Oh, yeah. Ben. Tyler's roommate. Sorry.

Lily nods. No wonder the name is familiar. *Tyler talked to you about me?*

The dots swirl on the inbox. *Yea. Says ur dun unless u text him about a million x 2nite. Best delete this, jus sayin.*

OK, she writes. *THX.*

She's starving, she has to study for the next set of exams, and she has to pick up the crumpled clothes off her floor. First, though, she needs to get started on those texts.

Lily sends off a few messages of hearts and a description of her workout. She tells Tyler how her room is neat now. *Pictures to follow!* she adds. It buys her a few minutes to pull out her books and set up for a study session. There are power bars in her desk – they'll just have to do as dinner.

James has emailed her his notes for their history exam. Lily owes him big-time, but she can't even think about it now. Instead she sends him a quick thank-you, pings Tyler a few more heart emojis, and settles into writing her outline for her exam. The power bar wrapper splinters under her fingers, a slab of protein rolled in cocoa and peanuts. Promising herself cheeseburgers and fries later, Lily spends the next hour reading for five-minute intervals and sending frantic messages to Tyler in between.

When she finishes her history coursework, Lily realizes she's going to have to run to the grill and pick up a jar of Nutella or boxes of Cheez-Its.

Her stomach thunders with hunger. She picks up her phone, steps over the clothes heaped like a zit on the floor, and heads downstairs. *Please forgive me,* she texts as she walks. *Please, Tyler. I never meant to hurt you. Just had to do schoolwork. You get that, right?*

The doors to the campus swing outward with a loud screech that makes Lily grit her teeth. June has brought longer days to Massachusetts, and the sun paints the sky with blood as it sinks beneath a bank of clouds.

Lily's phone vibrates. *It's me again,* Ben's Facebook message reads. *T says u doin ok. Nother 2 days and you'll B off the hook.*

An older guy walks by her on the sidewalk, stoops to pick up a paper coffee cup from the path, and throws it at the trashcan near Lily's dorm. The lid swings and crashes back into place with a sound like a slap. Even tiny sounds, it seems, have the power to turn her into a wreck.

Lily bites her lip and tries not to cry.

11.

Lily finds summer vacation means freedom from Prescot that quickly turns into her irritation at Mom and Dad just for being her parents. She escapes her house after a few days and goes to Erica's house for a few hours.

Her friend's backyard is landscaped to look like a miniature version of the gardens at Hever Castle: lawn mowed in diagonal stripes, and fruit trees as a border on the fence. Apple and pear saplings have been forced into woven arrangements by an anonymous gardener, and the branches interlace in braided designs.

Lily and Erica lie out on the smallest patio, the one with a pavilion to shade Erica's delicate skin. Lily lounges out of the circular shadow, squints at the sun, and hopes for an early tan. The bright light is purple against her closed eyelids.

"So awesome you're back." Erica sips her lemonade from two straws. "Life was a lot quieter without you around."

"Is that a compliment?" Lily takes a drink and stifles a shudder. It's far too sweet, the usual syrupy concoction Mrs. Winslow buys. She finds her own sports bottle and sneaks a drink of lukewarm water.

"Yes, of course, duh. I was so bored. And the girls at Snowe are such bitches – oh, my God. You have no idea how clique-y the school has become since you left."

"Oh, no. Really? Let me guess – Courtney and her whole crew."

"Yup. She's always nasty, but you know what? I just ignore her now." Erica scrolls through her phone as she talks. She laughs, types in a rapid response, and sets it down. "How can you stand the heat? I'm dying here in the shade."

The air is filled with a dry, crackly sound as though the backyard is on fire. When Lily looks around with eyebrows raised, Erica jerks her head at the huge oaks bordering the Winslow property. "Gypsy moths," she explains. "They're so gross, Lily, you have no idea. One plopped on my arm last week and I freaked out."

"Ugh. Knowing you, I bet you had to take seven showers." Lily dodges the dripping ice cube Erica throws at her and glances at her own phone. Time to check in with Tyler. *Just hanging with Erica,* she writes. *How's the swim team?*

He sends back a single *Hi* as a response. Lily has learned by now she can't let it go – he expects her to keep texting. Her mathematical mind has figured it's about a five to one ratio. She sends him five messages, and he'll send her a one-word answer.

More importantly, he won't lose his temper or shut her out for days on end.

Hope things are good. I miss you! PS – There are gypsy moths in the trees here. I think I can hear them chewing the leaves. So foul. Sun feels good, tho. Send you a pic of my tan later.

She adds a few more texts and leans back. "Ugh, so hot," she complains. "Want to go to the beach later this week?"

"Oh hell yeah." Erica smiles into her phone and takes a selfie. "As long as I can bring the umbrella and the big towel and the baby pool."

Lily grins. Erica's list of necessary items for the beach is extensive – her umbrella is so huge it takes three people to put it up, and she needs a blow-up pool filled with water to wash off the sand. It's a pain in the ass to load up her stuff and bring it all to the Jersey shore, but Lily's used to it by now. Besides, cool ocean breezes and boardwalk fries are too tempting. "Okay, we'll make it happen." *Going to hit the beach with Erica,* she writes. *Maybe tomorrow or the day after.*

She frowns when a long text comes back from Tyler. *Why you talking to her? Thought you were done with that crazy slut. You need to tell her to get lost. Too gullible. Anyone could tell you anything and you'd believe it. Unbelievable, smh. You're such a fucking idiot.*

Tyler, I told you she wasn't the one who sent those texts. She's fine – she's my friend.

By now she knows how to calm him down, even from miles away. Lily asks a couple of questions about his performance at school, how incredible his times are, what her coach in New Jersey has planned for the home team. It defuses him, and after he tells her about Rosemont's pool and how dumb her workout routine is compared to his, Lily feels he's forgotten about Erica and the beach.

Any parties tonight? she asks.

Why, you checking up on me? Being a jealous bitch? I'm faithful, I don't study with members of the opposite sex unlike some people.

No, she responds. *It's fine. Just hoping you're having a good time.*

There's a long wait. *Yeah.*

Her phone drops to the over-padded deck chair, loaded with the weight of their conversation. She knows she still has to go onto social media and Like all of Tyler's posts, respond to his comments and be his good girlfriend. Retweet his tweets. Heart his Instagram posts. But for the moment she feels crushed by the crunchy sounds of gypsy moths in the trees, the too-sweet lemonade, and the sun.

Yes. The summer must be the reason why she feels drained and limp.

A shout breaks through the gypsy moths. Erica's mom walks towards them with a pizza box and a pile of napkins. "Thought you might be hungry," she says.

"Pizza is so salty," Erica complains.

Lily gets up from the lounge chair and sits next to her friend. "Thanks, Mrs. Winslow."

"Why, it's my pleasure. I'll be back with more lemonade." Erica's mom sets a few paper plates next to the steaming box and heads back across the long backyard, a trim figure in tan and coral.

"Mom's lemonade sucks," Erica whispers.

"Oh thank God," Lily laughs. "I thought I was the only one who couldn't deal."

"Does she dump an entire bag of sugar in on top of all the high fructose? It's so sweet it hurts my teeth."

"Think we can water the trees with it after she leaves?"

"Maybe it'll kill the caterpillars." They both giggle as Erica digs in her bag for the hand sanitizer she carries everywhere. Lily smells lemons and - is it sage? Pine? – as Erica squeezes a glop and rubs it into her palm. She spends a long time on each finger. Lily sees Erica's knuckles whiten as she kneads the stuff into her palm.

"It smells," Lily comments.

"Mmm. I'll get a different kind next time. Lush instead of Bath and Bodyworks."

"Going green, huh?"

Erica laughs. "Sure. Let's go with that."

The lemon and pine smell lurks in Lily's nostrils as she bites into a sloppy triangle of pizza. The dough is undercooked except for the bottom, charred black from the oven. It's even worse than the pie at Nationals. Despite the Winslow's obvious wealth, Erica's mom always seems to serve the worst food.

Erica bites into her own slice and eyes Lily across the table. They stare at each other for a moment before Erica breaks into more giggles. "I know," she gasps. "It's terrible. We can always call for Chinese, though. And soda."

"Now you're talking my language." Lily stops chewing her slice and drops it into the grease Rorschach on her paper plate. "Lo Mein? Or Kung Pao chicken?"

"Both, duh. And egg rolls."

• • •

Ben, the guy from Rosemont, seems to have appointed himself as Lily's adviser. He sends her his email and, after a few half-hearted exchanges, asks for her phone number. With a shrug, Lily complies.

Tyler talks about u a lot, he writes. *But there's a bunch of girls who hang round our hall 24-7 and wait for Ty, I'd want 2 no if it was me.*

Lily adjusts her towel and rolls onto her stomach. She's showered off the sweat and chlorine, ready for a night of watching a movie with Vincent and the guinea pigs. *Thanks, but it's fine. I'm not a jealous girlfriend.*

Okay. He seems to consider before adding, *You should probably come visit so he don't forget u.*

We r talking about it. Her finger hovers over the screen before she adds, *Drop a few hints, k?*

K. Look 4ward to meeting u.

It's cold in the air-conditioned bedroom. Lily shivers, towels herself dry, and dresses in sweats and flip-flops. It's not a good look, but she can peel off a layer if she goes out after the movie Vincent wants her to watch with him.

When she opens her bedroom door, Vincent stands there with Ham tucked under one arm and Lettuce in his hoodie pocket. "How long have you been there?" Lily demands.

"Not long." Vincent shuffles into her room and sets the pigs down on Lily's discarded towel. They sniff at the wet spots, and Ham starts to chew the Macy's label. "I'll get their playpen in a second. Hey, can we watch Saw? And The Ring?"

"You'll have nightmares." Lily plops on the rug and starts to fiddle with Ham's ears.

"It'll be worth it, Lily. Please, Lily, please. Come on."

"Fine, I don't care." Lily waves her hand at the TV, a Christmas gift from a few years ago. Months of begging and pleading with her mom, plus long promises she'd keep up her grades and read her summer books every day won over her parents in the end. "Dad watching sports?"

Vincent shoots her a look. Of course Dad's downstairs, shouting at baseball. "Be right back with piggie snacks and the DVD's."

He crashes out of the room, a slender kid with massive feet. Both guinea pigs popcorn with fright as Vincent's sneaker connects with the doorframe with a thump. From the kitchen Mom yells they have to be careful and not bring the ceiling down for the Good Lord's sake.

While Lily waits, she herds the pigs onto the towel and away from the charger cords. Lettuce is in a sassy mood and jumps out of Lily's hands when she tries to catch the little furry football-shaped animal. By the time Vincent returns with a bag of Veggie O's and a few movies with lurid DVD covers, Lily has given up on the pigs. She wraps Ham in a towel, corners Lettuce behind the bed, and hugs her as punishment for being a pain.

"Did they jump all over the place?" Vincent rattles the bags, and both pigs wheek with excitement. "I think the playpen stuff's up here in your closet."

"You left it there." Lily goes to her closet, pokes about, and finds the guinea set-up, a wired hoop meant to corral the pets. Once it's ready, she plops Ham and Lettuce inside, and Vincent scatters a few treats for them on the layered towels. "They really want peeled grapes, you know."

"I know. Maybe when Saw's done."

She watches him open the DVD player and select the disc while she settles down on the ground next to the guinea pigs. As soon as the first scene appears, a face underwater and a key that gets flushed down a rusty drain, Vincent huddles against Lily's side.

"We should get popcorn and drinks," she suggests. "Piggies aren't the only ones who get hungry from horror movies."

Vincent winds his skinny arms around her waist. He argues that he's scared already and she can't leave. They wrestle a bit before settling into the story. After each graphic scene, her brother settles closer until he's draped over her shoulders and practically in her lap.

The doctor in the movie finds a phone in the room where he's held prisoner, and Lily gasps. "What?" Vincent demands, his eyes huge. "Do you think there's a monster in the closet?"

"No, silly. I just remembered I have to text Tyler."

"But you texted him before the movie started. I bet he's busy with college things."

Lily shoves him with her hip so she can access her phone. "He likes me to check in every few minutes."

"Every few minutes!" Vincent finds the remote and freezes the frame of the movie. On the screen the puppet with spiral cheeks shivers in time and seems to assess the audience right through the TV screen. "Do you have to do that when you have a girlfriend? Or boyfriend or whatever? Because I don't want to."

"No. Well, it's different for everyone. I mean, I've had boyfriends who just called me once a day or a couple times a week. I guess Tyler's one of those people who likes to know where I am all the time."

"Oh." Vincent turns back to the movie and points the remote at the Saw puppet. "Weird."

"You're twelve," Lily scoffs. "And you have no idea how it works yet."

Vincent presses Play, and the action returns to the loud argument between two men chained up in a dirty basement. "I may be twelve," he says finally, "but I still know what's weird."

Lily sends a few texts to Tyler, goes to Facebook and Likes his latest post. She scrolls through Twitter and responds to his tweets. In the middle of finding his latest Instagram, she pauses.

Is it weird? She's been so in the moment, so invested in Tyler's uncertain temper and his outbursts, she hasn't thought about her own behavior.

The air-conditioning kicks back on, and Lily shivers. In order to warm herself, she scoops up Ham out of the enclosure and snuggles closer to Vincent. He doesn't seem to notice, intent on the movie's latest bout of gore. He'll end up sleeping in their parents' bed. Lily will get blamed for it, but she's used to it.

Lily scratches Ham's butt, and the little animal purrs on her chest. If only people were so easy. Give them food, find their kick spot, everyone's happy.

On the screen, Dr. Gordon has a flashback: an almost-affair with a medical student. He's so intent on the relationship, he ignores his daughter when she cries about a man in her closet.

There's a chain bolted around one leg. Soon the doctor will consider sawing off his own limb so he can escape the nightmarish basement.

• • •

Vincent ends up in their parents' bed like Lily predicted. She follows as her dad carries the boy in, tucks him under a huge duvet, and turns off the lights. "Guess I'll wake up with bruises." Dad straightens up and puts one hand on his back. "Vincent's elbows are harder than pool cues."

"You can sleep on the couch if you want." Mom comes in with extra pillows. Her nurse's training lets her slide one under Vincent's head without waking him.

The phone in Lily's hand vibrates. *I miss uuuuuuu*

Hi, she texts back. *Just watched Saw with Vincent.*

College sucks. Evyone jst shady. Come see me bby

Lily chews the inside of her cheek. She can tell that Tyler is drunk again. Maybe one of his jokes didn't go over with the college crowd, or a girl found his beery, handsy ways irritating. Still, she'd like to see the campus and visit the pool.

"Can I visit Tyler?" she blurts.

"At Rosemont?" Dad wanders out of the bathroom, loaded toothbrush in his fist. "I don't think so."

"Why not?" Lily plunges into pleading mode, her usual method for getting what she wants. "Come on, it would be good experience for college visits. They have a great swim team there, and I want to see the pool. Maybe meet the coach. C'mon, dad, please? Please please please?"

"There's no way!" Dad explodes with wrath. "Go visit this guy in college while you're still a freshman in high school? Not happening."

"I'm a sophomore now, so I can go," Lily declares triumphantly. She sits on the bed near Vincent's lumpy feet to make it clear she won't give up.

Dad starts to brush his teeth vigorously. "No, you can't," he says around a mouthful of foam. She splutters, but he waves her off and goes into the bathroom. Lily hears the faucet run followed by prolonged spits and rinses.

She waits, a stubborn fixture on the bed, until her father comes out of the bathroom. He dries his hands in one of the crimson and gold fingertip towels Mom always tells them they're not supposed to touch. "Where would you even sleep? Not in his dorm room, I can tell you that. And," he continues as she draws in a deep lungful of argument, "not in a girl's dorm room down the hall either."

Mom snatches the towel from him and shakes it out. "I could go with her," she offers. "We could stay in a hotel together, the way we did when she was sick."

Her mom's unexpected support makes Lily look up from the phone and stop typing I love you's to Tyler. "Really?" she asks. "Mom, you're – oh, my God. That would be so amazing."

Her brother's legs twitch under the thick duvet, and Lily catches Mom's eye. They both snicker as Dad snarls, "I can't believe you're considering this!" He throws both arms in the air. "Not to mention, I don't even like him."

"Maybe Tyler just needs to see what a supportive, normal family looks like. I already told you his father is pretty odd. However," Mom adds, "he has to come for a visit here first."

"What?" Lily frowns and lets her jaw drop. "He'll never want to visit my parents – no way. Let's just go. You can come too, Dad, and meet him."

"No visit here, no trip to Rosemont." Her mother throws his crumpled towel into a blue canvas laundry bag.

Lily recognizes the tone of finality in her mother's voice. She gets up, jams her phone into her pocket, and leaves the room.

Is there a subtle sound as the door closes, the quiet slap of her parents' palms as they share a high five? Lily slams her way into her own room, bounds onto the bed, and finds her phone. Tyler has sent a few pics from the party, him surrounded by a group of girls. *They seem to like me,* he writes. *College rocks.*

Ignoring the picture, Lily writes back. *I'm so sorry, but my mom says I can't visit Rosemont unless you come here first to meet my dad. I know. 1950's much?*

The response is another shot of Tyler flanked by two girls, both laughing up at him. It seems he's over his depression. *You're missing out,* he texts. *You want me to leave all this to meet some parents? That is so stupid.* For a few angry thuds of her heart, Lily considers powering down her phone. Tyler looks so handsome, deep dimple in his cheek. It used to mean a secret smile, the one that was just for her.

Lily takes a deep breath, ignores the pain in her stomach that always seems to erupt when she's texting Tyler, and lists a few dates. She's learned by this point it's better to offer him some options so he feels like he's the one in control.

There's a long wait while she feels like she might jump out of her skin. Just as she's about to go and dig out some summer work to take her mind off the conversation, he texts that the end of July might be okay. *Guess I'll see you in 2 weeks or whatever,* he adds. *Go to bed, but don't forget to answer when I Facetime you when I get home. I want to hear you sleep. Want to know where you are. Always.*

Don't spend time with anyone else, he adds.

I'm the most important thing in your life.

Lily peels off her sweats and yanks one of the huge t-shirts she uses as pjs in the summer over her head. She brushes her teeth and drags a wet cloth over her face. Her heart beats as she slams into her room and thrusts her feet between the wrinkled, messy sheets.

Her anger ebbs. Before she turns off the light, she sets up Facetime so Tyler can see her the moment he calls.

• • •

Summer flashes by, layered with swim practice and gym workouts. It's difficult to find a day to hit the shore with Erica, but in the middle of August Maria gives the swim team a free morning. As soon as Lily hears, she texts Erica.

The beach is crowded by the time Lily and Erica arrive. Mom sets up an umbrella and opens her book, a novel with the cover image of a frantic female who steps out of a shadowy doorway.

Lily hasn't slept well. Tyler hasn't texted her a lot, although he still seems to expect her hourly updates. Swim practice has become a blur of rubbery limbs and cold caffeine. She wants to flop on a towel and lie in the sun for hours.

Erica sneaks into the shade of her mom's umbrella and gets out her own book. Lily sends off her check-in to Tyler, and he actually writes back with a big grin in a shirtless selfie. *Miss this?*

Of course, she replies. *Miss you so much, bby.*

It wakes her up, makes her slog off her exhaustion. Lily amuses herself by texting her friends from Prescot. She even shoots a quick Hi to Yasmin.

Disgusted, she throws the phone into her beach bag and hops up to drag Erica off her towel. "Come and boogie-board with me," Lily begs. "The waves are good, it'll be fun, c'mon."

"Might as well say yes," Mom comments. "My daughter won't give up until you do."

Lily pulls Erica's arm again, scoops up their boards, and heads to open water. The space between the flags is filled with kids and stately, elderly swimmers, but she finds an open lane just close enough to avoid the lifeguard's whistle.

Saltwater sprays her face as she splashes out with Erica close behind her. When they're far enough out, Lily holds her board and waits for a good wave. She catches it just right and smacks onto her stomach, rides the water all the way to the beach.

They surf for so long she's dizzy by the time Mom waves for them to come in. The sand and sky seem to swing around her, and the ocean's roar is still in her ears, as though her skull has become a conch shell.

She survives the usual sandy, sticky trip back to the SUV and sits on her damp towel to protect the seats. Mom stops for boxes of greasy food at The Lighthouse, and Lily wolfs down two hot dogs plus fries.

After they drop off Erica, Lily moves to the front seat. She ignores her mom's complaints about sand in the car seats, turns up the radio, and hums along to the music.

"You seem happy," her mom comments.

Lily doesn't answer, but Mom's on the right track. The sensation that rolls through her tired limbs and salty skin is weightless, floating, spacey enough not to have a name to tie it down to any emotion.

She stifles a burp, tells her mother to stop laughing. The car is filled with notes from a half-forgotten song.

It's been a great day, the best Lily can remember in a long time.

12.

After weeks of more begging, Dad relents and says Lily can visit Tyler at college. "As long as you stay with her," he declares.

"Absolutely," Mom agrees. "We'll go to Rosemont for the night, take Tyler out to dinner, and we'll stay in a hotel."

"You'll room with Lily?" Her dad shoves his sunglasses up onto the top of his head.

"Of course." Mom pours clear liquid into a cocktail shaker and adds ice.

Lily hugs her dad and flies upstairs to call Tyler and let him know she's going to visit. As usual, she gets his voicemail blaring "What?" followed by the pounding bass of alternative music.

"Dad's letting me come out to Rosemont!" Lily sings at the beep. "So excited to see you, can't wait, we're spending the night too. Well, at a hotel. Me and my mom. But you and me'll spend time together, which is the important part. Right?"

Lily presses End Call and jumps off the bed. She changes into her last dry practice suit, humming one of the old songs from her mom's radio station, and giggles. Tyler would make fun of her if he could see her now.

He finally calls back after practice. "Yeah, okay," he says in her ear. "Guess that'll work."

"Okay!" Lily flops back on the pillows and crosses her ankles. "I can't wait. It's going to be so amazing to see you in two weeks."

"Two weeks?" She can hear the anger in her voice, and her gut twists. "No way. Not happening."

With a huge effort, Lily manages to control her own temper. "We already agreed on the date. My mom took off work and booked a hotel. It's all arranged."

"By who? Who arranged it? Not me, that's for sure. You think you can control me? Fuck off. You're so stupid sometimes. I hate that. It's like you want to have the final say on my life."

If she cries he'll hear the tears in her voice and get even angrier. Lily swallows and says, "You told me the date. I told my mom. I gave you a couple of dates and you said the end of July." She stops, unable to continue. It feels like someone has jammed a hot poker down her throat.

"So that makes it okay to just fucking waltz into my life? Into my school? What if I had plans? God, you're so fucking spoiled." Tyler doesn't yell. His temper makes him quieter and more deadly.

Lily's arm falls to the quilt, her fingers still clutching the phone. She sobs, her chest heaving with the effort to keep it down so he won't hear. "But I'm your girlfriend," she whispers.

Mom talks to her supervisor as she drives, her Bluetooth wobbling in one ear. "I already ordered palliative care," she says to some unknown associate on the phone. "The family's all on board except for the father. Between you and me, he's been a pain in the ass. He'll come around, though, once he sees how quickly she's gone downhill..."

Lily tunes her out and scrolls through her phone to shots of her and Tyler at the beach. They stand hand in hand in the waves. He talks, she laughs at what he says. Even though she's a tall girl, Lily is dwarfed by his height.

There are other pictures – in the backyard with him in the background, her in a cocktail dress with his arms around her from behind, a shot of Tyler's ring on her finger, the two of them at a restaurant with Vincent and her parents. They all look stiff and uncomfortable, as though they're wax statues.

And another of his flushed face, jaw slack, lips damp and loose, and eyes closed with pleasure ...

Lily glances at her mother and closes the camera app. Her heart thumps pleasantly against her chest. After Tyler's visit to New Jersey, Lily prays they're in a new phase. Moving forward, they can work out the way they don't talk to each other, the way he puts her down when she tells him how she broke the 24-second mark in her 50.

After all, he's agreed her mom should come to Rosemont too. So what if he gets cranky or demanding? His team is in the top ten in the nation, and he's working his butt off on a scholarship. No wonder he doesn't always have time for his girlfriend.

Plus Lily promises herself she can take whatever Tyler dishes out. She's tough. As a swimmer she's able to hold her breath until her head spins, and she can jump back into the pool after puking up her guts.

Yeah, she can deal with a few insults. After all, they're only words. It's not like Tyler hits her or anything.

"We should be there in a few minutes." Mom points in the direction of the passenger window. "God, look at that house. The brickwork is incredible, isn't it?" Lily hums in agreement, although she has no idea what her mother means. She has to admit the houses near Rosemont are huge, and the lawns out front are the size of small countries. "Although," Mom adds with a sigh, "they say the heroin problem here is out of control. The best public schools in the system, and 35 percent of the kids use drugs."

The words squirm into Lily's mind like snakes. She doesn't want to think about kids so rich and bored they want to poke opiates into their skin for a thrill.

Lily's sport keeps her focused, not only on the black line painted on bottom of her lane but also the future. It's the next five seconds, making it to the turn or touching the wall before her competitors do. It's dragging herself out of bed when it's dark outside and icy rain stripes the windows while everyone else is asleep. It's who she is.

God, Lily prays suddenly, let me keep swimming no matter what happens.

• • •

Lily has to sign in at the dorm, a brick building hidden at the back of campus. There's a student behind the desk, a girl in a bohunk dress with a messy bun. When she rises from the desk to point out the stairs, Lily sees she's got Birkenstocks on tanned, shapely feet.

Mom trails after her and protests they need to stick together. "I think we're parked illegally," she adds. "Might get towed. We have to go and move the car first. I didn't realize you wanted to just kerblam straight upstairs to his room."

"No one visits their boyfriend with their mom," Lily hisses. "Seriously? I won't go into his bedroom – I won't even sit down in a chair. We're just going to have a quick reunion and head out to a great seafood place he told me about. With you." Her mom's mouth opens, and Lily adds, "I promise. Mom, you can trust me. Go move the car – I won't die without you for twenty minutes."

"I do trust you. It just 18 year old boys I don't trust, especially around my daughter."

"It's daytime, mom. We're in a dorm filled with people." The Birkenstock girl watches the entire scene with great interest, and Lily nudges Mom with her hip. "Go move the car, and I'll meet up with Tyler. It'll be fine."

"I'm pretty sure sex still happens in the daytime in a dorm filled with people," her mother snips.

"Really? Really?" Lily feels embarrassment crawl up her neck, a deep blush of shame.

"There are advisors on each floor to make sure students and visitors stay safe," Birkenstock Girl chirps.

Mom seems unconvinced, but she heads to the rotating door. "Be right back!" she adds.

"Just said that fifty times," Lily mutters as soon as her mother disappears.

"The stairwell's right down there. Elevator's broken, again, ugh." Birkenstock Girl pauses. "I'm right downstairs if you need me. I'd go up with you, but my manager's a bitch about us staying at the desk, and I just can't lose this job."

"I'll be fine," Lily insists.

The third floor hall is painted gunmetal gray and lined with doors. Most of them are open, revealing messy beds and empty bottles. Music spills out of one room labeled Crack Club, and as Lily passes, a guy falls out, followed by a barrage of pillows. "You suck, Blowfish!" a deep voice shouts from inside the dorm room.

Lily slithers past the kid to room 589. It's closed. Tyler is in there, she thinks, maybe changing after practice. He's going to open the door and... Her stomach jumps with pleasure and nerves as she knocks. Maybe he'll give her a big kiss or pick her up and whirl her around like one of those romantic couples in a movie when they reunite after a world war. She pushes her hair behind her ears and fingers the gift she brought for him, a box of his favorite cookies.

A few minutes tick by, and she frowns. Is he on the phone? Or watching a YouTube video with ear buds in and the volume turned up? Maybe he lost track of time studying... She knocks again and, after there's no response, pounds on the door.

Loud footsteps echo inside before the door flies open. Lily's smile dies as she sees the person in the dorm room is a stranger. There's no doubt he's a swimmer, not with those wide shoulders and serious lat definition. Longish hair stands up in spikes. He resembles a startled hedgehog.

They stare at each other for a few seconds. "Yes?" he says.

"Uh, hi." Lily feels her heart pound. "Is Tyler here?"

A girl joins the boy in the doorway and winds her arms around his waist, lays her head on his shoulder. "Don't tell me you're Lily," the boy says.

Feeling as though she's about to get sick, Lily nods. "Yeah," she manages to say.

"He's such a dick," the guy says. "Sorry, I'm Ben. We've texted, right? Nice to meet you in person." The girl pushes him, and he adds, "This is Bree."

"Ben and Bree," Lily repeats mechanically. "Hi. So, is Tyler here?"

Bree examines her thumbnail. "Went to a party."

"What?" Lily feels tears prick her eyelids. "But he..." The last thing she wants is to break down in front of this girl. "Sorry. Didn't mean to bother you. Guess I – okay." Feeling as though she's embarrassed herself enough in front of Tyler's roommate, Lily heads back to the stairs. Crack

Club appears to have evolved into a full-blown party, complete with beer and marshmallow guns.

Lily hides in the angled stairwell and crouches on the top step as she blots her eyes on the hem of her halter-top. There's a lump in her throat that tastes like salt and rust. She feels in her pocket for her phone, pulls it out, and types. *Where r u Im hear u said 6*

The music from the Crack Shop bounces off the chipped paint on the walls. Lily waits, but there's no response. Her only option is to find her mom, admit Tyler has ditched her, and head to a hotel room where she'll go insane until he calls.

Lily will have to slink past Birkenstock Girl again. Alone.

And Lily remembers Bree. She's seen the girl's picture before on Tyler's Facebook profile.

"Hi." Ben appears in the doors to the stairs, making her jump up. He's alone.

Tyler still hasn't responded. "Hi." Lily puts away her phone and blurts out a watery laugh. "I'm so sorry I bothered you! Had no idea you were there with a girl. Didn't mean to be a..."

"A cockblocker?" Ben laughs. "Don't worry about it. Bree's just a friend. She went in there to hang with that bunch of tools." He jerks his head in the direction of the Crack Club. "Anyway, I wanted to tell you I called Tyler. He got held up at the party, but he'll be back really soon. Well, soon. Like, in an hour."

An hour. Lily stifles her dismay and manages to smile. "Oh, sure. Yeah, probably he got talking to a couple of guys and forgot the time. Or maybe there's a pong table? He loves pong. Or were some of his teammates there? Maybe they have to go over training schedules and stuff." She stops and closes her eyes for a second. "I'm – just tell me to shut up."

Ben grins. His weird hairstyle suits him, the streaked blond spikes against freckled milky skin. "No, you're good." His eyes flick over her as she stands up. "You're a swimmer too, right?"

"Yeah. You?"

"Isn't it obvious?"

Lily laughs in relief. He's a lifesaver. She knows she's being dramatic, but if she waits with Ben, she won't have to crawl past Birkenstock Girl or call her mom to come and pick her up like a second-grader at a bad birthday party. "Thanks for the rescue. I'm gonna go hide in the library or on campus until Tyler texts me. So, if he calls or anything, could you just let him know I'm here?"

"Fuck that." Ben holds out his hand, and she grasps his forearm to get hauled onto her feet. "Hang out with me. I'm just chilling anyway. We'll leave the door open," he adds when she begins to stutter, not sure what her mom would say. "C'mon. We can even sit in the hall if you're nervous."

"I'm not nervous, it's. Just. Well." Lily doesn't know what to say.

He guides her past the Crack Shop. "No, I get it. It's dumb for a girl to go into a room with anyone she just met. See? Look, door open. Check it out. Got these really comfy seats I can bring out into the hall. Blam, one for you, and there's one for me. I'll sit wayyyyy over here. Done. You're safe."

Lily sinks into the creaky chair and smiles up at him. "You're being so nice, and I'm being paranoid."

"Just let me get my laptop." Ben subsides into the chair, wiggles on it a few times. He seems to test whether or not it'll buckle under his weight. "Guess I could actually work while we wait."

She pulls out her phone – it's what people do in awkward situations, right? Stare at a tiny screen so they don't have to interact? – and scrolls through email, texts, Instagram updates. There's nothing new. 2048 doesn't appeal, and her required summer book requires way too much concentration. Idly she asks Ben what he's working on, and he tells her it's a stupid essay for a stupid American Lit requirement.

"I wrote one of those a few weeks ago." Lily tries one more message to Tyler: *I am literally hanging outside yr room with yr roommate right now.* "About Flannery O'Connor."

"No way – same!" Ben sits up, and the chair shrieks in protest. "What'd you write about?"

"A story called The Life You Save May Be Your Own." Lily refuses to ponder the irony of the title. "My friend and I brainstormed a theory about human hearts. I know it sounds pretty barbaric, but our theory was you could dissect someone's heart and still never find out what's really going on inside..." She breaks off. Ben stares at her, his mouth open.

"This is – damn. So awesome. Mind if I use your idea? I mean, I'll riff off it and find my own sources and quotes and shit."

Lily holds out her arms. "Be my guest. Happy I could help, especially after you rescued me."

Ben shoots her a look as he types. "Yeah. About that. Ty's my boy, right? I mean, there's such a thing as guy code. I'm not saying what he did was right, but..."

"Wait. What did he do? What are you talking about?"

He flushes and bends over the keyboard. "I mean, this. Whatever. Not like I'm perfect either, right? I can be a jerk too. Probably all guys are."

"Oh." She breathes out. "No big deal. I was freaked out just now when you found me on the stairs. New place and everything, you know?"

It makes sense. This is college, after all, not high school, and probably there's a whole new set of rules. Relationships are more casual. Mistakes happen. Parties erupt out of nowhere – the Crack Shop is proof. Underneath it all, she's sure Tyler is a good guy. The ring on her finger says so.

Ben gives her two thumbs' up. "Most girls would call and scream at him or make a scene. Tyler hates that. He told me the other day. You know the girl who was just here? Bree?"

Now he has Lily's full attention. "What about her?"

"She went off on me and Ty last week. Said we were players, said we didn't know our asses from a hole in the ground, told me to go fuck myself."

"Wait." Lily leans forward, and her chair groans. "Why?"

He shrugs. "Who knows? You drink a coupla beers, stuff gets said, I don't know. Point is, Tyler told me she's a freak and he can't stand her loud mouth." A phrase on the screen seems to catch his attention, and he frowns at the words.

Down the hall, a shirtless guy jumps out of the Crack Club. He clutches a crinkly orange object in one hand and, as Lily stares at him, tears it open to chug the contents. They appear to be desiccated worms. "Raw ramen!" he yells.

Lily catches Ben's eye. "Uh, don't let me keep you," she says. "Sounds like the party's starting to blow up."

Ben nods, his expression serious. "Because I really want to go and eat uncooked noodles."

"Snort the flavor packet!" a girl inside the Crack Club yells. The shirtless guy rips a tiny square and holds it to his nose.

"Now you're really missing out," Lily adds. "Hey, that might be Shrimp flavor, you know."

"Did you just..." Ben stares at her for a second before bursting into high-pitched giggles. It's infectious, and Lily starts to laugh.

"Shrimp - so stupid!" she gasps, which seems to set him off again. "Why is this funny?" They calm down, and Lily blots her face with the mistreated halter-top. "I needed that," she adds.

Lily's phone vibrates, and she pulls it out. Ben, along crunchy Ramen dude, has saved the day. Now she just needs Tyler to arrive, and her visit will be perfect.

However the text isn't from Tyler. *Think you can escape me, bitch? I'm still here.* Whoever has sent it is using an unknown number.

"Lily?" Ben's voice is gentle. "You okay?"

Her phone chimes with another text: *The visit with your bf won't help. He's screwing around with other girls. Remember when you're at your next meet.*

She holds out the phone, and Ben's hand covers hers so he can see. "Damn," he says. "This is some nasty shit."

"Hey!" The shout comes from down the hall. Tyler, his hands curled into fists, stands by the stairwell. "What the fuck are you doing?"

One of the Crack Shop partiers switches off the music. A face haloed with golden ringlets pokes out. It's Bree, obviously consumed with curiosity. Mr. Ramen is right behind her, his face still covered in Flavor Packet powder.

Ben drops Lily's hand, closes his laptop with a snap, and stands up. He fumbles the rusty chair closed. "Sorry," he mutters, but it's not clear if he's talking to her or Tyler.

"Hey!" Tyler yells again. "What the hell? What are you doing?" He must be seriously pissed off if he's raising his voice.

Lily stands up so fast she gets dizzy and nearly falls. Next to her, Ben quickly picks up his chair, throws it into room 589, and scuttles down the hall towards Crack Club.

"What am I doing? I'm waiting for you." Lily feels anger like static in her head. "You told me to be here at 6. I've been here for nearly an hour. An hour, Tyler." She feels she's about to explode. "You're the one who invited me here. It's not like I just…just…just…"

"Just…just…" he mocks. "And if you're sitting in the hall to flirt with my roommate, you don't get to complain. I had to go and meet with my coach, and it turned out there was an important event, which I had no idea would happen, and I couldn't concentrate because I tried to get back here to you. And when I finally do, I see you and Ben all cozy, holding hands and shit."

"He was looking at my phone! And he helped me!"

"Not what I saw. In any case, why did you come up here? You should have called me, waited downstairs, and when I got here I coulda showed you around like I planned. But you ruined it."

Tears of frustration slip down her cheeks. "I didn't know," she begins. "I tried to text you a couple of times."

Tyler shakes his head. "Do you really think a text would get through in a party? You know what you look like right now, all red-eyed outside my door? Like a dumb 15-year-old kid out of place." He punctuates each word with a stab of his finger in her face. "You're so lucky to have me.

Your college boyfriend. What would you do if you were all alone here on campus? Wander off to the bar? Try and pick up a guy, maybe a couple of guys? Jesus. And you're so loud, you made a scene. In my college. And you have no idea how hard I worked to get here."

"I'm almost 16," Lily mumbles. Her mind whirls, trying to pick apart the rapid-fire accusations he hurls at her. "And you just said you were with your coach, not at a party."

"With my coach at a thing. Jesus, can't you hear? Are you deaf?"

She doesn't know where to begin. He's wrong – she does know how hard he's worked to get a spot on an NCAA Division 1 college team. Every swimmer knows about the constant struggle to make a mark in a not-very-popular sport. No one really comes to watch swim meets, after all. The competitors push their bodies through the water for their parents, their coaches, and in the end, for themselves.

Lily crosses her arms tightly. Her stomach hurts, but she doesn't want to show him how scared she feels. "Look, Tyler. Can we just take it down a notch? I'm sorry I got frustrated, but you have to understand how it felt to arrive in a strange place expecting to see you, and instead I had to hang out with your roommate, a guy I never met before. My mom's gonna kill me if she finds out, by the way."

"What, you might get grounded? Lose your allowance? Get sent to your room?" His eyes are dark slits. "My spot on the team could be in jeopardy if I don't jump through the hoops, don't go to the parties and give campus tours."

"Okay. I'm sorry, I didn't realize it was such a big thing. Ben just said it was a party, so I pictured you at a mixer or frat house. I had no idea you had to go to sports functions."

"But that's just it." He crowds closer. Tyler smells like beer under the cologne she gave him before he left for Rosemont. "You immediately thought the worst of me. Not cool. And now you're in my face with your high school stuff, and I just don't have the time or the energy. Do you know how hard it is to go to college? How much work it is? Not to mention the schmoozing and meetings. You. Have. No. Idea. In fact, I wonder if we have anything in common now." He adds a few comments under his breath. Even though it's too quiet to hear, she flinches. Everything he says is like a red-hot brand on her skin, leaving scars no one will ever see.

"So, what – we have to break up now you're in college?" Lily's still dizzy with the turns the conversation takes. She's on a carousel that spins faster and faster until she gets sick or falls off. "Right?"

Her stomach jolts again, an electric bolt of pain. She realizes a break-up might be not be the worst end to this conversation. Don't throw up, Lily thinks. Just don't throw up here in front of him.

He hisses and bends forward, pulls her to his chest so he can kiss her. "I fucking miss you so much, and when I get back from a dumb social event I see you flirting with my roommate. And now you're about to break up with me?"

Tyler's voice is in her ear, and she can't think straight, and she's so sorry if she hurt him, and she wants to get away but has no idea where to go. "I'm not breaking up with you." Lily squeezes her eyes so she won't cry, not anymore. Not for this.

His chest expands as he sucks in breath, as though he's about to say I love you, or I hate you, or just one of his barbed remarks that always seem to turn her inside out.

A voice, bright with excitement, emerges from the stairwell. "This looks like a tender reunion! How are you, Tyler? I managed to find a parking spot. Of course it was miles away, and I had to walk all the way back, but it was worth it to see such a beautiful campus. Do you love it here?"

Her mother. Of course.

Lily watches as Mom walks past the Crack Shop. A marshmallow pops out of the room to hit her butt, and she skips with a little squeak before scurrying over to them.

There's a huge smile on her face. "Well, what do you think?" Mom nudges Tyler's arm. "I've delivered her to you." Lily turns to the wall to wipe her eyes as her mom adds, "So, ready to go to dinner, you two?"

Lily nods. She can see her mom, the hallway, and even the Crack Shop over Tyler's broad shoulder, from where she stands pressed against him. It's as though he is now the frame around her entire world.

"Good to see you, Mrs. Batista." His voice is smooth, as though Mom's arrival is the greatest thing in the world that ever happened. They might be on the steps of a museum, all three of them, in a civilized conversation about art and world politics. "I hope you don't mind if I get changed quickly first. I'm starving."

13.

Lily wishes she could have just one more of those summer days spent at home, even though they seemed endless and boring at the time. July and August have melted away like ice in a soft drink at the shore, and she's back at the Prescot pool enclosure.

There are concrete tiles under her toes instead of sand. It's sophomore year and she's a year older, but nothing has changed.

Lily finishes her text to Tyler: *Hi bby - just finished practice– about to get dressed and head 2 dry land.* She overhears Haddigan's voice, echoing around the locker room. "Yeah, come over at eight. Tell Staci and James, okay? I've got soda and pretzels, and Yasmin said she'll bring healthy stuff – fruit or kale chips. Oh, I know. But, whatever. See you then, m'kay? Love you."

Obviously there's a party in Haddigan's room. Lily hasn't heard about it until now, but everyone on the swim team is crazed with fall swim season and 10th grade classes.

She climbs into dry sweats, bundles her damp hair into a messy bun, and cinches it with a tie from her wrist. By now, it's a reflex to check her phone and text Tyler. She tells him she's dressed and about to leave the locker room. The battery blinks at 23%, and her stomach sinks. She'll have to find a way to send him constant updates, or he'll go batshit.

"Texting your bae?" Haddigan laughs. "Each time I see you, you're like this…" She mimes holding the phone, shakes her wet hair over her face as she scowls at the screen. "Sorry girls, just have to tell Tyler I need to pee!"

"Shut up." Lily tickles her waist, Haddigan's kryptonite. "Walk me to the gym for dry land?"

"Can't. I have run to the library to put my name down for a peer tutor – the engineering elective is kicking my ass."

Haddigan gives Lily one of her toothy smiles, swirls her long ponytail over one shoulder, and grabs her swim bag. It isn't until the locker door swings shut Lily realizes Haddigan hasn't invited her to the party or even mentioned it.

It must be a mistake.

• • •

The sun's out today. Might go for a run later. Just finished breakfast. Heading to Lit class.

Ugh, so sick of poetry from centuries before I was born!

Can't wait to see you next weekend.

I think there's a party here tonight. I won't go if it makes u uncomfortable, tho… Let me no wut u think.

Love your new Facebook update. Already Liked and commented. Will share it if u want me 2.

Lit class done. Yay! Now about to go to Advanced Calc.

Sorry – couldn't text in class. Prof was all over us. Lunchtime. Warm enough to be outside. PB&J – woo hoo! Exciting! What are u up 2?

Chapter 13.

Tyler, are you there?

Ty?

• • •

During the block set at afternoon practice, Lily feels as though she's on top of everything for once. Her laundry is ready and actually put out for the service. She's signed up for a work group in her Historical Lit class, since the Odyssey might as well be written in the original Greek as far as she's concerned. All her texts have gone out, since Tyler expects to be notified before and after each class. He hasn't written back, but Lily knows he has a lot on his plate at college.

The water parts before her like chlorinated soup, her hair a familiar weight at the back of her neck. Robert doesn't say anything, but she knows he's pleased with her time – another .02 seconds off her best freestyle practice time.

Still, it's swimmer's etiquette to drag her body out of the pool, to complain about how much practice sucks, to ask if she can leave early. Of course Robert says no and tells her to get her butt into the gym.

"Heavy on the squats!" he yells. The order echoes in the huge space. Overhead, the metal beams shiver with reflected light from the pool. With a wave to indicate Yes, Lily opens the door to the locker room so she can change for dry land.

Haddigan and Staci stand by one of the lockers. Lily opens her mouth to say Hi and ask them what she can bring to the party, even though they haven't mentioned it to her yet.

"You mean she doesn't know?" Staci murmurs.

"I just can't watch her text her boyfriend all night while the rest of us hang out. It's sick. Do you realize he has her class schedule? He makes her check in. And if she doesn't tell him where she is, each moment of the day, he gets pissed…"

It's obvious they mean her. Lily feels rage and shame course through her veins.

Haddigan has no idea what she's saying. Tyler is concerned, that's all. He wants to keep her close because Lily's so important in his life – he's told her so. He's even hinted at marriage. No, more than hinted – he's come right out and declared she's the one he wants forever.

Haddigan's a bitch, and Staci is clueless, and Lily has no need for their negativity in her life.

Making as much noise as she can, Lily stomps past the two girls without a glance in their direction. Her locker door, when she bangs it open, makes a satisfying clang. She strips off her suit and lets it fall onto the floor.

Determined to make the scene even more awkward than it already is, Lily pulls out her phone and opens the screen. The battery is at 3%. *Phone about to die going to do squats text u soon*

The text, when she hits send, minimizes as the screen goes black. Did it go through? she wonders. Oh God, please please please let it go through.

• • •

Without her constant texts to Tyler, Lily feels isolated and unsure what to do next. She rushes through her workout, skips dinner, and opts for quick leftovers in her room. There she plugs in the phone.

As soon as it comes to life she calls Tyler on Facetime. There's no response. Sometimes he makes her wait for hours, repeating his name until he sees she's invested enough in him.

Lily's become used to it. Probably a lot of boyfriends do the same thing to their girlfriends. With a shrug, she opens her laptop and logs into the group chat for Lit.

When the student group opens, James puts up an outline of the expected assignments with a few suggested themes. The students read through the workload and let James decide who will do what for the papers they'll have to write.

He, Lily, and the other participants reach a conclusion on one of the essay questions and divide the mythology research into manageable chunks. The chat comes to an end, and Lily opens a new tab to start work on her section.

She jumps when she sees Tyler's blank gaze like paparazzi inside her phone. "Hey!" Lily hopes her voice sounds normal. "Didn't realize you were there. Sorry. I got sucked into a shitpile of work for…"

"Obviously. It's so nice to get a call in the middle of a team meeting and be ignored. Wonderful, just fantastic."

Lily clicks her tongue. "I just said I was sorry. It's not like I did it on purpose. I have work here too, you know."

There's no way to recall the words once she's said them. A fleeting grimace – is it anger? joy? – passes over his face. "Oh, is that so? Well, I tell you what. You can just wait and see how long it takes me to answer."

"What?" He's just as difficult to read as epic poetry. "Tyler, what do you mean?"

The screen on her iPad shakes and resolves to show a corner of his dorm room. "Tyler?" she asks. "Tyler, you there?"

The phone pings to life with a text. *Yeah. Good. Keep the attitude up. See where it gets you.*

"Tyler?" Lily's chest aches as she realizes he won't answer, not until she's done her penance for acting out. "Tyler? I'm sorry, baby. Please forgive me. I didn't mean it. Baby, no. Don't do this. I have so much work, you have no idea. I can't spend time… I mean, I will spend time on you of course, but it'll put me behind and with double practices I'll never be able to catch up."

Her room looks out over the campus, dark blue and gold in the late hours of autumn. She still doesn't have a roommate, which means extra space for Lily's clothes, books, and swim gear.

But it also means she's cut off as though she sits in a castle turret and waits for a rescuer. Nowadays princesses don't wait – they rush out, slay the dragon, start a charity to help disadvantaged children. When they were still roommates Yasmin often talked about Queen Rania of Jordan's work to promote women's education and micro-finance. Lily, however, is stuck in her room, silent except for her voice as she pleads over and over for Tyler to forgive her. If he does, if he answers, at least she'll know she's alive, not just existing.

"Tyler?" Lily pleads. "Just answer. Tyler, are you there?"

Out in the blue and gold there's a party going on. Staci and Haddigan hang out with a bunch of people, talk about movies, and braid each other's hair. There's food, laughter, music.

Lily scrubs the corners of her eyes with one sweatshirt sleeve and goes back to her research on the geography of Odysseus's voyage home. After an hour she manages to get into a rhythm: find a reference, cut and paste, plead with Tyler to forgive her. Work, write, beg. And repeat. Lily sorts facts, posts back to James and their digital group.

Her voice grows husky, but she still talks to an empty screen.

Maybe Tyler's left the room. Maybe Ben and Bree are there Perhaps all three of them watch and laugh as Lily apologizes over and over again. There's no way to be sure.

She is certain, though, about how furious Tyler will be if she stops begging him to talk to her. He'll shut her out, lock her into a cold, acid pool of his rejection.

Lily jumps when the phone rings, and she puts aside her notes on the Greco-Roman wars. Relief cascades through her – Tyler's forgiven her quickly this time.

But it's Erica's picture on the screen, freckled and with that signature gap-toothed smile. When Lily answers, Erica jumps right into a long story about a dance at their old school, how she was supposed to go with a guy she met at practice, but he ended up ditching her for another girl.

"Hang on just one second," Lily says. She waves at the iPad and speaks to Tyler's dorm room – conversation with an empty space. "Hey, baby, I'm still here. Erica just called me."

"Oh, are you Facetiming your boyfriend? And meanwhile I'm blabbing about this dumb guy I just met? Ugh, I'm such an idiot." Erica laughs. In the background Lily can hear the bathroom faucet.

"No worries. Tyler and I just stay on Facetime while I do homework. I think he's hanging with the swim team, so don't worry about it." Lily makes herself breathe, slow the desperate tumble of words.

"I'm so glad to hear from you," she adds. That much is true. In Lily's dark, isolated dorm room, Erica's bright face is beautiful. "So this idiot from the swim team showed up with another girl from school? Even though he knew you'd be there?"

"Yeah." There's the whoosh of bathroom soap followed by more water. "Crap, my knuckles are bleeding again. And do you know who he brought instead?"

"Who? Don't tell me it was Courtney."

"Yup. Can you believe it? That squirrelly bitch who used to tattle on us in fourth grade – for things *she* did!" Erica's voice is indignant.

"You're so better off. His loss. Wait, hold on." Lily waves to Tyler's dorm room. "Still here, catching up with Erica! Okay, then! I'll check in again soon!" Her voice sounds like the tones of a chipper nurse who is about to give a reluctant patient a spinal tap.

Erica hesitates. Lily can hear the check in her friend's breath. "Is he even there? How long have you said his name to him like that? Did he answer you at all?"

"Oh." Lily waves one hand in the air. "It's – this weird thing we do. I kinda pissed him off, so he just wants to know I'm here for him. Don't worry, he'll pick up in a few minutes. I bet he'll be back soon."

"But…" Another moment passes. Outside, on the campus, a few kids run around with sparklers. One of the on-site teachers opens a window and yells. There's laughter in his voice, as if he acknowledges the beauty of their silliness. "Lily?" Erica repeats.

"I'm still here."

"You know what?" More running water. "I'm gonna ask my mom if I can come up and visit this weekend. Cool?"

Lily sucks in air, tastes cinnamon and burning leaves. "Oh my God, I'd love it. You have no idea. Do you really think she'll let you come?"

"I don't care." The thump of more soap squirted out of a pump container onto already clean hands. Lily can hear the liquid, the squish of wet palms rubbing together under the faucet. Erica's voice is grim as she adds, "I won't ask. One way or another, I'll be there." Lily brushes her hand across the screen as though she could touch Erica across the miles as they say goodbye.

As thrilled as she is about Erica's visit, she still has to do her – her duty. "Tyler?" Her voice cracks. "I'm still here. Ready to talk whenever you are." She'll work for another hour, pack up her books and get ready for bed. The iPad will sit next to her pillow, an open window so Tyler can keep watch.

She may be physically alone, but Lily has a ghost to keep her company.

The assignments curl and burn under her steady fingers on the keyboard. It's almost midnight when she closes the computer, brushes her teeth, and slips between wrinkled, messy sheets. Tomorrow, Lily promises, I'll make the bed.

The iPad is on her pillow. "Going to sleep," Lily slurs.

"Why?" His face appears in the screen. "Sleepy?"

Lily mumbles how tired she's going to be for practice and class.

Okay, Tyler answers. Of course, I forgot what time it is. Sleep well, and good luck in the pool. Kill that practice. You know I got your back. I'll be the loudest one on the sideline, cheering you on as I watch you compete. So proud of you, Lily.

"Hey!" Tyler's shout wakes her. Those supportive words, the ones she needs so badly from her boyfriend, have been nothing but a dream. "Hey! Didja forget about me? Where the fuck are you, Lily? What are you doing, Lily? Didja fall asleep? You better not. Not now."

"Sorry," she says. Lily fights to keep her eyes open. Tyler's image on the screen wavers in front of her, his mouth opens and closes. "You're nothing but a stupid loser," he says. "You choose school over me, sleep over me. Call that supportive? Cause I sure don't."

Lily feels a hot, red balloon inflates inside her chest, and she wonders how this can really be her life.

• • •

"Grilled havarti and apple, please. On wheat." Lily orders a drink at Tribeck's counter. Behind her in line, she smells lavender and lemon.

Erica smoothes more hand sanitizer onto her fingers like invisible gloves.

At the register they scuffle over payment. Erica declares her mom has given her money for lunch, and Lily insists she's the host. In the end Erica says she'll pay for dessert. "If you're still hungry," she adds as a guy with dreads and a pierced septum slides a huge sandwich onto Lily's tray. The cook at Tribeck's grills them with real butter from local farms, and the cheese is smoked with cherry wood.

"I'll still be hungry." Lily leads them to an outside table under a hummingbird vine trellis and slides into the cast-iron chair. As soon as she's settled, Lily sends a text to Tyler to let him know where she is.

The girls eat in silence, punctuated by the crunch of kettle chips and fresh coleslaw. "This is so good. I love it here." Erica leans back in her seat and sips an iced coffee.

"Where's your mom - at the hotel? Or did she decide to go shopping?"

"Is this even a question? Shopping, of course. She's decided she needs a new purse. And shoes! Did I mention the shoes?" Erica pushes her plate aside and feels in her pocket. Lily already knows what she needs - more hand sanitizer. "Anyway. I have gossip…"

"Ooh." Lily picks up the untouched half of Erica's sandwich and bites in. "Tell me," she says around ham and arugula.

"Actually, it's pretty sad. Courtney lost her shit."

"Ugh." Lily pulls a face. "Do I have to be sorry for her now?"

"No, but get this. I heard she slapped that guy I told you about, the one I was supposed to meet at the dance. She hit him at Starbucks, hauled off and slapped him. I missed it, but Toni told me later. Yes, that Toni – we text and stuff now."

"Really?" Erica used to hate Toni, one of the girls who cornered her in the bathroom the day she and Lily met.

"Really. Things are different in high school, you know?" Erica puts away the bottle and opens the kettle chips on her tray.

Lily frowns, swallows the rest of the sandwich, and takes a sip of fresh lemonade. "What happened with Courtney? I mean, she was always a classic Mean Girl, but slapping the guy she dates? Was it self-defense?"

"No, not at all. And get this. Will, the guy I told you about, was covered in bruises. She'd been hitting him for a week, and he never told anyone. Not even his parents."

Lily drops her sandwich onto the plate. She knows abuse happens in all forms. Parents abuse kids. Kids don't take care of parents when they get old. There are boyfriends who hit their girlfriends, and vice versa.

Lily feels like she's jumped into a huge pool in a lead-lined scuba suit. Little prickles cascade down her spine, and she has to pretend to wipe her mouth in her napkin to hide behind.

Because what she feels is jealousy.

Lily is jealous of the boy who wears Courtney's attacks on his skin, his abuse written in dark splotches of blood like alien hieroglyphics. Now his parents will take him to a doctor or a famous specialist for therapy and make sure he stays away from Courtney's right hook.

Maybe he'll change schools. He'll get sympathy. He'll get help. But, Lily considers, not all bruises appear on your skin:

Being forced to stay awake when you're exhausted.

A constant search for validation.

The struggle to stay positive when you're alone.

The horror of getting used to insults so you almost expect them.

These things don't appear on your skin. Insults don't bruise, neglect doesn't break your arm. No one can see what lies in your heart.

Because when you're wounded on the inside, no one knows about it.

She blinks her tears away so she won't break down in a New England sandwich shop. "You look tired." Erica, as usual, appears to read Lily's thoughts. "Practice kicking your butt?"

"Yeah." Actually, practice has been a distraction, a haven from the hellish dreams when she finally falls asleep. She has a new nightmare of a huge eye watching her as she swims through the endless dream-mazes. It blinks, disappears, and leaves her alone in cold, dark silence. A few times she's woken with tears on her cheeks.

If she opens up about any of this to Erica, Lily knows she won't be able to stop. Her voice will dissolve in sobs, and she'll ugly-cry right there in the middle of Tribecks' patio on this beautiful autumn day.

And there's more. If she talks about the whole situation with Tyler, it will become real. If Lily speaks the words in her heart, she'll give isolation and exhaustion real power over her life.

Instead, she makes herself giggle at Erica's jokes, steals a chip, and talks about how much she misses New Jersey. She mentions how lame Prescot is lately, how her classmates have become weird and stuck-up.

Lily laughs and talks, waving her hands for emphasis. She catches a glimpse of her reflection in Tribeck's glass front, a pretty girl with bright hair, athletic build, and good skin. She's amazed at how carefree she looks.

Please save me, she thinks. It's a silent prayer. Maybe the friend who knows her so well will see the scars no doctor can find, the hidden heart that lies underwater like a dreadful treasure.

She finishes her sandwich and eyes Erica, who is applying more hand sanitizer under the table. Even if Lily did reach out to her friend, what would she say?

Would Erica even believe her?

14.

As fall gets colder, Lily feels like she lives inside a glass aquarium. She can see the other students at Prescot as they meet up for lunch, hang out after class, arrange ski trips and parties, but she's separated from the laughter and brightness of their lives.

Lily's day is layered with class, practice, and Facetime with Tyler. He tells her he's her protector against isolation.

There's always a message to send, a Facebook post to Like, unspoken questions she has to answer. Where are you? What are you doing? Are you faithful? She's forgotten what it's like to be alone without his voice in her head.

She understands the rules he's put in place for her: Always be accessible. Keep Tyler updated of every action, even if he complains you text too much. Be beautiful. Be perfect. Don't ask questions. Don't tell him how much your stomach aches. Illness is disgusting. Say his name over and over on Facetime, even if he doesn't answer for hours.

"Tyler? Tyler? Tyler, are you there?"

She's not allowed to have her own life, or opinions, or dreams. The thought of an hour to herself, a free zone of time without the constant pressure to check-in, is lovely and impossible.

Fantasies like these are dangerous, and Lily does her best to stay away from them. She concentrates on the good things in her life: Erica, Vincent, the guinea pigs. And Tyler, of course. *Can't wait to see you,* she texts him and tries not to wonder if it's true.

To make things worse, Lily's swim times continue to swing up and down, with more bad days than good ones. Split seconds creep back onto her time. Her vision seems clouded, fogged with exhaustion.

Robert glares from under his haystack eyebrows from where he towers over her at the side of the pool. She leans on her elbows, lets the weight of her skull bow forward in defeat. 23 seconds, once in her grasp, now seems out of reach.

As she swims, the water seems to thicken like amber around a trapped insect. When Lily retreats to the locker room, her arms and legs shiver from the effort of moving.

Dry land isn't much better. Lily checks the plates a few times to make certain no one has snuck a few ten pounders on as extra ballast. Invested in lifting weights, it isn't until the end of the workout she realizes Haddigan is on the bench next to her.

"Hey." Haddigan grins, as if Lily is the one person she hoped to see out of the entire student body. "Lats are kicking my butt today."

Lily exhales with pure relief. She isn't crazy. She's not isolated. Everyone has a rough time now and then. "Mine too! And that practice today, ugh. My times suck."

"We're nowhere near tapering yet. It'll be fine, you'll see."

The words of support let the knots in Lily's stomach dissolve. "Want to hang out after dinner tonight? I've got to finish that physics paper, but after we could go get ice cream."

"Sure." Haddigan stops when Lily's phone goes off with a blare of rap music.

Tyler's alert. "Sorry, Haddy, sorry." Lily scans the text about how his team is lame and college sucks. Lily sucks her lip as she writes a few words of consolation.

Haddigan sits up and slings a towel around her neck. "Think I'll go in to the trainers for more adjustments. You have class, right?"

Lily nods. "I'll call you later." Does she sound too eager, like a kid who pulls on mom's skirt? It's impossible to tell. Haddigan's face stays calm as she waves goodbye and disappears through glass doors, another lost opportunity for friendship.

Already Lily's phone is blowing up with demands from Tyler. He knows her schedule and has timed her day to the minute. *Are you on your way to get changed? You should be done with practice, right? Text me as soon as you get to class. Don't forget. Text when you're done. Text. Text me. Text.*

Lily's appetite has died, murdered by the constant, dull ache in her gut. The dreams of the watery maze continue to overwhelm her at night, and when she wakes it's as though she never slept.

Prescot's campus, painted in red, yellow and orange, wavers in front of Lily as she walks to class. The half-eaten power bar in her hand tastes like sand. Cronuts, bagels, egg sandwiches – none of the breakfast options at the grill tempt her.

She stops at a water fountain, drinks until her stomach swells. Maybe she's just dehydrated, a common side effect from her sport – swimmers all sweat, of course, but they can't feel it in the pool. Lily, like everyone else on the team, has to concentrate on her fluid intake.

The loss of appetite, the weird dreams, her swim times – she can blame them all on dehydration. It must be the answer. Lily stands up, sends another text to Tyler so he'll know where she is, and goes to class.

In the middle of the group exploration of Life at Versailles under the Sun King, Lily gets up to go to the bathroom. When she returns, Yasmin is in the middle of an intense, whispered conversation. "She wants to hang out with us tonight. I heard Haddigan talked to her this morning. But we just can't watch her go down like this. Have you seen her? She's on the phone all the time with him – I think she has to text him before and after each class. It's painful to watch…"

Staci flicks her eyes sideways at Lily and nudges Yasmin, whose whisper cuts off like blood flow under a tourniquet.

• • •

"They just don't get me, y'know?" Tyler slouches on his bed in the Rosemont dorm and flips a pen between long, shapely fingers. "Jealousy, probably."

A flush of love pierces Lily. Why has she ever doubted him? He's the one who understands her, ever since the very beginning. Everyone who's not Tyler thinks she's crazy and 'painful to watch.' She wishes she could reach into the iPad screen and touch the wrinkle between his brows. "It's the same way here. And my 50 went above 25 seconds again."

"Oh, I hit that time in 8th grade. Anyway. The coach says my time isn't where it should be. So dumb. Of course I'm better than the rest, goes without saying, but his expectations are ridiculous. What, am I at the Olympics? And Ben thought it was so funny when the asshole coach chewed me out. Like he could ever hope to reach my level."

Tyler flips the pen onto the bed and leans back against a pile of pillows. One is marked in blue and orange with the looped swirls of Prescot's logo, the cushion she sent him for a three-month anniversary gift.

"Maybe he just doesn't understand how hard it is to be the best." Lily crosses her ankles and smiles into the iPad screen.

"How would you know? You've never been number one." Tyler flings the pen across the room. She hears a clunk as it hits the opposite wall. "Anyway, I've gotta get out of here."

"'Kay." She nods, prepares to end the call.

"I've got somewhere to be, Lily. Jesus."

"No, it's fine! I told you, do what you gotta do."

"Yeah, right." Tyler frowns, rubs the back of his neck with one palm. Did a former girlfriend tell him his muscles bulged when he bent his arm like that? "Meet me in Jersey. Soon."

"Oh! Uh, okay. Actually, I have a trip home planned…"

"Perfect. Change it to the 11th." He leans forward, and the screen fades to black without a good-bye.

Lily taps one fingernail against her teeth. The night stretches out in front of her, blank and dark. She sends Tyler the date of her upcoming visit and slumps back in the desk chair. If she goes home to meet him, will he actually show up? Or will he yell at her for being demanding when she asks about it, the date he has requested?

It's not like she has a choice. No need to even think twice. If she doesn't appear in New Jersey on the 11th, Tyler will take it out on her for weeks.

The other dorm room bed is empty since she still doesn't have a roommate. There aren't even sheets on the bed, just a gray mattress stained from where a former student must have spilled makeup or fruit punch.

The dark screen of her laptop reflects the vacant bed. Lily kicks the desk. Should she head outside, prowl the floors, find Yasmin and Haddigan? "Hey, guys! What's up? I was heading downstairs and heard music, so…"

Instead, Lily pulls out her phone and scrolls through her texts. Although Tyler once said he fixed the Erica problem, she still has the hate texts from freshman year where she saved them in her message archives. *You're a bitch. You can't even talk to me now, bitch? Hope everyone finds out what a slut you are, bitch.*

Erica now has a different number. The messages she sends are typical: *What's up for the weekend? Had a blast at your school – still drooling over those sandwiches. Wish you lived closer. So proud of you, tho! Love you, bby.*

Lily feels a spike of curiosity. There's no way the same person could have written both sets of texts. Erica would never call Lily a bitch. Ever.

There's a little 'i' button beside the archived messages, the first ones she got. Lily clicks it to see the information, a number she once knew by heart as well as Erica's name.

She can't resist pressing the green Dial button. The other end rings several times, a muted sound like a ship's horn lost in fog.

Lily's just about to hang up, when the line clicks. "How did you get this number?" a voice demands.

"This is Lily." She hasn't thought it out, what she'd say if anyone picked up. "Who is this?"

No response, just silence on the other end. A few seconds pass, and Lily hears another click followed by a long hum. The other person has ended the call.

Every instinct tells her the voice belongs to the person who sent her the hate-texts, and that's not even the worst part. Lily recognizes the voice.

I've heard this person before, she thinks. Female. Older. But where?

The answer teases her until she gives up and goes to bed.

Beyond her window, there are sounds of music and stupid party games. Laughter chases Lily into her dreams. There, she swims alone in the underground maze, watched by one unforgiving eye.

• • •

Bubbles in the hydrotherapy whirlpool burst like tiny grenades with a whiff of chlorine. Lily lies back in the swirls of water to chase health and happiness. Deep down, she knows the cure for her slow freestyle times and choppy swim strokes won't come from whirlpools or deep-tissue massage.

No one can see what lies in your heart, not even if they crack open your ribs and dissect it.

What lies inside Tyler's heart? Lily knows he wants to win when he competes, just like her. They both live with endless laps and impossible workouts. Other than that, she's not sure of what drives him.

Control? Yeah, definitely that.

It's been a terrible morning in the pool. Her shoulder aches. She knows her sprint stroke is wrong, the dolphin kicks didn't work out the way Coach wanted, she's far off her best times, her mind's not in the game. With a sigh, she gets up and dries off, still in her suit. One of the chiropractors hands her a dry towel and tells her to wait for a check-up.

"Hey." Robert sinks into the metal chair beside hers. "Trainers are all backed up, huh? Competition season is nuts." His eyes close as he rubs them with large thumbs. "Lord, it was hard to get out of the bed this morning. Seems to get tougher each year, and it was bad enough when I was young and foolish."

Lily lets her head clunk against the chipped wall inside the trainer's room. She's in for a Talk with a capital T. "Have I done something wrong?" The question sounds clipped, annoyed, as if he's a huge interruption instead of her coach.

His eyes measure her, dark brown pupils rimmed with red. "I want to show you this." He tilts up one butt cheek as he feels in a back pocket with a hand the size of a tennis racket, withdraws an ancient wallet, and flips it open.

There's a picture of a woman inside a plastic sleeve, skin lighter than his, with a smile so wide it crinkles her eyes. She wears a summer dress patterned with daisies, cut straight across her neck. It exposes more amber skin, smooth and young even in the old photo.

"Your wife?" Lily guesses.

"Yeah."

"She's pretty."

"Was." Robert touches the picture with one careful fingertip before he places it back into his pocket. "Was pretty. She passed two years ago."

Lily frowns. She's not sure where the conversation leads – it's as mysterious and eerie as the underwater maze in her dreams. Long moments tick by. "Sorry," Lily mutters. Across the room, Haddigan laughs and chats with the trainer who's stretching her out.

Robert waves away her lame sympathy. "I went to hell when it happened. It was a car crash – can you believe that? Just a dumb accident, the kind of tragedy that happens to other people. The sort you hear about in the news. Except this time it happened to her."

The floor is freezing under Lily's feet. Robert describes his reaction, how he hid in their house. "Couldn't even leave our home to get a sack of groceries," he says. "Ate through all the cans and jars in our cupboards, even went to pick berries in the woods when I got hungry. Really. Our daughter used to call all the time, but I stopped answering the phone. Didn't want to talk to anyone."

Her eyes prickle, and Lily ducks her head so he won't see. Robert gazes across the room. "She was lucky," Lily blurts. He raises his heavy brows, and her cheeks heat up with embarrassment. "I mean, your wife. She was lucky to have you."

"You might not have said that two years ago. I was a real mess. Didn't sleep, started hallucinating. Saw things that weren't real." His lips compress. "They say it makes you stronger, right?"

The metal chair creaks as he stands and looks down at Lily. "You take the time you need," he says. "Don't fight the water, and don't fight yourself anymore. You're young, strong, and you've got real talent. I know that for a fact."

Lily murmurs a lame, "Okay." When she looks up, the corner is empty. Robert is gone. The trainers and Haddigan chat about something, maybe school or parties. Lily hears Haddigan's soft laughter, the joy of a girl who has nothing to lose.

Stop fighting. The concept is new, surprisingly simple. Maybe she can show up for practice and take it easy, find her way back through the maze.

It'll take hard work. She doesn't mind that, though. It's just the way things seem so difficult lately, and there's no reward in sight.

There's no more time to waste. Even though her shoulder still aches, Lily decides to get out of the sweaty, underground trainers' room.

"All done?" Haddigan calls out. "Wait for me – let's walk to class together."

Lily grins and waves. Maybe it is just that easy. She slips on her shower sandals. They slap against wet tile as she heads to her locker, opens the lock with a practiced twist of her wrist, and pulls out her gym bag. As it thumps onto the wooden bench, the side pocket emits a beep.

Tyler. There's a sharp twinge between her ribs as Lily takes out her phone and views the long line of texts. *Where are you. I'm sick of waiting. Tell me what's up. And - This is my last message I'm sick of it goodbye.*

Lily's hands shake as she writes frantic messages – *Sorry, I had to get hydrotherapy, My shoulder is killing me, Please don't be mad.* The desperate little bubbles wing towards him, but there's no answer.

Her shower is quick, a mad dash in and out of the warm water. Conditioner squeaks in her hair as she towels dry and types another text.

No response.

Tyler will keep her in silence all day. He's got a number in mind, an abstract figure. As soon as she sends the requisite amount of apologies – is it 50? 100? - he'll forgive her and it will all be fine again between them.

It's no big deal. Lily can get her body to practice every day, so she can

164

survive this.

She watches the screen as she rinses chlorine out of her ponytail under the sink faucet and dresses in thick sweats. Outside the long Prescot lawns will be glassed over with frost. The athletes' footprints in the silvery grass will map out their dedication when Lily heads outside.

The locker room is silent as she sends one final text to Tyler and repeats how sorry she is. Lily picks up her gym bag and looks around.

There's no one else. Haddigan must have left. Did she come in, see Lily hunched over her phone?

The flame of relief Lily feels when her phone finally vibrates is extinguished when she sees it's from Courtney, of all people. Lily hasn't talked to the girl since she left for Prescot.

Have you seen this link? OMG, I'm so embarrassed for you.

Lily blinks as she pushes through the heavy gym doors into the chilly Massachusetts morning. The URL Courtney has sent is a Tumblr link. Lily spends her time on Instagram and Snapchat, if she goes on social media at all. Between Tyler, schoolwork, and swim practice, there's hardly time to go and reblog pictures of cute actors.

An unflattering photo of Lily coming out of the pool is capped with a headline: This Lily Batista Chick Is a Bitch.

The title is a smack in the face. Lily sucks in cold air and scrolls through the Tumblr feed – five posts, all put up on the same date. *Lily thinks she's so hot. She got into Prescot by cheating.* This has been retweeted and Liked by twenty people. One person has added *I hate girls like that.*

Who put it up? And why? It isn't until she's halfway into Lit class Lily realizes she forgot to get breakfast. For a swimmer, skipping meals is bad news. Already she's down thousands of calories.

At Prescot the students don't have to get a pass to leave the classroom. Lily gets up in the middle of a discussion about chivalry in European ballads and heads to the bathroom. Locked in a stall, she sniffs and finds half a power bar in her purse. The food tastes like plastic.

To send a text is against the rules, but Lily does it anyway. *Tyler, are you there? Please just answer.* She breathes out a watery sigh and adds *I need you. I really, really need you right now.*

There is no response.

15.

After the early ice of Massachusetts, New Jersey seems too hot and humid for November. Dad's car passes groups of people out for a walk around their neighborhood: kids jeering at a boy on a scooter, a few girls intent on their phones screens. They all wear padded jackets and, in the case of the girls, furry earmuffs. Lily, by contrast, has peeled off her sweatshirt. Even though she's down to her cami, the muggy atmosphere of the car is stifling.

In the front, Dad talks to a client through his dash interface. He uses phrases Lily doesn't understand, things like VoIP and Internet Protocol. In the rearview mirror his face is red with anger as a big work deal goes south. "For Chrissakes. I already talked to China about this whole meeting. Tell Jerry to stop dicking around or we'll look like a bunch of assholes."

Bored, Lily scrolls through her texts to Tyler. It's a long line of promises and apologies from her, short bursts of complaints and expletive-heavy insults from him. The yearlong conversation is pathetic. There's no other word for it.

She can't lie to herself any longer.

All the messages are from her. Tyler hasn't responded since the day Robert talked to her about the death of his wife.

Dad finishes his call and starts in on the questions about her swimming, practice, strokes, taper, future meets. Lily answers her dad, although she concentrates on her useless apologies to her boyfriend.

I'm so sorry.

I didn't mean to do anything.

Please don't cheat on me.

Lily wrote the last one after midnight, hazy from a few Tylenols she took to ease the pain in her shoulder. At the time it seemed logical, but now she sees the words make her seem young and inexperienced, a girl who has to beg for her boyfriend's attention.

Automatically, she answers her dad's questions. Yes, her swim times have been okay. (Not true.) No, she doesn't have a lot of homework. (Also not true.) Yes, she's kept up in all her classes. (Sort of.)

The questions are worse when they get in the house. A slew of cousins and aunts gather by the garage door as though they've waited for her. The instant she walks inside, an uncle shouts, "Hey! Lily's here!"

She's surrounded.

Vincent's face, hovering at the edge of the crowd, brightens as soon as he sees her. Lily excuses herself and squeezes her way to him, and they hug briefly. Her brother's grown, although his ribs still feel like bird bones. "Skinny," she says in his ear.

"You're skinnier," he retorts.

It's easier with Vincent at her side. Lily's able to sneak past the kitchen, where Mom chats with another group of relatives. She waves a martini glass in the air to illustrate a point. As Lily and Vincent head towards the stairs, a wave of pink liquid splashes onto their mother's shirt. She doesn't even notice as she continues to laugh with an aunt about how much the holidays suck.

Ham and Lettuce are stashed in Lily's room to keep them out of the way of all the guests. The guinea pigs get jumpy around too many people. Lily scoops up Ham and collapses on the bed. "Whew," she sighs.

"Yeah." Vincent folds his legs into a pretzel and sinks onto the floor. "It's been like this all day."

"When's dinner? Guess I have to put on jeans or a skirt." Lily has no idea what she's packed to come home for the Thanksgiving break. Her bag might be filled with car parts for all she knows.

"You have a while." Vincent crashes on the mattress next to her and scratches Ham's back. The pig responds with a loud purr before chattering his teeth.

"He must be hungry. Go steal a bag full of lettuce?" Lily bats her lashes and nudges Vincent's hip with one toe.

She doesn't have to ask twice. He gets up and heads out, closing the door with a click.

Lily's phone is on 17%. The charger is in one corner of her sports bag, underneath a pile of t-shirts and crumpled heat sheets.

She plugs in the phone and scrolls through the texts. Nothing new pops up except Happy Turkey Day! from Erica along with a long line of X's and O's.

"This is ridiculous," Lily mutters. She's grumpy after the car ride and onslaught of relatives. Her index finger stabs Tyler's info, and she hits the Facetime button. Downstairs she hears a burst of loud laughter.

There is a click, and the call picks up. Lily sees nothing, just a square window framing a patch of carpet. "Ty, are you there? It's Thanksgiving, and I'm home. You're probably at home too. Come on, Tyler, it's time. Either you're gonna break up with me, or we'll figure this out. But you can't just shut me out."

A text pops up at the top of her phone. *Keep it up.*

"Why?" Lily closes her eyes and forces herself to take a few breaths. She's relieved to finally get a text from him, a sharp stab to the heart. He's answered her, yes, but it means something she can't confess to herself just yet.

Wanna see how long you'll keep texting. To see if you're real or not. Or if you're one of those fake-ass girls I meet all the time.

Ham shifts on Lily's chest and begins to whistle whataweek, whataweek, whataweek. Outside the door, Vincent's footsteps thud up the stairs. "Okay. Listen. I'll text and take your test or whatever, but right now I gotta go be with my family."

Knew you couldn't hack it.

Her little, interior voice kicks in. Lily's used to cold pools on frosty afternoons and climbing back into the water after she's puked up her power bar breakfast. The inner monologue is her competitive spirit, and it makes her want to win, to ace Tyler's 'test.'

"I'll hang in. You'll see." She's just able to press End before Vincent comes in with a wad of green vegetables.

The guinea pig, an inert football on Lily's chest, starts to wriggle and becomes a ball of fur and claws. "I think Ham and Lettuce can smell the food," Vincent sniggers.

"Ow!" Lily manages to scoop up the pig and deposit him into the wide cage. The animals dive into the bowl, their wide ears making them look like miniature elephants without trunks. "Damn, he scratched me."

"He scratches everyone. We need to trim their claws." Vincent settles back on the floor and studies the guinea pigs. "Mom's loud."

"I didn't even say hi to her. Better get changed and go down there."

Vincent mumbles he'd better get out and starts to scramble to his feet, but Lily rushes to stop him. "Wait! Don't go yet. I – I'll do my makeup first. Stay." She's surprised at how much she's missed her baby brother.

"Yeah? Sure? 'Kay." He hangs his head over the edge of the cage and pokes the pigs' bowl. "This stuff looks too green. The store didn't have the right food." From the back, Vincent's neck looks slender, almost fragile.

"The piggies'll still eat it…" Lily doesn't pay attention as she sits on the bed to type in another text. *Still here! I didn't give up! Happy Thanksgiving!*

Maybe if she acts cheerful, as though she didn't have a care in the world, Tyler will go back to how he used to be. Her breath catches as she remembers him, tall and gorgeous, his bronze skin catching the light in the huge arena surrounding the competition pool.

Their best day together: his head bent over hers, the spark in his eyes as he put the ring on her finger. She caresses the tiny circle and the sapphire in its center. At least she still has it, a magical artifact, to let her know it all was real.

There's a knock on the door, and it opens slowly. "You never said hello." Mom comes into the room, sits on the bed, and slings an arm around Lily's shoulders. "Ugh, I'm tired already and we haven't even started to eat."

"How long will everyone stay?" Lily can't stand the thought of polite chitchat as she passes endless clusters of casserole dishes and serving platters.

"I don't know." Mom leans her head on Lily's shoulder. Warm breath gusts against her neck, tainted with vodka. "We have to go down and socialize. Your grandfather has asked when you'll get here about a thousand times already."

Lily loves her grandfather, a silent man with a quick smile who seems to come alive when he sees her. "Okay. I'll come down like this…"

"You look pretty, you always do." Mom drags the sports bag across the quilt and scrabbles inside. "But you know your grandmother expects you to change into real clothes."

"Ugh." Lily stretches her eyes. "Guess I need a little privacy…"

Mom gets up and beckons to Vincent. He doesn't argue, just climbs to his feet and follows their mom out to the hallway. As the door closes, he raises his hand in a quick, shy wave.

But when she's alone, Lily doesn't bother with clothes, even though she's still in shorts. Instead, she pulls out her phone and types, *Did you eat your turkey yet? Is your phone turned off? Forget how to read? If you don't hear from me for a while, I have to do the family thing.*

And – *Tyler, please. I'm sorry.*

• • •

"Tyler."

It's after midnight. Downstairs the hum of voices dies down as the last of the relatives leave. Lily managed to stay long enough to say goodbye to her grandfather, itching to get back upstairs. In the pocket of her jeans is a flat packet of twenties, his parting gift along with the whispered advice to go and buy something nice for herself, not for anyone else.

"Tyler," she says again to the dark screen. "Tyler. Are you there? Ty, I won't go anywhere. You know me – you said we were alike. I'm the one who gets you. Out of all those students who go to Prescot, you told me I was the one who understood. I haven't changed. Have you?"

"Ty. Ty. Ty. Ty."… She's said his name so many times it sounds like a word from a foreign country – North Korea, or maybe Jupiter. The view on her laptop doesn't change, but there's a ding on her phone. *Keep going,* his text reads. *Fate may be rewarded.*

He means faith, not fate. The mistake is endearing, as though he just came to life. She's talking to a real person, not just a machine.

"Tyler," Lily repeats. "Ty. Tyler."

Outside, the wind curls around the house like a woman who fights for her lover's attention. A far-off car honks, maybe to say goodbye before the driver heads onto 195.

As the sound dies away, Lily hears whispers in the hallway outside her room. "You hear it?" her dad hisses. "Just let me go in there and put an end to this whole stupid thing. I can't stand that boy. He really pisses me off, thinks he can take advantage of our daughter, I will not put up with it. He's lucky I don't get in the car, drive over to his house, and punch him out."

"No." Mom's voice is blurred, but urgent. "It'll be fine. If we make him upset, he'll take it out on her. Don't you see? Maybe if we have him over or something later with our family. He's fine when he's happy. Just – just let me talk to her."

"She's not the problem here!" Dad whisper-yells. Lily can picture how red his face will get from rage.

"I know, but if we barge right in, we'll just create a Romeo and Juliet kind of situation. Tell her she can't see him any longer, and it'll just get worse. Can't you see? Don't be stupid."

"You're stupid."

Their voices die out, and Lily slumps against her headboard. This is all her fault. She's the epicenter of a hurricane.

Hurricane Lily, who spreads destruction wherever she goes. Worse than Superstorm Sandy.

The blankets feel oppressive, pooled around her hips as though a shadowy jailer holds her by force. Lily bounces out of bed, runs to the bathroom, and swallows water straight out of the faucet. She gasps for breath and braces her hands on both sides of the sink, staring at herself in the mirror. Clumps of hair stick up at random from her scalp, and there are bruises under her eyes from lack of sleep, purple crescents of exhaustion.

Jitters run through her body as though she can't catch her breath.

Already she's taken too long. Lily dries her face on the hem of her shirt, snaps off the light, and heads to her room.

"Tyler," she says to the blank screen. "Tyler. Are you there? I'm still here. Tyler." A sob erupts from her mouth, a wobbly bubble of grief, and she collapses on the pillow.

There's a light tap on her door, and Lily manages to grind out, "Come in." Whoever it is tiptoes inside and closes the door. A moment later the bed dips – too much to be Vincent, not enough for Dad.

Her mother.

Her fingers shake on Lily's cheek. "You know what?" Mom's voice is blurred. "I need some work stuff, and apparently we have a few holiday parties. So. Do you want to go shopping with me tomorrow?"

The offer makes Lily open her eyes and slough off her exhaustion. She pushes up on one elbow and squints at her mom. "Really? I have practice, though. And Erica said I could come over."

Mom smiles, a determined and bright crescent in the dim room. "I know. But we can steal an hour in between, head to the mall, try on inappropriate shoes, have an overpriced coffee – what do you say?"

Lily considers the little square of money from her grandfather. "Sounds good. Really good."

"Okay." Mom swipes her face with one sleeve. "Bring extra clothes to practice, and we can sneak out as soon as you shower."

"Yeah."

The bed moves as Mom stands up. "I'm excited," she says, before opening the door.

"Me too."

• • •

The wind kicks up overnight and drags in a storm with intermittent, spiteful bursts of rain. It sprays Lily as she walks up to Erica's door. She doesn't have a jacket since the air is hot and sodden with humidity, "an unseasonably mild Thanksgiving weekend," the radio announcer blares joyfully.

Mom waves good-bye from a nest of gold and pink shopping bags as Lily rings the doorbell. "Have fun! Don't stay on your phone the whole time. Talk to people."

In the guts of the house, Lily hears a deep bong-bong. Erica's mom opens the door to reveal golden oak floors lined with Turkish carpets. "Oh," she says. "Lily. I didn't know you were coming over today."

"Erica invited me..." Lily isn't sure what to say next. She's saved by the appearance of Erica in the foyer.

"Okay. Well, welcome." Mrs. Winslow smiles and waves her inside.

"I streamed The Descent for us," Erica whispers into Lily's ear as they walk up to her room. "It's so creepy."

Lily mutters scary movies always make Erica hide under the blankets and beg Lily to tell her what's happening on the screen. It always ends up that way – she's worse than Vincent. "I kinda have to keep in touch with Tyler while we hang out. Do you mind?"

"Mind?" Erica pauses beside her room. The bears and medals they collected as kids are displayed on shelves and frames in neat rows, unlike the tangle of stuff in the corners of the dorm room at Prescot. "Of course not. He's your boyfriend." She plops into a leopard-print beanbag on the floor, and Lily squishes beside her. "Bet he's still in the middle of adjusting to college."

"Yeah." Lily nods. Erica's validation makes her feel her life actually makes sense. After all, Tyler must be going through a lot of changes, not only with classes and a new swim team, but also there's a completely new group of people he has to get to know, to work and swim with every day. Of course the Rosemont experience is making him cranky. "Yeah, you're right." She leans her head on Erica's shoulder, cool in the darkened room. The air conditioner's running, even though it's Thanksgiving weekend.

"Still, it's weird. Why isn't he hanging out with you? You'd think he'd want to be with his girlfriend for the holidays."

"I'm kind of on probation at the moment." Lily drags down the corners of her mouth. She sounds like an idiot. "You know, it's like you just said! He's all worked up about school, and to be honest his dad is kind of a nightmare, one of those creepy survivalists, and Ty has to deal with it all. I don't want to stress him out on top of it."

"I know, but…" Erica clicks her trackpad to pause The Descent. On the screen a group of actresses freeze in the act of climbing down ropes into a dark cavern. "I'm your friend. So, guess what - you're my priority. You get stressed too, right? You've got problems, not just this guy. I care about you."

Lily considers and waves at the laptop. "Mind if I use this for a second? I want to show you what I've been dealing with." When Erica raises her eyebrows and lifts her palm to signal have at it, Lily minimizes the movie screen and opens a new window. She has the URL memorized: Tumblr@LilyBatistaIsABitch.com.

As soon as it comes up, Erica frowns and leans forward. "Oh, my God," she says. "Oh, my God! Lily, you've been – holy shit. When did you find out about this?"

"Courtney texted me the link."

"Are you kidding? Ugh." Erica gasps and reaches out to grip Lily's arm. "Oh, my God," she repeats. "What if Courtney's the one who high-jacked my number and sent those mean texts? We're in a couple of classes together, so she could have stolen my phone. I think she's all about computer programming, too. So, she could've hacked into my phone. If she punched her boyfriend, she's capable of anything."

It doesn't add up. "But why?" Lily flicks through the Tumblrfeed. There are no new posts, just comments and reblogs on the old ones. "We hardly knew each other. I don't think I ever talked to the girl unless we were put on the same project or whatever."

"I don't know. People are freaks. Look at me - I wash my hands every five seconds. I'm surprised you put up with my nonsense."

Lily rolls into her, and they wrestle, trying to push each other off the beanbag. "Don't even start."

Erica giggles and shoves back. After a few more scuffles she scrolls the trackpad. "Still, we should get this site taken down. Look, there's a Report link. And, while we're at it, you need to seriously think about your relationship with this guy. You've texted him at least five times since we came in here – yes, you have."

With a guilty start, Lily puts away her phone. Erica has it all wrong. "You just don't understand."

"Lily." Erica's voice is soft. "Has he replied? At all? Even once?"

The phone screen is filled with the blue bubbles of Lily's desperation, her pleas for Tyler's attention.

Erica's right. There's no response.

Under her cheek, the beanbag chair rustles with Styrofoam pellets. Lily reaches out a finger and closes out the Tumblr page. She can't look at it anymore.

On the screen, the Descent actresses continue their climb into the dark pit and laugh about how there's only one way out once they enter the cave. They have to go through the darkness underneath to make it to the other side.

"I just mean you should think about the situation." Erica leans her head on Lily's shoulder and pops open her bottle of hand sanitizer.

"Did anything happen to Courtney?" Lily asks.

"She doesn't go to school anymore, if that's what you mean. I think she was expelled."

"So Will's safe from her?"

"Well." Erica spreads the sanitizer between her fingers, chasing invisible germs. "As safe as he ever can be, I guess."

• • •

"I just drank too much vodka! I'm so sorry. Guess the holidays snuck up on me, and before you know it there was a huge turkey in my refrigerator and no other food. Thank God for Wegman's." Mom's chatter blends in with the usual oldies station on her SUV, one hit wonders from decades when Lily didn't exist: songs about tying a yellow ribbon and a horse called Wildfire.

"Mom," she says suddenly. "Think I should break up with Tyler?"

The car jerks so suddenly Lily is thrown forward against the belt. "Sorry," her mother says. "I'm so – really? You think you might break up with him? Oh, honey, I'm beyond happy. You just don't know. It's been a nightmare, to be honest. A very dark time. I – you've just made me so happy."

Guess the answer's yes, Lily thinks. Even from several states away, Mom has picked up on the situation. "I didn't say I'll definitely do it."

"No, I know." Mom reaches out and touches Lily's knee with one perfect, manicured hand. "Just the fact you've thought about it at all, though, is … oh shit."

They pull up into the driveway. There are two figures beside the open garage door.

One is her dad, teeth bared in his VP of Marketing smile.

The other is Tyler.

16.

"Blow off practice." Although Tyler's breath is warm in Lily's ear, his voice makes her shiver. "We can marathon Netflix all night and order in pizza or Chinese."

He'd be furious if she told him how much her stomach hurts. Hidden in the cuff of her sweatshirt, Lily digs one thumbnail into the palm of her hand. The pain keeps her grounded. Later, if she wears long sleeves, no one will see the bruises. "C'mon, Tyler." She clears her throat. "I have to go to practice in the morning. You know how it goes – take off one day and it's easy to keep skipping. I hate to leave you, but I gotta do it. If you know what I mean." Please, please, please let him understand. Of course he'll understand – he gets her. Right?

"I forgot you were perfect. Too bad your 23-second goal is tied to your workout. Didn't I tell you real talent is in the DNA? And, end of the day, there's nothing you can do about it no matter how many laps you do. Swimmers like me don't have to be boring and show up to the gym all the time." He sucks his teeth. "God, it must suck to be a loser like you."

Lily wonders if Tyler's doing as well as he says he is. It's obvious he's gained a few pounds. The once-elegant muscles in his arms seem softer, less defined, but he brushes it off as his version of the Freshman Fifteen. "Plus," she adds, "my dad would never let you spend the night."

He sucks his teeth again and flops back against the plaid couch. They're in her basement, the best place to watch TV. Lily freezes on the cushion next to him, afraid to say anything else. On the big screen, colored images move and blur together. There's thwarted romance behind a series of killings, and – aliens? Lily raises her sleeved fist and, when she's certain Tyler isn't looking, wipes tears from the corners of her eyes. The frame of the couch shakes as he shifts to pull out his phone and tap his fingers against the screen.

In the movie, the main character screams. She's just found a dead body in the closet.

"You haven't been on Instagram for a while. Have you even seen any of my posts?" Tyler's brows inch down over his straight nose, the kind of profile found in museums or on the back of coins.

Lily jumps and digs out her own phone. She scrolls down his feed to Like and comment.

Already a few others have checked in. Lily recognizes a few of the names from her Rosemont visit, including Bree. *Hi cutie,* she's written. *Can you come over when you get back?*

Depends on my mood. Tyler has added a few smiley emoticons.

"What the hell is this?"

He grabs her wrist and peers at the screen. "What?"

"This."

Lily jabs at the Bree comment in answer, and his jaw drops. "Are you kidding me? It's bad enough to date a high school student without the little petty jealousies. You just told me I can't spend the night at your house. Ridiculous, I'm 19, and now you're in my face about this college slut? She hooked up with my roommate, which you're well aware of, since you enjoyed hanging out with Ben so much. Don't even. And," he adds as Lily opens her mouth, "I have to put up with those assholes from Prescot all up in your business. So really it's your fault if I text another girl. Think about, if you're not too brain-damaged."

She feels her mouth open in complete astonishment. "What - who are you talking about?"

Tyler's voice takes on a high, sarcastic tone. "Hi, I'm James, let me help you study, I'm so perfect, your boyfriend is shit, let's go to the library and make out." His body twists like a snake about to attack, and he grabs the remote to click off the movie in one perfect motion. He lands on top of her, and his swimmer's thighs bracket her hips. "Is this what he did to you in the bookshelves?"

His kiss is the climax of the attack. Lips and teeth bite her neck, jaw, cheek –not an expression of love but part of his crazy accusation. Tyler breaks away after the attack, his face unreadable in the shadowy room.

Upstairs a door opens, and the stair lights to the basement snap on. Tyler swings off Lily and turns on the television. By the time Mom comes in with a tray of drinks and snacks, the movie is back on and he's in his place.

"Thanks, Mrs. Batista." He reaches for a plate of cookies.

"You're welcome. It's almost time for Tyler to go home, Lily. Getting up for practice will be impossible if you stay up any longer."

On the screen, the heroine is brought in for questioning at the police station. After all, the corpse has been found in her home. The logical explanation is she must be guilty.

• • •

Maria, Lily's coach in New Jersey, slaps a practice sheet onto the final kickboard and stands up. "You look excited to be here." She heads back to the tiny, glass-walled office the coaches share at the Y.

Lily sucks in air before starting the last of her 200's. "Last 25 of each 200 monster kick!" Maria calls from her office.

As Lily enters the water, her arms feel like she's wearing kettle bells. Mom slouches on the uncomfortable bleachers and looks like she doesn't feel much better.

At the end of the painful 200's, Erica swims up to Lily and rests folded arms on the edge of the pool. "Ugh. I need breakfast. Want to go to the diner after this?"

"I do, but Tyler's in town." Lily ducks her head under the water, ashamed of being that girl. She always said she'd never be the one who ditches her friends as soon as a guy shows up. "Uh, maybe all three of us can go out." As soon as she says it, Lily knows it's a bad idea.

"Sure." Erica gives her a bright smile and heads back into the lane.

Lily fights her way through the rest of the practice sets. It's one of those days where when swimming seems impossible, and the only thing getting her through is the constant voice in her head. Right now, in

Sarasota or York or Wilton there's a girl who shows up for practice. She works harder than you. She busts her ass on sets and dry land. You might have to swim against her at the next meet. Pain is temporary – victory lasts forever.

Her legs tremble as she hauls herself over to her mother's side and collapses on the bench. "Ow," she says.

"Me too." Mom hands her a water bottle and a power bar. "Eat. Drink. Don't faint on me, okay?"

Lily nods and chews. The air, as usual, is chlorinated and humid. As a result, most of the parents look a little frizzy, although her mother's French braid is smooth on her seersucker shoulder. A burst of affection runs through Lily, and she leans her head against Mom's knee.

"Hey! Your hair is still wet!" Her mother wiggles the thigh Lily's using as a pillow.

"Sorry." A moment later Mom's fingers stroke Lily's thick, dark-blond strands. "Can we go out to breakfast with Erica?"

"Sure." Mom's reply is immediate. "Maybe we can all go to the mall again, too."

"Hm. Guess I should see what Tyler wants to do first."

Mom's hand in Lily's hair pauses for a second. "Thought you were going to…" Her voice dies out. The moist air swirls around them as a group of the older, male students come in with an instructor – water aerobics. Across the room, inside the coach's office, a phone rings. The water aerobics students splash each other in the pool.

"Hey, Phil, last time I saw a submarine as big as your gut, we were in the Korean War," one old man laughs.

"Haha, you're a funny guy. A real Bob Hope, you are."

In her lane, Erica reaches the end of a lap and makes a face at Lily, jerking her head in the direction of the men. Maria's firm voice can be heard over the chaos followed by the ding of the old-fashioned phone in the coaches' office, as she hangs up.

The scene is familiar and safe. Lily settles against her mother's shoulder, almost asleep. Across the pool, the boys in her old swim team climb out of the pool as they finish their final laps. She's known them for years, went to their birthday parties, been asked out by a couple of them. Pete, the tall guy with tanned skin and hair bleached silver from his lifeguard job, kissed her after a successful meet a couple of years ago.

What would her life been like if they had stayed together? She can just imagine hanging out with his large, friendly family, lifeguarding with him on the beach.

"I'm dead." Erica plops on the bench next to her and jerks Lily out of the hazy dream. "Totally dead. Those final laps killed me."

"I know. Right? Here, need water?"

Erica waves a bottle in Lily's face in answer. "Hi, Mrs. Batista," she adds.

Mom smiles and waves. "Breakfast," she whispers, and cuts back to a long harangue about IV's.

"So up for the diner right now. Eggs and pancakes and bacon and waffles – I want it all." Erica towels her hair roughly and peeks between the folds. "Uh, not the Blue Palace, though. Heard they had a rough health inspection."

"You are the only person I know my age who keeps up with health inspections." Lily nudges Erica and jerks her head at the locker room. "Ready?"

They both stand up. Mom clicks off her phone, tells them to hurry up. It's all normal, just a regular vacation day away from Prescot. Lily knows every tile in the Y: the best water fountain, which bleachers creak when you sit down.

Lily's sniffs the familiar old rubber and chlorine of the pool enclosure as armor against her growing isolation at Prescot. She's so intent on those details she nearly walks into the tall figure by the door, standing in her way with folded arms.

He's just as dark as Pete, but without the blond hair. The result is shadowy, mysterious – almost scary. Lily's heart thumps quicker when she sees the glitter in his eyes.

In front, Erica stops. "Oh. Tyler. Hi."

She doesn't like him. Lily's sees it written in every line of Erica's body – the way she stiffens and hugs the big swim bag in her arms.

The usual quick upward jerk of his chin is Tyler's only response. He waits until Erica goes into the locker room and bends closer to Lily's ear. "Thought you were done with her."

"She's my friend. I mean, we've been friends for, you know, forever. Plus she practices here, so I can't exactly avoid her. Not that I'd want to, anyway…" Lily's foot itches, and she lifts one leg to scratch her toes.

"You should have blown off practice, just like I said. Didn't I tell you? I'm always right. If you weren't such a spoiled idiot, you'd actually listen to what I say. Words, Lily – they mean things." Tyler's mouth spreads with triumphant confidence. "Anyway, go get changed. I got the truck outside."

Lily feels his hand, warm and insistent between her shoulder blades. She has no time to respond before she's propelled into the locker room.

• • •

The green and brown boxy truck belongs to Tyler's father. There are plain boxes stacked in the back, bungeed to the metal sides and floor. She knows they contain MRE's, a water purification system, and a small tent.

Tyler swings into the driver's seat, slams the door, and pulls out a laptop. "Okay. Don't want this to go over wifi, so I've saved it to the hard drive. Here."

Puzzled, Lily leans over the center console. There's a screen grab of what looks like code. "What is it?" she asks.

"See this number?" Tyler runs the pointer over one line of the code. "Now, watch." He pulls up another png. "Notice anything?"

"They're the same number. Where'd you get this stuff?"

"You kidding? My dad knows all kinds of hackers. They're always breaking though government firewalls. Pathetic." It's not clear if he means the insult for the hackers or the CIA computers.

He grunts and returns to the first document. "Guess what this code is for? The hate blog you found."

Lily feels her stomach sink, as though she's about to jump off a bridge. "And the matching numbers?"

His grin returns. "IP address. My dad's guy used his software to get through their firewall to track it. even though the phone's source changes with different routers, the NAT translates it to this." He stabs two identical strings of numbers and letters. "You know what this means, right?" The pointer clicks back to the second doc. "It's all laid out here. Shows the time, date, location, everything."

"What does it mean?"

"Yeah, well." Tyler closes the laptop, moves his seat back, and folds his arms. "You already know what's up, right? Finally making the connection? Your little friend in there, the one you were so cozy with on the bleachers, she's a hypocritical bitch. It all comes from her phone number, the one you first showed me last year. Like I said, I'm always right."

• • •

Lily has to call her mom and explain what happened, why she left with Tyler instead of waiting. "Are you at home?" Mom demands. "I just got here. Erica was none too pleased, by the way, and I don't blame her."

Tyler reaches Lily's house and parks in the driveway just as she's able to hang up on Mom's play-by-play accusation. The garage door is closed, its white paneling a blank screen of irritation.

His kiss is demanding, all teeth and tongue. As soon as Lily gets into it he pulls back, leans against his door, and takes out his phone. The screen displays a girl Lily doesn't recognize. "Yeah," he answers.

Lily hesitates, climbs out of the high seat and jumps down from the truck. Don't date anyone with tires bigger than you, Erica once told her on a sleepover. They giggled under a blanket fort together that night, strung out on sugar and friendship.

She could confront Tyler and demand to know who's on the other end of the line. Already Lily knows what would happen. She can map out every word of the future conversation. Her question would be met with his disgust and accusations, a long litany of her faults.

As usual, she'd be the one who was wrong.

Her ribs ache. She can't breathe. Lily closes the door, watches Tyler back up the truck and head onto the street until the sound of his engine dies away.

In the end, it's easier to avoid the fight. If she demands to know who just called him, it will turn into a long ordeal and, in the end, become her fault. Lily opens her mouth, and her exhale sounds like a sob.

The path to her door is greased with new rain. Overhead, clouds glower and bunch in weird shapes: a heart. A knife. A turnip.

When she opens the door, Vincent sits on the steps. Ham and Lettuce are on his lap, side by side like two fur footballs. As soon as Lily comes in, he raises one finger to his lips.

Her parents are in the kitchen. Their voices are a strained chorus of dismay. "But why did you let her leave with him?" her dad whispers. She can picture his face turning red as he asks.

"You don't understand. It's just easier for everyone in the end if I go along with it. She's not going to leave him, and he tortures her if I interfere."

"What? 'He tortures her if you don't interfere!' Did you hear her the other night? 'Tyler. Tyler. Tyler.' I was ready to jump in the car so I could go and punch him out. It drives me insane."

A clink of glass on glass. Mom's making herself another drink. "She's my daughter too. All I can do is my best to make the situation as easy as possible …"

Dad hushes her. A door opens, shuts, and the kitchen grows quiet. Their parents must have gone out to the patio.

Vincent's eyes are huge behind his glasses as he strokes the calm, sleepy guinea pigs. Lily plops next to him on the step and feels as though she's the one who's just been punched.

Her relationship with Tyler affects her entire family. She, Vincent, and even her parents are connected with invisible lines like butterflies in a web.

Maybe being a family means you all drown together.

Those aching, desperate thoughts fade with the soft wheeking of the pigs in Vincent's lap. His team sweatshirt smells like detergent when she wraps an arm around his shoulders.

The tiny moment is an island of calm. The website, Prescot, her swim times, and – and Tyler. The peace is shattered when the kitchen door slams again. "Lily!" Dad calls. "Where are you? Lily!"

"I'm here."

He strides into the foyer and holds up his phone. "Did you see what your boyfriend just tweeted? About how sexy his fellow students are! Do you know a girl called Bree?"

Lily sighs. "Yes, dad, I do."

Mom hovers in the background. "Did you meet her when we visited?" She lifts her glass and drinks.

"Yes, mom, I did."

The glass falls from Mom's hand and smashes on the floor. The sound makes Ham squeal and jump like an exploding popcorn kernel. Lily's horrified to see tears in Dad's eyes. Her father should be a rock or a fortress, and instead she's made him cry.

"He ignores you," Dad chokes out. "I heard you the other night – must have said his name a thousand times. Fucking treats you like shit... Sorry, Vin. I didn't mean to curse. Like crap. And look at what he writes about this girl – how nice she is, how beautiful, amazing body, smart..."

He trails off as Lily takes the phone and reads the thread. Tyler and Bree have a trail of flirty messages back and forth. The exchange reminds her of how he used to be with her, funny and attentive.

Mom disappears into the kitchen, and Dad purses his lips as they hear ice and more liquid slosh into a glass. "We should clean up the hall first!" he shouts.

"Maybe if we're nice to him," Mom replies from the kitchen. "I told you his father was a head case. Maybe Tyler will be the way he used to be – such a polite boy when I met him."

Vincent shrieks. "Shit! Ham peed on me!" Out of nowhere, he bursts into tears. Lily hasn't seen him cry since he was in first grade.

"Just because I cursed doesn't mean you're allowed to." Dad blinks and points to the stairs. "C'mon, buddy. Let's get you and the pig cleaned up."

Lily sits on the steps, frozen with horror. Vodka seems to have become Mom's drug of choice, her dad can't handle the situation without cursing, and Vincent has regressed to his seven-year-old self.

"Here." Mom waves a roll of paper towels as she enters the hall and gets on her knees. "Could have told him I'd have this cleaned up in no time." Her words come out in breathless spurts. She pulls off a wad of towels and swipes vodka off the wood floor in sloppy ovals.

On the steps, Lily crosses her arms over her stomach. Her insides ache, but whether it's from hunger or nausea is hard to tell.

"I have to do homework." Lily scrambles up to her room. From the bathroom, she hears Dad rumbling to Vincent about curse words and guinea pigs.

The quilt Lily's grandfather brought her from a vacation in Spain is soft under her cheek as Lily comes apart. It not just tears, more the sensation of her body dissolving into molecules and atoms.

When she's empty and undone, Lily sits up and draws in a long, shuddering breath. There's no more avoiding what she knows, way deep down, what has to be done.

It's time.

Her phone is in her pocket. She takes it out and scrolls through the Twitter messages between Bree and Tyler, a flirtation spelled out in pixels for the entire Internet to read. Even with the decision she's about to make, it isn't easy to read the tender messages. He jokes, *You're so cute, like a kitten or something,* and Bree flirts back, *Aw! Look who's talking sexy...?*

Lily taps his number and anxiously waits for Tyler to answer as the phone rings. He rejects her call. She tries again and again but he refuses to answer.

It leaves her no choice. Lily's hands shake as she types in the text message. *I'm sorry, Tyler, I can't take it any longer. We're done.*

One of the biggest decisions of her life only requires a few keystrokes. She stares at what she's written and feels blank inside.

In the bathroom, Vincent insists he never meant to say a bad word, that it was all a mistake.

"I know," her father soothes. "I know, buddy."

"But I really didn't, dad!"

Unable to think of any reason to hold back, Lily presses Send and falls back on the bed, breathless from what she's just done. Her grandfather's quilt feels like the satin pillow under a suicide's corpse.

Lily chokes on darkness, feels as though she's six feet under the ground. Her heart thunders, and she tries not to cry out and upset Vincent. The kid's been through enough for one day.

Erica picks up as soon as Lily punches in her friend's new number. "I can't do it," Lily whispers. Rolling off the bed, she pads to the closet, steps inside, and closes the door. In the darkness, she sinks to her knees and sobs. "Can't do it, Erica. Can't do it."

Lily relates the break-up in hiccups. When she stops to suck in musty oxygen, Erica asks, "Why should you do anything? Whatever it is, I mean?"

"I'm talking about school. Prescot. I just broke up with Tyler and I can't go. I can't leave."

"There are schools here."

"Yeah." Lily nods, even though her friend can't see. "You're right. I could – I could – but it's the middle of the year ..."

"You can figure it out. And guess what. I'm proud of you for breaking up with Tyler, I mean. I didn't want to say it before, but he's a dick. You're so much better off, and I know it was hard, but you did it. You did it, girl."

Her heart pounds in Lily's chest. She can't breathe right after crying. Even her skin hurts, as though there's acid in her veins. "Erica?" she adds, afraid to ruin one of the few good things she has left.

"Yeah?"

"Tyler said you were the one who started the hate site about me on

Tumblr. Sorry, you know I wouldn't… but I don't know what is up or down … I just…"

"No." Erica's voice is firm, filled with conviction. As soon as she speaks, Lily believes her. "I promise I didn't start the Tumblr. If I ever found out who did it, I'll kick their asses. That's a promise."

"Okay." Lily apologizes until Erica tells her to stop and go talk to her parents.

It's good advice. Lily's made her decision, and now she has to act on it. Life is about to change. She stands up, opens the door, and feels the rush of fresh air on her face.

Already there are five texts on the phone screen from Tyler. Lily can see the words, although she tries not to read them. They might suck her back into the shadowy, nightmare maze where she'll drown. *What do you think gives you the right and you're gonna be sorry and it's your loss and it's all a joke, don't you get it, the Twitter thing is just a joke. I told you I texted her because I couldn't see you all the time. So in the end, this is all on you. It's all your fault.*

As she watches, another message pops up. She can't help seeing the words: *You just failed my test.*

17.

My new boyfriend – so hot! Jealous much?

Lily can't believe Bree's post has gone up so fast. The girl has changed her profile picture to a shot of her and Tyler kissing at what looks like a party. Behind them, rowdy undergrads lift red Solo cups. Ben's hanging over Tyler's shoulder, face split in a wide grin. Obviously, the roommate doesn't care his hookup has moved on.

Lily knows the kiss is Tyler's 'In Your Face' tactic. She could do the same thing for revenge by calling James, Pete, or any one of a dozen guys she knows. *Wanna hang out?* A few hours later, she could post her own make-out session on Instagram.

The thought exhausts her.

But Ben was the one friendly face at Rosemont. When Lily was lost, abandoned by her boyfriend, Ben was the one who came to her rescue.

Lily flops back on the pillows and throws her phone on the bed. She squeezes her eyes shut and tells herself the tears are for Ben and the lost possibility of a new friendship. Crying over Tyler is a waste of time.

A tap on her door makes her sit up, scrub her eyes, and suck in a painful gasp of air. "Come in," she says, trying to keep the sadness out of her voice.

Mom opens the door and trips over a pair of jeans on the rug. She grumbles about the messy room but trails off when she looks at Lily's face. "Crappy day out, huh?" She sits next to Lily, and the bed dips under her. "You need to go back to school. No, I don't mean Prescot. We know you can't leave New Jersey at the moment. I'm talking about school here. We have to re-register you before the state comes after us for being delinquent parents."

"Mom. I don't want to – I gotta go to swim practice." Lily's phone vibrates, and she can't help picking it up. Erica wants to hang out later.

They 'need to talk.' She types Okay, cool and tries to listen to the rest of what Mom tells her about school records and paperwork. Lily interrupts after a few minutes. "Jesus, mom. I can't…"

"What you can't do is sit up here, day after day, surrounded by dirty laundry." Mom sniffs and kicks a pile of wilted t-shirts. "You wear sweats all the time, you never go out…"

"I was at practice this morning!" Lily sits up, outraged.

"Besides practice, I mean."

"Erica just texted. We're gonna hang out later."

With a sigh, Mom gets up and heads to the door, still nagging as she opens the door. "Bet she's coming here. Right? God forbid you actually leave the house. We all want to support you, Lily, but I swear you've got a butt-shaped dent in your bed. Not even kidding."

With a frustrated howl, Lily bounds off the mattress and stabs Erica's number. "I've got to get out of here," she says as soon as Erica answers. "You still want to get together? Okay good. Not my house – not yours either. Food court? After practice? Okay, perfect. See ya."

Lily hangs up and drums her fingers on the edge of the dresser. In the depths of the mirror, her reflection looks back – pale-skin, messy hair, lips cracked with dryness. She can't remember the last time she put on makeup.

Her depression wafts her into the bathroom, where she trails a washcloth over her face. There's moisturizer in a glass jar by the rack of toothbrushes, but Lily can't summon the energy to put it on. Instead she rakes fingers through her hair and scowls.

Before she can go and climb into practice gear the doorbell rings. Lily hears Vincent murmur to Ham or Lettuce – "It's just a guest, silly piggy, not an axe murderer, just chill."

Bright voices splinter downstairs, followed by loud feet thumping the staircase like scales played on an oversized piano.

"Lily!"

Erica's voice. Lily sticks her head out of the bathroom and sees her friend, all glammed out with a new haircut and sparkly shadow on her eyelids. She's wearing mascara and lip gloss as well. "Why are you all decked out?" Lily asks. "Is there a new cute coach I don't know about? And I thought we were going to meet up at practice..."

"I just couldn't wait to tell you." Erica threads her fingers through Lily's to pull her inside the bathroom. "Mom just got the letter today. I've been accepted to Prescot. We head up there next week."

"What?" Lily shakes her head. Taking entrance exams to get into private school was such an intense process, complete with exhaustive interviews and long essays. She and Erica went into the ordeal, certain they would both get accepted.

They knew they'd go to the same school and be roommates. It was supposed to be magical. Lily's acceptance into the finest private school in the country when Erica got nothing was a setback to their friendship, but they managed to handle it. They'd always been best friends, after all.

Erica and Lily. The two names always went together.

And now Lily's the one at home, not even re-registered in her old school yet, about to be left behind as Erica waltzes off into the horizon. "Are you serious?" Tears prick Lily's eyelids. Crying again – she's always teary lately.

"Yup. I guess they had a vacancy when you left." Erica peers at her. "Hey, you're not mad, are you? You don't know what it's been like, ever since you left. Mom's been on my case all the time. She goes on and on about swim times and grades and self-confidence, and how it's all my fault I didn't get in when you were accepted. It's like she can't shut up. And Dad just looks at me and shakes his head, like I'm such a disappointment..."

She leans over the sink, squirts liquid soap on her hands, and starts to scrub. The overhead light blinks, and Lily remembers the mirror image of this scene, the day when her mother told Erica's family about Lily's acceptance. No one had said a word.

Erica had been the one to break the awkward silence. She jumped out of her seat, threw her arms around Lily's neck, and whispered congratulations.

When it's her turn, Lily discovers she can't be as gracious as her best friend once was to her. She's too raw, too broken. "Great," she snaps. "I just got home and you're about to take off. I'll be all alone now, no one to hang with, have to practice with those idiots at the Y." The tears course down her cheeks. Erica stops scrubbing her hands and stares at Lily's reflection.

The mirror shows Erica's glamorous makeup and sleek hairdo. Next to her stands a pale, disheveled stranger, eyes swollen from this next bout of misery.

No wonder Tyler has a new girlfriend.

• • •

It's easier at swim practice. Everyone's underwater, so they all look the same: flat hair jammed into rubber caps. Wet skin in wet suits. Outside, the weather has turned cold, so the atmosphere inside the Y is steamy.

Lily cuts the water, intent on her new stroke style. After battling through her final lap, she climbs out of the pool and tents her body under a towel. The bench creaks under her weight, and she wishes she could fade away, a phantom in the fog.

"Tough practice?" Mom's stare is vague, unfocused.

"Practice was fine." The cement is rough under her wrinkled toes.

"You know, you could at least…" The accusing tone in her mother's voice vanishes as a pink and orange figure emerges from the swirling humidity. "Betsy. How are you?"

"Wonderful." With a bright smile, Erica's mom leans against the thick metal bar separating bleachers from the pool. "You've already heard Erica's news, I'm sure."

When Mom opens her mouth to reply, Lily interrupts. "Erica's been accepted to Prescot, mom. She told me tonight. I didn't have a chance to let you know."

The bench creaks again as Mom crosses her legs. "In that case, congratulations. I'm just sorry our girls couldn't be there together."

The way her mom talks makes Lily lift her head. *Just. Sorry. Our. Girls.* The words are blunt. Mrs. Winslow doesn't seem to notice as she sits next to them on the uncomfortable bench and crosses lean, tanned legs. She looks like a starlet on the red carpet. "It *is* a shame, isn't it?"

Lily pulls both arms close across her chest. It's not just her imagination. Her mom and Erica's mother don't like each other. How did she miss it, after all those years?

They've all gone to meets, practices, birthdays, and barbecues together, both families as part of a whole. The mothers kiss each other on the cheek when they meet at parties. "How are you?" they say. "Oh my goodness, there you are. How are you? You look amazing…no you…" The words are always spoken in the high register of long-lost girlfriends who meet after years of separation.

And yet Mom's face is frozen in a defensive attitude, while Mrs. Winslow's chin juts out. The two finish the battle of their conversation, and Erica's mom gets up to prance off.

Lily looks up. "Sorry," Mom says. "Hope I sounded normal. Ugh. To be honest, she can be a real bitch."

"Don't use that word," Lily begs. "I hate it."

Mom's fingers tremble on Lily's wrist. "Sweetheart! Did Tyler ever call you that? Oh my God, I bet he did. I'm – I apologize." Her mouth staples into a hard line.

Bitch. Lily has heard it so often it nearly became meaningless. Thinking about it now, she's shocked at herself. How could she have become so complacent? He was her boyfriend, and he consistently called her names – hurtful, degrading insults like little sneaky barbs hooked into her lip. Lily was the fish on his line, continually thrown back into the ocean again and again. She kept swimming back, kept biting the same hook even though she knew it would tear her apart.

Even after the break-up, what would happen if he walked through the mist and sat next to her at practice? Attacked with his biting, demanding kisses?

Suppose, she wonders, he shows up at the Y. What would she say if he asked her to come back to him?

Lily tries to tell herself the answer would be No.

• • •

The car's door latch is slippery with ice. Winter has hit New Jersey with a vengeance. Lily blows into her cupped hands, jogs in place, and waits for Mom to come out of the Y. As usual, her mom has stopped to talk to a group of swim parents.

"How was practice?"

"Jesus." Lily jumps and sees Erica right behind her. "I nearly peed my pants. Sneak up on people much?"

Erica pulls the green crocheted scarf tighter around her neck. "Still mad at me?"

"I'm not mad. It's just." Lily's anger is visible in the cold night, a cloud of frustration and lost hope. "Going to a new school sucks, you know? I thought at least I'd have you." The thought is too big to put into words. Erica's a light in the darkness, and Prescot's about to swallow her up. Lily knows she'll be terribly alone without her friend.

"It was so easy for you." Erica shivers. "You don't realize it, but Prescot accepted you right away. Remember when you got your email saying you had a slot at the school? Your mom was so happy, you were thrilled, your dad told everyone at the Y. Even Maria put the news up in her office, and she never cares about anything." Lily barks out a short laugh. It's true. Maria only talks about practices and meets. "When you left, ugh. It was horrible. I think my mom went crazy for a while. She wouldn't talk to me, wrote thousands of letters to the Dean…"

"Seriously?" Lily is shocked. She never bothered to ask how Erica felt when the time first came to go to Prescot. The two of them talked on the phone constantly after the move, but only about dumb stuff like who was in their classes and how practice was that morning.

"She just wouldn't let up. Nagged at me to eat more, eat less, wear the right clothes, swim faster, make the National Team, wash my hands, don't wash them too much, don't take so many showers. It sucked." Erica's face crumples.

Lily dumps her swim bag on the ground and pulls Erica into a hug. "Sorry," she whispers into her friend's moss-colored scarf.

Quick footsteps echo through the lot. Both women, Lily's mom in her Uggs and Mrs. Winslow in high heels, walk up to the car. "I just heard!" Mom says. "Congratulations, Erica – I'm so happy for you."

Mrs. Winslow's glove – beige leather with brown fur trim – caresses Erica's coat sleeve. She says Erica's test scores were the highest in the region, the letter from the Dean was simply lovely, just filled with compliments, Erica will be the best student they ever had.

Mom nods and murmurs, "How nice." Her key fob clicks, and the car chirps in response. Lily climbs in beside her mom, waves goodbye, and shouts promises to call Erica soon.

In the car, Lily's phone vibrates. A hot surge of hope courses through her chest. Has Tyler sent an explanation, an apology, a declaration of love?

It's none of those. Yasmin, of all people, has sent a series of texts.

Hi.

School sucks!

Miss us?

Lily thumbs the screen, but it's not Yasmin she wants to text. After months of talking to Tyler before and after each class, sleeping with him on Facetime next to her on the pillow, she feels cut off. Her body is an amputated limb inside a stainless steel surgery pan.

I miss Tyler, she thinks. Hot tears roll down her cheeks, a final act of her body's betrayal. In that dreadful moment, Lily would give anything to be back with him. She would deal with his insults, put up with all the online flirtations, and write text after text. He could call her a stupid bitch. She would say his name for hours until he finally decided to talk to her.

Anything to fill the void her life has become.

"'Lovely letter from the Dean.'" Mom snorts and slams her palm on the steering wheel. "Go to hell."

18.

The lunchroom in Lily's new school is loud and smells like baked beans. She sits by herself in one corner, hunched over a turkey wrap from QuikStop. Across the room, Sonya chats to a group of students. Their faces are bright with laughter until Sonya catches Lily's eye across the room. The girl lifts her chin, turns away, and whispers to one of the girls.

Lily lets the wrap drop into her napkin. She's had enough soggy lettuce for one day. Obviously Sonya has taken Courtney's empty throne as Head Mean Girl. Lily slumps and pulls out her phone - at least she can stay in touch with Erica.

In New Jersey the weather stays on the wrong side of freezing. Icy rain slants into Lily's boots and shirt collar, and it seems the days stay sullen and dark. At Prescot the lampposts would be lit to make the campus glow like a golden tree ornament as the students headed out to chat or make study group plans for later..

The overhead neon tube flickers. Lily fiddles with her phone and decides to write an email instead of interrupting Erica's day with a text.

• • •

Hey girl,

Just wanted to say hi and see how things are going. Here life is horrible, haha. I don't mean to sound sad, but it's just hard to start over in a new school.

Guess you know what I mean, although the girls at Prescot are nicer. (At least I hope so for your sake!) You weren't kidding about Courtney's old crew, except Sonya is Queen Bee now. It's like I'm a leper. Those girls act like I have the plague.

God, I'm sick of myself and my dumb depression. I'll be back to normal soon, I promise. But right now life is just...tough.

And there's no one to talk to.

• • •

Lily stares at the words on the screen, certain she should delete everything she just wrote.

"Chlorine!" Sonya has come up behind Lily's chair. "Does anyone smell nasty YMCA chlorine?"

Startled, Lily brushes the touchscreen and her email disappears. She didn't even get to sign her name.

"Yeah, gross pool water. One of the swimmers probably peed in it too!" One of the followers hoots with laughter, and the group cracks up.

Don't cry. Not over a bunch of brainless idiots. Lily concentrates on her phone and looks at her text messages. Tyler's name is at the top of the list, still her most-used contact. Such a constant presence leaves a hole in her life now that he's gone. She wants to hear the voice in her head, see the words in a message, sit and say his name all night until he's decided she's suffered long enough.

You're never good enough.

You're an idiot.

You're a waste of space.

What you do means nothing.

I'll always be better than you.

You failed the test.

And her voice: "Tyler. Ty. Ty. Ty. Tyler. Tyler, are you there?"

The table is empty except for her and half of a mass-produced sandwich. At other linoleum islands, kids talk about the weekend, games, sports, movies, and hook-ups.

Across the lunchroom, there's another kid who sits by himself, just like her. Lily recognizes Will's black hair flopped over his forehead. Is he hiding another bruise? Despite everything, is he back with Courtney?

Like him, Lily's got no one to talk to in the overheated cafeteria. Tyler may have been a disaster, but his skin was warm against hers. His voice was deep in her ear. She was never completely alone when she had him…

No. When he had her.

Lily blinks and feels like she's swallowed ground glass. She forces herself away from her contacts before she writes a messages and texts it to him. No, she thinks. No, not that.

Her phone shudders, and Lily jumps. Did her thoughts swim through the air and land in his ear?

There's an email in her folder, a response from Erica. But when Lily opens it, three tiny words float in pixilated space.

Who is this?

• • •

The time in afternoon class crawls past. Lily's head aches from boredom and exhaustion. If James could see her heart now it would be black and crawling with maggots.

Broken. Cracked. Diseased.

She feels shattered. Her new high school's standards are much lower than Prescot's, but Lily can't summon the energy to raise her hand in Trig and Advanced Bio, even when she knows the answer. It's easier to hide behind inside her oversized sweats and watch other kids get the praise.

After school the students climb on the bus. A pretty redhead waves to her, a former teammate from the Y. Lily's got a ride with Mom, so she can't sit next to the girl, or ask her about her swim career, or start a new friendship.

Overhead, dark clouds glower and promise more icy rain. When her mom arrives, Lily climbs into the back of the SUV. Even though she dreads her mother's questions - How was your day? Meet any new friends?? – Lily's gloom increases as her mother punches in a number and starts an argument on the in-dash phone with a coworker. "I submitted the paperwork already," she snaps. "Yes, I told Don. He said it was fine, told me to call Dr. Yi. It's all taken care of, so I don't see the problem."

You're never good enough.

You're an idiot.

You're a waste of space.

You failed the test.

If she texted him, Tyler would get right back to her. It would be contact, a way to avoid the black hole inside her chest. Even his many punishments, long bouts of silence, were themselves a kind of communication. I'm testing you. I want to see how strong you are, see how long you can last. It's for us. You have to put up with it for us. I'm here, you just have to win me. But you're such a stupid brat, you'll probably mess up again.

And now there's nothing. Lily feels she floats in deep space, an echoing vacuum about to suck out her guts. It's like a cult follower forced out of the group, having to search for a new existence. It's like standing in the cold rain as she looks through the windows into a room warmed by fire.

The afternoon is already so dark Lily can see her face in the glass, white skin and hollow cheeks. Maybe she's got a terminal disease. She'll be a young, beautiful corpse. Tyler will come to her funeral and cry over the open coffin. "I should have treated her better," he would say. "I should have begged for her forgiveness, should have told her I loved her."

Lily watches the grainy ice on the glass and tries to keep herself together.

Practice, when she arrives, is a nightmare. Several of the lights have blown out, and the Y is darker and colder than usual. Lily has to fight against the water to reach the end of the pool, where she can lift her head and gulp icy air into her lungs.

Maria's frown isn't necessary. Lily already knows her times continue to get worse.

Out of the pool, her legs shake. She nearly trips on the way to the locker room and has to reach for the side rail. "Whoa!" Pete's voice, behind her, is cheerful. "Watch out, Batista!" Fingertips on her elbow, five constellation points of warmth. "Hey," he says in a lower, more intimate tone. "You okay?"

Lily's so cold she can feel the hot tears before they cascade down her cheeks. "I'm fine," she manages to say.

"Yeah, I'll say." Pete winks outrageously. "Still got the same number, right?"

The photo of Tyler kissing Bree floats between them. He can go out with other people – why can't she? "Yeah," Lily answers. She takes a deep breath and forces herself to engage. "Gonna use it?"

"I just might." Pete's fingers slide off her flesh, and he winks.

Lily escapes into the locker room. Her wet feet make no sound in the puddles on the floor, and she wonders if the pool water invaded her ears as well as her life, her mind, her heart.

Shivering violently, Lily dives into the nearest shower. She still wears her practice suit. The water on her skin doesn't feel like anything - not hot, not cold. All she can sense are shudders electrifying her body down to muscle and bone.

• • •

Pete doesn't wait long. When Lily enters her bedroom, three missed calls from his number show up on her screen. She plops on the mattress and chews one thumbnail as she listens to his messages. "Hey Lily. Missed your blue eyes when you were away! Big party tonight at my house. Wanna come over?"

It's the very last thing she wants, but after Sonya's remarks in lunch and Lily's own dark solitude, maybe she should go. If she got out of the house, escaped her messy room and lonely life, she could forget Tyler and lose everything in one night of alcohol and loud music.

As she taps Pete's number to call him back, Lily flips through the clothes in her closet. It's time for a shopping spree. Most of her shirts are from meets or swim teams.

"Lily!" Pete sounds like he's already started on the beer. "Can't believe you called, that's just so awesome." He shouts away from the phone, probably to some of the guys in the room. "Hey, shut up you assholes! I got a hot one on the phone."

Instantly Lily regrets the call. "Uh, so…" she falters. "What are you doing?"

"What are we doing?" he yells. From the background, there's an answering roar of drunken laughter interspersed with several filthy comments. "Get your beautiful butt over here and you'll find out. Hey

Lily," he adds before she can answer, "what are you wearing? Wanna give us a show so we know what to expect?"

The crowd jeers, and someone off-screen shouts "Nudes! Nudes! Nudes!"

Lily realizes she's frozen inside her closet, one hand fisted on the hood of an old Prescot sweatshirt. Horror and shame pour into her lungs. She's drowning. "I don't know...Pete? Can we talk in private?"

"Talk in private!" Pete screams. The party woo-hoos, and some joker adds a line about getting off in the bathroom and to clean it up when he's done.

She still can't move. Lily hears the quick patter of his footsteps, a door opening and closing with a crash. "Yeah," he whispers. "I'm alone. Getting it out now."

Lily shuts off her phone, throws it onto the floor, and covers her face.

The carpet, when she comes back to reality, is rough against her cheek. Lily lies on the ground of her bedroom. She's run away from everyone – Pete, Maria, her family. Now it's just her and the carpet, soaked with tears she can't seem to stop.

Because none of them, not even Vincent, are what she wants. Her desire for Tyler is a fist in her gut that overwhelms school, friends, family, even her sport. It's all meaningless without him. Pete's betrayal is the final seal in her despair.

Tyler may have been hard to deal with, but he never called and expected Lily to show off in front of a crowd. It was the opposite with him – Lily was precious, sealed away from the world in a glass case. He told her she was his future. They were going to get married one day. He gave her a ring. So she had to text him a lot – what was the big deal?

Why did she ever break up with him?

Lily crawls over to her closet and finds a box she hid from herself after the break-up. The flaps are duct-taped shut, and she breaks a nail as she rips open the carton.

Inside are the precious souvenirs left over from a relationship.

A valentine he wrote: *Hey, idiot. Guess I gotta give this to my dumbass girlfriend.* Later, when she complained, he told her, "It's just a joke. Jesus Christ. I thought you would understand. Give me a fucking break, guess you don't have a sense of humor. What, you're so in love with me one little insult makes you sad?"

"No." At the time, Lily had forced herself to smile. "No, of course not. I'm fine."

At the bottom of the box, under his college sweatshirt, Lily finds a tiny, velvet box. She picks it up and holds it against her cheek. For a moment she's back at Prescot, warmed by the sun as Tyler handed her the ring.

She'd give anything to feel his smooth skin against hers, taste his rough kisses, hear his husky voice over the phone. It's the sound she misses, not his words: "You're too sensitive. Any girl would be happy to go out with me, and I chose you. And you're gonna to give me shit about what I do? Or don't do? Cut it out. You have no idea what you sound like. What you look like. So ugly when you yell, your face turns this weird color, it's disgusting."

She *has* to see him. Lily sobs as she scrambles for her phone where it's landed in a pile of her sneakers and scrolls to Facebook.

The picture with Bree is gone. Tyler's profile is a publicity shot of him in the water mid-butterfly. Long, powerful arms propel his body down the lane.

Lily sits up, frowns, and scrolls back until she finds a link to Bree's page. *Single again,* the girl has written. *Guys are such players! So sick of bullshit!* Her friends have added messages of encouragement under the post: *You don't need him, His loss, You tell him what's what or I'll make him stop talking shit.*

So Tyler and Bree have broken up. His feed, when Lily scrolls back to the page, says nothing about it. Instead, there are posts about how much practice sucks and how there's not enough time to do all the damn homework the profs pile onto athletes. He'll be an Olympic swimmer one day. Why the hell should he worry about crap like physics?

Before she can think, Lily has typed out a text. It's simple, friendly, no more than a question: *How r u doing?* The words float on the screen as her finger hovers over Send.

Should she? It would be so easy to return to the way things were, to have a direction. Go to school, text Tyler, go to class, text Tyler. Tell him how great he is. Agree she needs to work on her athletics, her looks, and her study habits. It would mean a return to being inferior, sub-human... Sobs rip out of her throat, and all Lily can think about is Tyler. She wants – no, she needs – him back in her life.

"Hello?" Mom stands at the door. Lily looks up, and her mother's face crumples. "Oh, my God. What – what happened? Oh, baby. I'm so sorry. I should have been here..." Her words die out, and she comes into the room.

"I'm fine." Lily's words burn her throat. "Just leave me alone. Get out."

"I can't. Sorry, but I just can't do that." Mom's voice comes out as a strangled whisper, and she slumps onto the bed. "You're so pale. How long have you been crying?"

Lily's mouth quivers. "For the past six months, I think."

"Oh." Mom collapses onto the bed and hides her eyes in one sleeve of her turquoise sweater. For a minute they stay in silence: Lily on the floor, her mother coiled on the quilt.

She has to say something, anything, to make Mom get out so she can be alone and send the text to Tyler. If she makes contact with him and wins him back, everything will be fine again. "I'll be okay. Promise. I just have to work harder, you know, try to fit in at school."

"No. You can't do this alone." She covers her face with both hands and mutters something about needing a full glass.

"A full glass of what, mom?" Lily feels fresh tears on her lashes. "Vodka? That's how you handle everything, right?"

"I thought we could help you through this by being a good family, but it's not working." Mom sits up, thrusts fingers through her thick hair, and twists the dark mass over one shoulder.

"It's all my fault. Right? Dad curses all the time, you drink too much, poor Vincent burst into tears the other day, and it's all because I brought this poison into our house. Just say it – this is all because of me." Lily's forgotten the fallout from her relationship, how months of catering to Tyler's demands made everyone in the house, not just her, go south. Lily's chin trembles as she holds up the phone so her mom can see the unsent text. It's the last attempt at reclaiming a system of torture so old and familiar it's almost become comfortable.

Mom breathes out as Lily erases the words on the screen, brings up the list of Contacts, and blocks Tyler's name. He's no longer her jailor or her refuge. With slow, careful movements, she gets off the bed, crouches close to Lily, and puts one arm around her shoulders.

"I love you so much," her mom murmurs into Lily's hair. "Too much to sit by any longer and watch you crumble into pieces. You're staying in our room tonight, and tomorrow I'm taking you to a doctor."

Lily starts to protest, but her mom shakes her head. "No, Lily. Baby, I can't lose you. We have to go and find you real help."

19.

"I guess Tyler just wanted more than I can give." Lily pulls her knees to her chest, uncomfortable even on the padded leather sofa. Across a low table, Dr. Nnamani nods. "He was never satisfied. I tried to support him as much as possible – tweet the meet results, Like all his Facebook posts, and always be there with a supportive comment on Instagram. But it was hard. I was tired from staying up all night…"

Dr. Nnamani raises one finger. "Could you just tell me more about why you were up all night?"

Lily attempts a light-hearted laugh. It comes out as a miserable squawk. "Oh, you know. Boyfriends, right? They always want to know where you are, or what you're doing. Tyler used to Facetime me all night. We'd put our iPads on our pillows and fall asleep together. But," she adds, "he got mad at me for things I'd done. Often I didn't know what they were. He wouldn't answer when I asked him. I'd have to Facetime him and say his name, over and over, until he forgave me and he'd talk. Then we were fine again."

"Did you ever discover what he thought you had done wrong?"

The sofa is cold against her neck as Lily slumps back. There's no real answer.

"Let me ask you another question, if you don't mind?" Lily shrugs, and Dr. Nnamani writes a few words on a legal pad. "Can you go back and tell me Tyler's demands, but from your viewpoint?"

The questions are too difficult. How can she find the right words to describe such a slippery situation? "I tried to support him the way he wanted," she repeats. "Once, over the summer, I decided it was time to break up. But it felt like he could read my mind. As soon as I made my decision, he showed up at our house. It was – freaky. Scary."

"It's true some people are very good at predicting others," the therapist comments, "and often abusers have that ability. They concentrate on their victims and look for any little sign of strength. In their minds, personal growth is extremely threatening. We'll go over this in-depth, but I'd still like to concentrate on you. You changed your mind when he appeared on your doorstep?"

Lily nods. She was so weak. All it took was one little visit and she gave up any idea of leaving Tyler.

"Your viewpoint." Dr. Nnamani repeats.

Lily bows over her knees so the therapist can't see her expression. Her palms are slick with sweat, even in the chilly office. "I was tired," she mumbles. "Got exhausted. I'd try and try, and it was never enough. Told him he was the greatest boyfriend ever, the best swimmer I ever met, and it didn't make any difference. He wanted sex but not to kiss me unless it was making out and a blowjob. I felt disgusting. If I had been prettier, or older, or a better athlete, he would have wanted me. We could have gone back to the way it was in the beginning.

"Things were perfect back then." Lily's eyes are starting to fill with tears as she talks. "He was so supportive, so sweet at the start. I'd never met anyone like him. But when he went to college, it all changed. If I didn't text him before and after my classes, he'd go ballistic. Knew my schedule, too. One day I forgot to charge my phone, and he didn't talk to me for six and a half hours afterwards. Said it was my fault. I had to keep sending him messages all the time until he agreed to answer. It was a constant test, and I didn't know the right answers. Like a horrible nightmare when you go into a class and there's a big exam, and you realize you haven't cracked a book all semester? You ever dream that? Because I lived it."

Overhead, a distant machine hums. Maybe it's the heat, kicking into action. Lily feels wiped out, drowning under the weight of her words. Until they are spoken, she's had no idea how lost she felt.

"Thank you for telling me this." Dr. Nnamani makes a few more notes and rests her chin on one index finger. "Do you mind if I ask how these events made you feel?"

The breath in Lily's chest stutters. "Feel right now? Like I'm in the ocean and there's a tidal wave coming at me. No way to escape."

"That's helpful, but can you tell me more about the past when you felt you had to text Tyler all the time and Facetime with him all night? What were your reactions? It might be easier to start with your physical response."

Lily feels numb, a limp balloon filled with sadness.

"Nothing?" Dr. Nnamani clears her throat. "Any sickness, pains, trouble sleeping, eating…"

"My stomach." The words punch out of her from a place Lily almost forgot. "My stomach. It hurts. All the time."

"I see." The therapist's voice is gentle. "For how long has this gone on?"

Lily knows exactly when it started, but it's difficult to say. Once Mom read her The Little Mermaid. In order to be with the prince, the mermaid had to turn her tail into legs. Each time her foot touched the floor it seemed as if she trod on sharp knives, or so the story went.

"Tyler," she whispers. "It started the night I met Tyler."

• • •

Therapy has to fit between school, homework, and practice. There's no time for anything else, so perhaps it's better Lily doesn't have a social life. A good day is when she makes it through a couple of hours without crying. A really good day means a phone call from Erica or a few words with swimmers at the Y.

At practice, Maria insists again on breaking down Lily's stroke. As a result, swimming is a gray flow of worsening times and constant repetition. When Lily complains, Maria brushes her off and says the times are exactly where they should be, tells Lily not to be worried.

Each day Lily gets up at 5 AM, looks through the window at a black sky, and dresses in her suit to go and practice. She can barely remember why she does it.

The sets Maria has on the practice sheets are intense and make Lily ache right down to the bone. When she reaches the edge of the pool, she has to grasp the edge with slippery arms and fight for air. Her breathing sounds like death, and she wonders if she's about to puke up her breakfast.

Again.

Maria squats between two of the practice boards, pristine in a white cotton shirt and khaki pants. Lily can see the creases on the coach's knees. "You have a visitor," she says.

Is it Tyler? Lily can feel panic in her chest. Before she loses it, a large shape blots out the watery light from the neon tubes above. Dark skin, even teeth, grizzled black hair threaded with gray.

"Your stroke looks good." It's Robert. He grins at her and steps back as she climbs out of the water. "Don't look so shocked – I'm in Jersey for a clinic."

"Oh."

Water slides down Lily's skin when she climbs out of the pool to shake his hand. When she shivers he pulls a squashed, lumpy object out of a bag. "Here. Brought you this as a reminder." It's a big orange and black towel: Prescot colors. The school crest floats in the center.

Lily pulls it around herself and relaxes in warm, dry terrycloth. "Thanks. The new stroke looks okay, huh? My times are crap, though. Sorry – I mean they're not good."

His deep, rich chuckle echoes through the open space. "Of course your times are crap. I'd be kinda worried if they weren't. I see you've got a new, longer reach, especially in that last set. In a year you'll be at the top of the pack." Robert nods when she frowns. "Now, I'm not talking smack here. Next year you'll win state championships. Two years, on a college team. Six or seven out, you'll be at the Olympics."

Warm salt tears mix with pool water on her face, and Lily blinks. "You really think so?" Her voice is a whisper. To make the Olympics is a hidden dream, one she's kept secret from everyone.

Not even Erica suspects how much Lily wants it.

"Yeah. I do. Plus, your stroke isn't the only problem. Right?" Robert's brown eyes are focused on her so completely it's as if no one else exists.

"You're working on freestyle, but it's not the most important thing right now. 'Fact, you could walk away from this pool right now, never come back, and I'd still think you were the strongest athlete I ever met."

The towel slips. Absently Lily hitches it up. "What?"

"Your stroke is slower because you're starting from scratch. Same with you. Things are tough right now, but in the end you'll emerge stronger." Robert's laugh is short, as though he's just surprised himself. "You know, like a butterfly."

• • •

In the Y showers, Lily bends her head under water not hot enough to warm chilled skin. Her phone rattles on the ledge and brings her out of a dream about the Olympic Village.

Quickly she turns off her shower so the phone won't vibrate into a pool of water. It slides in her palm, and she steadies it with one finger. At first Lily doesn't recognize the name on the misty screen. She blinks away drops of water from her eyelashes and peers at the screen.

There's an email from Nolan, Erica's cousin. She hasn't thought about him for months. Lily loops the Prescot towel around her and holds the corners with her teeth. She opens the email, praying he's not about to ask her out on a date. It's the last thing she needs in her life at the moment.

He doesn't mention possible dinners, movies, or hangouts. Instead Nolan has written a single question: *Have you ever seen these?*

There are several attached docs.

Lily wipes her hand on the towel and looks at the docs. They are copy-and-paste texts of two emails with an added note from Nolan at the top. *Received them today. Know anything about it?*

The first is far too familiar. *Hey, bitch. Remember me? Couldn't cut it at your fancy school, right? And your swim times keep going up – at fifteen you're already done. Do us all a favor and quit.*

Lily wipes her eyes and sucks in air through her nose before she reads the message below it. It's an email addressed to Nolan. *So sorry about the last message! Total mistake – could you delete it, please? And don't forget to*

stop by for dinner, soon. I have a big birthday present with your name on it!
The message is signed Aunt Betsy.

Coach Robert's orange and black towel slips to the wet floor. Lily flings it over one shoulder and runs to her locker, rotates the combo lock and lets the door slam open. Sweatshirt and sweatpants hang from the hook in the back. Lily wrenches on her clothes, head shaking.

It can't be, it simply can't be. Why would...?

As soon as she's dressed, Lily grabs her bag and marches out of the locker room. Dad is on the bleachers, hunched over his laptop and barking into his phone, "Third quarter's gonna be shit. I've got to go to Cleveland right after our meeting..."

"Dad, you have to take me to Erica's house. Now." He looks up, mouth open and eyes unfocused. "I know, I'm sorry. But I have to talk to her mom. It's important."

Dad's glance darts between her face and his laptop. Perhaps what he sees in her eyes convinces him, and his face creases into his usual grin. "If you say so, Sunshine."

He hasn't called her the old pet name in years.

• • •

The Winslow home is as lovely as ever. When she presses the doorbell, a deep tone sounds in the belly of the large foyer. Instantly Diamond, the terrier, starts barking.

There's a sound of footsteps. "Hush, you silly dog," a woman says. Lily knows whose voice it is, and her palms grow slippery.

When the front door opens, Mrs. Winslow has Diamond tucked under one arm. "Lily!" She raises perfectly groomed brows. "I didn't expect to see you until – how nice. Please come in."

Lily doesn't answer. She holds out her phone, the email from Nolan on the screen.

Overhead, the clouds race over the weak sun and a sudden spiteful wind spatters rain onto Lily's already-damp hair. Erica's mom is frozen at the open door. In her arms, Diamond growls. "I don't know why you're showing me this," she begins.

"Don't." Lily feels her lips tremble. It's all too much, the practices and school and therapy and Tyler – and now this. "Just don't, okay?"

"Jesus." Mrs. Winslow's smooth forehead puckers. "Guess you can come in. We should talk."

"Why?" Fury makes Lily's lungs burn as if the winter storm blew flames instead of gritty ice. "Why? Can you just explain? I've gone through hell, you have no idea, and it just really sucks. What you did. I accused Erica, see what I'm saying? Your daughter! You made me think my best friend hated me. And for no reason..."

"No reason?" Mrs. Winslow's voice rises to a screech. "You are the reason! Don't you get it? The only reason Erica made it into Prescot is because you left. And you're so perfect. Good grades, spot on the National Team, pretty face, perfect body. How could Erica ever compete?"

Lily doesn't know where to begin. "So you had to insult me? Bully me? Just to get Erica into the right school?"

The woman's shrug is elegant even with the cold rain on their skin. In the driveway, her dad waits behind tinted glass. Lily can almost sense his gaze. If Mrs. Winslow starts to yell or even gets violent he'll burst out of the car in Lily's defense. She's secure in his support, but for this moment, she doesn't need it.

"I would have been so happy if Erica could have come with me. We could have gone to Prescot together," Lily declares.

She can't bear to look at Mrs. Winslow's face any longer. Lily steps back, nearly stumbles off the sandstone steps. The humiliation is the last straw after practice, her talk with Robert, the confrontation with Erica's mom. She has to escape and pray Erica will still be her friend when this is all over.

Just as she slides into the passenger seat, Mrs. Winslow shouts a few words. "Are you going to tell? Are you going to tell Erica what happened? I'll say it's all a big lie! She'll never believe you!" The woman's face is crimson from yelling so hard.

Lily doesn't bother to respond. She closes the door and buckles her seatbelt. Dad puts one arm on her seat back to back away from the luxurious house. In the doorway, the little dog twists in the woman's arms, leaps onto the steps, and dashes after the car.

In the rearview, Erica's mother grows to a tiny dot and disappears. The wind buffets the SUV, and with a crash the rain begins at last.

20.

Lily's whole family attends the first big meet of the spring season, the Northeast High School Regionals. Her mom nudges Lily's shoulder with hers and grins. "Feeling good?" she asks.

"Yeah." Lily's new stroke has become second nature, part of the athlete's vital muscle memory. As a result her swim times have slowly been getting faster and have once again dropped below the vital 24-second mark. Each day brings a new achievement, faster kicks and smoother hand entry.

Vincent holds up the retro Instamatic camera he got for his birthday. "Smile." Lily bares her teeth in an exaggerated grin, and he clicks the shutter. A tiny rectangle slides out, and he blows on it before handing it to her. She looks different in the ghost image as it emerges, a girl made of ink and film.

This new girl isn't happy, not yet, but she's not tragic either. Lily stares at the photo of a person she thought was lost forever.

A high, bright voice breaks into her thoughts. "Oh my gosh - it's totally her!" Three girls in black and orange swim caps rush up the bleachers and apologize as the squeeze past spectators and other competitors. "I told you she'd be here." Erica nearly trips over the last seat and lands in Lily's lap. "Missed you so much!"

Staci and Haddigan stand behind her. "Hey guys," Lily says. The moment couldn't be more awkward, and she feels her neck prickle with sweat.

Her former teammates smile and say hello. Lily remembers how nice they were, always so sympathetic and willing to help. In the end, she was the one who drove them away. Haddigan and Staci will never be her close friends again thanks to Tyler.

If she went to parties at school or even just hung out like a normal person he wouldn't have been able to control the situation. She nearly trips on a step as realization crashes over her. He had to drive away James, of course, but also her girlfriends. No wonder he hated Erica so much and did everything he could to prove her guilty of those hate-texts.

Lily still hasn't told anyone what Erica's mother did with all those emails and texts.

Erica's face is dimpled with her smile, and the Prescot team flanks her. To take her aside now and lay the whole thing on her shoulders would be a shitty thing to do, at least at the moment. Lily decides, not for the first time, she just has to wait.

Haddigan fiddles with her usual braid and asks a few formal questions about Lily's home team. It's always going to be like this between them. The lost possibility of friendship with her and Staci makes Lily suck in a breath – after everything that's happened, Lily regrets losing them the most.

Erica makes it better by asking Lily to visit the Prescot team's bleachers, jumping up and down on her toes with eagerness. Lily turns to her mother. "Is it okay?"

Mom checks the heat sheet, crumpled in her left hand. "I guess. You have to swim soon, though."

"We'll bring her right back." Erica drapes an arm around Lily's waist and tows her down to where the Prescot team huddles.

There's a tall boy by the steps, his back to Lily and the Prescot girls. He talks intently to Robert.

Lily recognizes him right away.

Tyler's back from college on spring break, so he's still in street clothes, jeans and a tight-fitting shirt. His shoulder-to-hip ratio is ridiculous, and for a moment she feels a pang of pure lust.

He waves one hand in the air, making his biceps bunch and smooth muscles slide under the brown skin revealed by his rolled-up sleeve. Apparently Tyler's trying to explain something, and it looks like Robert wants no part of it as he turns back to the male members of Prescot's swim team.

Lily is aware of damp concrete under her feet, the lines of antlike swimmers pacing each other in the pool, the muted and relentless overhead lights. In her ear, Staci murmurs how sorry she is, how she had no idea Tyler was going to show up.

"No," Lily interrupts. "It's okay." Because this is just another hurdle, one of those barriers she has to move beyond before she can continue.

Continue to swim, to go to school, to simply be.

His eyes catch hers, and triumph swims in those beautiful depths. Tyler's lips part, but Lily has learned enough to be on the offense. "Hi." She marvels at her own casual tone.

Before he can respond, there's a low voice in her ear. "Hey," James says. "Lily? Is that you?"

James. He's there at the meet – she has no idea why – and he's just saved her again.

She feels his strong arms pull her close. "I missed you," Lily whispers into his neck. "You just don't know."

"Missed you too," he replies.

"We all did." Staci joins them on the step. James mumbles an apology and lets go of Lily. "It's okay," Staci adds, smiling up into his face. "You two were friends before we happened."

"Wait." Lily can feel Tyler's eyes on her, but suddenly he doesn't matter. "You two are together?"

"Oh, yeah." James grins and rubs his neck. "Yeah, we are."

Staci wraps her arms around his waist. "I should have told you right away. Sorry."

Stepping back, Lily realizes she's happy for both of them. Hard working and supportive – they're perfect together.

"Guess you just lost your other boyfriend." The words are typical of Tyler, as immature and hurtful as always. Coach Robert crosses his arms and tells Tyler to back off, but naturally the guy doesn't listen. "Right?" he whispers, just loud enough so only she can hear it. "You're a loser again. That sucks." He punctuates it with a smile.

Lily feels a horrified kind of sympathy for him. It's an alien emotion leached from her bones, from her life with a wonderful family. After all, in the end she gets to walk away from him and concentrate on her brother, her parents, and her friends. She'll tell Staci how awesome her news is about

James and how much Lily has missed Prescot.

However, Tyler can never leave the dark pool in his mind. He'll continue to exist inside the trap that makes him hurt other people over and over again until they are scarred the same way he is.

She could try to explain to him how his wounds stay inside her, never on her skin, always hidden beneath her flesh. But he'd twist the conversation like a pretzel, and endless Moebius strip of accusation and insults. "You're not sorry, you're salty," he'd reply. "Already got a girlfriend. What do you got? I'll tell you what you got. You got nothing. Maybe another medal you can hang up at the school, not even in your house. Later, loser."

In the end, Lily realizes there's nothing to say to Tyler. In her mind, she's dealt with everything he threw at her, and she survived. Even now she thinks he's the best-looking guy she's ever met, but she's still okay.

He pauses on the steps, a slight furrow on his brow. Maybe Tyler waits for an explanation or for her to beg him to take her back. He's probably certain he's won yet again, as if life is nothing more than an endless competition.

Lily won't get an explanation either, not from him. In any case, it doesn't matter. Despite Tyler's attempts to separate her from the world, Lily is the winner.

Staci tugs her onto the bench and holds up her phone. "Picture!" Several other girls drape themselves over Lily's shoulder and smile up into the camera. Lily looks into Staci's phone, sees the freedom in her own face.

By the time her eyes refocus from the flash, Tyler is gone.

His presence is no longer a weight. Lily can concentrate on her warm-up and events. There's no need to flutter around him, say he's going to do great.

No matter how hard she worked to be Tyler's girlfriend and support him, it would never be enough. It's a race no one can win.

Maybe he's watching her as he returns to the bleachers. And maybe Bree or his new girlfriend is with him. She sits and watches while he moves like a shark through the sea of girls.

His new girlfriend, if she exists, is ready to praise him and be beautiful, all for him.

The thought doesn't make Lily feel jealous. No, it's just the opposite. She wants to go into the crowd and find the girl Tyler's dating. Lily wants to tell her to leave him, run far away, and never look back.

And this is the saddest part. There'll be new girls in Tyler's life, and none of them will listen to the warnings until it's too late.

Lily can only continue her own story and reach out to help other victims of people like Tyler. If she races fast enough and studies hard enough, one day she'll reach the heights and be able to help those victims, the ones with hidden scars on their hearts.

She feels this new resolution shoot through her as she hugs Erica one last time.

• • •

It's time for Lily's last event. She joins the other swimmers in her heat, girls from all over the Northeast. They move in a loose group near the starting blocks, roll their shoulders in one last attempt to loosen up. The usual butterflies flutter in her gut, more from the desire to win than true nerves. She's a fine instrument, a miracle of determination and survival.

The block is rough under her feet. Her skin is smooth, shaved in the hotel room to maximize her taper. Lily bends her head, arms pointed at the water. Her dive comes after the starter's beep in perfect timing.

Choppy water pulls her in and under. God, it feels good.

And for one single moment, under the water, before her body kicks into race mode, she's in a cold and quiet place. It belongs to no one except her, and fierce joy races through her blood.

She owns this moment, this event, this mind, this body.

Cutting through the sparkly surface of the water, Lily races herself into the future.

END

To my readers: if you have suffered abuse, you can reach out
to the abuse hotline at **thehotline.org**.

You can also call them at **1-800-799-SAFE (7233)**.

loveisrespect.org is a site geared specifically to teens.

(Please be careful using these resources. Find a neutral computer
or phone that can't be tracked by your abuser. The organizations have
guidelines to keep your browser history clean from searches or links to
these help sites.)

Abuse is insidious, often robbing victims of their self-worth and
identity. If you feel that you are at fault or were the cause of your abuse,
please know that you are completely innocent. You can get more help and
advice from NAMI, a mental-health advocacy group available at nami.org.

In order to write *A Cold and Quiet Place*, I had to thoroughly
research the world of competitive swimming. Several athletes and their
families helped by inviting me to meets, practices, and to their schools. To
those incredible young swimmers, thank you.

I also researched the dark issue of emotional abuse. The victims who
gave me insight into their painful histories are true heroes, and without
their bravery this book would not exist.

Lisa Daly, the artist who formatted this print version, donated her
time to make *A Cold and Quiet Place* happen. Therefore, I'm sending her
usual fee to the National Abuse Hotline. Lisa, thank you for your beautiful
art and generosity.

When I first contemplated writing this book, I met a father whose
daughter had gone through prolonged and horrifying emotional abuse. "If
I can just save one girl," he told me, "just one girl. That's all I want."

Perhaps you are that girl.

www.ingramcontent.com/pod-product-compliance
Lightning Source LLC
Chambersburg PA
CBHW072236170626
46813CB00003B/1254